THE VICTIMS

ISIDORE OKPEWHO comes from Abraka in the Urhobo Division of Midwestern Nigeria, but grew up mostly in Asaba, where he attended St. Patrick's College. At the University of Ibadan he established a distinguished record, completing the Honours Classics course in three years instead of the usual four, and winning the Classics Departmental Prize and the College Scholarship. He graduated in 1964 with a first class Honours Classics degree (the only one so far in the history of the University), also winning the Sir James Robertson Prize for best classics student and the Faculty of Arts Prize for best student in the Faculty.

He is currently a publishing executive, working in Nigeria, has written a long Latin satirical poem which appeared in Ibadan University's *Phrontisterion*, articles and reviews in that and other journals, and is working on a second novel.

The Victims

A novel of
polygamy in modern Africa
by ISIDORE OKPEWHO
with an Introduction
by SUNDAY O. ANOZIE, PH.D.
University of Texas, Austin

ANCHOR BOOKS

Doubleday & Company, Inc.
Garden City, New York
1971

THE VICTIMS was originally published in Great Britain by Longmans Group Limited in 1970. The Anchor Books edition is published by arrangement with Longmans Group Limited.

Anchor Books edition: 1971

For Catherine and Theodora

INTRODUCTION

The African novel of the late fifties and early sixties was dominated by the theme of the conflict of cultures. The New African Novel of the seventies, heralded by the publication of such works as *The Beautyful Ones Are Not Yet Born* by Ayi Kwei Armah, and *Bound to Violence* (*Le Devoir de Violence*) by Yambo Ouologuem, can be said to have two main characteristics which distinguish it from the "Old African Novel." The first is the tendency to turn away from the fascination of the past and the too often idealized historic vision of Africa. This may have been necessary during the period of the struggle for political independence, as a reaction against the colonial conspiracy to deny Africa her legitimate contributions to world culture and civilization. This historic vision characteristic of the Negritude school of thought in general is hardly necessary now. The achievement of independence by several African countries has created new social, political and economic realities which call for realistic confrontation and even a redefinition of social imperatives in Africa.

A second characteristic of the New African Novel is, thus, the rise of a new form of social realism based upon the study of particular characters in particular social situations. The exponents are not satisfied with a simple and objective portrayal of the relationships between the individual and his society in Africa, but wish to discover the deep philosophical systems implicit in any given human or social condition with which they may be concerned.

One of the books to set the tone for the New African Novel of the seventies is *The Victims*. Its author, Isidore

Okpewho, is a Nigerian and, like most present day Nigerian writers, he studied at the University of Ibadan, from where he graduated in 1964 with a first class Honours degree in Classics. Included in his brilliant academic career is a number of awards for his original verse compositions in Latin. Okpewho then, like the late poet Christopher Okigbo, came into creative writing via a long and painful apprenticeship to the Classical Muses and after a studious cultivation of interest not only in people but also in their mythologies, their religious systems of thoughts and beliefs, and the roles these often play in shaping their destinies. This adds an extra dimension of interest to *The Victims* and may help us to understand the way in which the author deals with a more familiar and local situation.

Indeed this first novel contains both structural and thematic evidences of the influence of its author's classical studies. Okpewho possesses a fastidious precision of style and an attentive ear for the differences in local dialects and speech often faithfully reflected in English. He also writes with a deep sense of the dramatic. Each action in the novel is charged with suspense and interest and so constitutes a social drama which, in turn, is carefully woven into the main plot:

> When Obanua and his first wife got tired of hitting and tearing each other they fell back each to some kind of support, panting furiously like fallen lizards and blowing their noses and glancing at each other from time to time with caution and hatred and shame. He had come home drunk and weak, but not so drunk tonight to offer some fight to a woman. . . .

It is, however, in the development of the plot and mood suggested in this passage, in the description of landscape and, above all, in the treatment of the theme of fatalism and error of judgment that the author of *The Victims* most displays the influence of the classical concept of humanism and tragedy. The novel itself begins with a description of weather conditions in a language not unsuitable to a heroic epic:

It was a rough, stormy night. Gusts of wind howling and tearing, alternated with brief intervals of false calm, and the fear of the rain was stronger than rain itself. The night was gone by more than half. . . .

To intensify this fear of the unknown which threatens the very existence of Obanua's house, this passage is followed by the comments of the two witch sisters who tend a solitary fire—and a one-eyed cat. They provide both the prologue and the epilogue to the story, and thus play a role similar to that of the Chorus in a classical Greek play, who intervene at given and often strategic moments of the tragedy, armed with special insights. In order to heighten its thematic effect, Okpewho invoked the caprices of the tropical climate, often poetically imbuing it with human qualities—"The amber-coloured sun, with a mischievous grin now and then on its face, was gradually burning the youth out of the day."

The story of *The Victims* proper is set in Ozala, a small Igbo village in Midwestern Nigeria around 1964–65, the "victims" of the title being members of the same ill-fated household. Part of Okpewho's aim may consist in examining a basic human paradox born out of the demands for adjustments within, and the conflicts that often arise from adjusting to, a given traditional system. For this the author elects the most potentially obvious situation—the traditional system of marriage based upon polygamy. The African institution of marriage known as polygamy has been the subject of so much comment, both in European works of anthropology based upon Africa as well as in modern fiction written by Africans, that only a few remarks may be necessary here.

In fiction, African writers have tended to idealize this traditional institution, sometimes portraying a family based upon polygamy as a conflict-free zone. Thus, in Flora Nwapa's *Efuru*, for example, the heroine is made to recognize her barrenness, and encourage her husband to take a second wife, who turns out to be her own housemaid. Okpewho's *The Victims* shows that this is not the entire picture—there is more to polygamy than a harmonious and peaceful coexistence of all the members involved. Besides the individual psychology and value-orientations, there is, for instance, the capricious and often inscrutable demands which each traditional society makes upon its members in terms of ethical conformism. Thus, in a novel like Achebe's *Things Fall Apart*, what binds Okonkwo's family together is the common fear which the wives entertain of their husband's temper, and the respect and authority which he commands in the family; that the wives are thus unable to manifest their subconscious personalities and wishes in open rivalries and disputes with one another may be seen more as an artistic comment on the character and psychology of the hero, rather than as a sign of weakness or a lack of individuality in traditional Igbo wives. The picture, as presented to us in *The Victims*, of women-in-marriage sharing a common husband, appears to be truer because it is, perhaps, a more dynamic one. Obanua's two wives, Nwabunor and Ogugua, are shown as two different individuals who are separated from each other not only by age, experience, physical and psychological makeups, but also, and most importantly, by their innate procreative capacities as women. A clash between two such polar tendencies—traditional and extro-active—is bound to be frequent and inevitable. To intensify this situation the novelist has entrusted the entire explosive environment to the charge of a husband like Obanua, whose lazy and lacklustre personality does not command any respect in his family, much less rule it, and whose escapist trips through alcohol, debts and gambling, while understandable in a man placed in his situation, make him nevertheless look like the fool in the Igbo proverb who leaves his burning house to chase rats. The only moderating influence on Obanua's two wives is that exercised either by his neighbours, as is commonly the case, or by his aging mother, who also assumes full control of the house and makes all decisions, including the last and fatal one to repatriate sick Nwabunor to her own village.

On the other hand, few Western anthropological accounts of the African traditional institutions of marriage have gone beyond seeing in polygamy, as in many other tribal customs, a primitive practice consisting in the "purchase" and "use" of women as chattels either to flatter a man's sexual appetites or to enhance his real or presumed social prestige and respect in his clan. Often the positive aspects are ignored. For instance, polygamy might be considered in relation to the kinship system prevailing within a given matriarchal community in Africa, or as a complicated social, economic and sometimes political arrangement aimed primarily at reinforcing social order and stability by, among other things, limiting the incidence of divorce and prostitution among women and, in communities where it may be considered a serious infraction, the presence of illegitimate children. Thus, in spite of the lighthearted and cynical suggestion contained in Obi Egbuna's novel *Wind Versus Polygamy* that this traditional system of marriage poses a serious threat to modernization in Africa, it is possible to say that polygamy did provide an effective instrument of human ecological control in a culture where environmental and human pollution in one form or the other was not unknown.

In Okpewho's novel, the main characters are portrayed as victims of two types of tragedy by "pollution"—not of man's ecological space, as the term itself may now connote in any industrial country of Europe or America, but rather pollution of man's ontological or existential space in a pre-industrial, tradition-oriented society. In this sense, the first type of "pollution" is that for which the prevailing system of ethics and beliefs—with its contingent social structure—itself is responsible because it imposes on the individual total submission and conformity. Within such a rigid, conservative system the individual has hardly any freedom of choice and very few alibis. A married woman does not escape from the duty of child-bearing upon which the society counts so much for the continuity of its members in time and place. If sterility in a woman is also considered as a social stigma and an object of communal gossip, a mother with only one child may sometimes seek

xi

refuge in the traditional belief that, her physiological situation notwithstanding, she is not after all incapable of bearing another one—hence the origin of suspicions and the search for explanations. These few remarks may help to understand the peculiar predicament of Nwabunor, the chief protagonist in *The Victims*:

> For nine more years husband and wife lived without another. That time was scarcely a happy one. She cried and cried, and he sulked and left her in the house and stayed out long. Fear, suspicion and distrust tormented her mind and nothing seemed the same again. Gradually her faith in God began to give way to a conviction that something was behind her ill fortune. And one day he announced to her that he was going to take another wife.

This passage, besides stating the cause of the strained relationship between Nwabunor and her husband, Obanua, after the birth of their first son, also reveals a traditional system of thought according to which every event or situation in life can be explained, causally, in terms not of chance or accident nor even through empirical observation, but rather in reference to some metaphysical design or conspiracy of forces beyond the individual. Hence the logic of intentional causality, common among traditional societies in Africa and which is often interpreted as witchcraft and sorcery, may indeed be considered as part of that superrational intuition which constitutes the basis of any authentic science or cosmology.

If the first type of "pollution" relates to the influence, arbitrarily and tyrannical, which any given traditional cosmology invariably exercises upon the lives and beliefs of those who participate in it, the second type may refer to the tragedy, whether collective or single, which may occur as a result of the means, both manifest and non-manifest, which the individual employs in order to free himself from the tyranny of conventions. This latter notion of tragedy is central to the Igbo traditional world-view upon which *The Victims* is based which recognizes not only prescriptive ethics but also the principles of reciprocity and individualism. Why is it that moving from two different directions—commitment on one hand, withdrawal or escapism on the other—Nwabunor and Obanua both end up, as the closing chapter of *The Victims* reveals, with an identical fate of insanity? The answer may be simple and direct—each of these two principal characters makes a choice that implies, by its very freedom and individualism, tragic inevitability.

Since Okpewho writes with a deep sympathetic understanding of the psychological motivations of the actions of his central characters, Obanua's error of judgment, at the opening of the story, does not lie in his new habit of staying out late, which began as a mere sign of silent protest against his wife's inchoate sterility—a domestic situation most likely to invite scandal and, as already mentioned, shame and gossip from neighbours; the error lies instead in his unaccountable choice of Ogugua as the second wife. This idea is fully implied by the novelist himself when he says:

> Not even Obanua could explain why he married Ogugua against even the protests from his own mother. They were both citizens of this town, Ozala, where she did not have a good reputation. She had proved a very difficult daughter to her parents, very independent-minded and caring not the slightest bit for their word. At the age of seventeen she had got herself involved in a love affair with a Portuguese merchant . . . who ran a goods transport between Warri and Ozala, and had borne him these twin girls.

It should be quite obvious, even from this passage, that if Obanua's decision is right according to tradition, his choice of Ogugua is wrong by the same standards. Obanua's decision therefore contains an element of fatalism due precisely to the paradox just indicated. Okpewho merely hints at this paradox, which is real in a tradition-directed society, tending to exploit it artistically but not developing it, although the treatment of such a paradox constitutes a major success in two novels by Chinua Achebe—*Arrow of God* and *Things Fall Apart*. For instance, whereas the author of *The Victims* seems to suggest that there is, in the Midwestern traditional Igbo society, no clear line of demarkation—implying a good deal of flexibility—between the individual's exercise of the freedom of choice and the collective application of restraining measures, Achebe seems to tell us in his first and third novels that, among traditional Igbos living on the eastern bank of the Niger, the individual can exercise his freedom, without incurring collective sanction or disapproval, only within certain prescribed limits of legitimacy. However, this difference in point of view may be more of a temporal rather than situational nature. For, writing about much more recent times, Okpewho may have only wished to exploit artistically the conflict between Nwabunor, a tradition-determined character, and Ogugua, who represents the modern, emancipated woman. Hence as the story unfolds itself, we find that not only her knowledge of the ways of the world and her open and adulterous carryings-on with Gwam, a local party supporter and a great scoundrel, but also the total unruliness and the kleptomanic tendencies of her two mulatto daughters are used to provide a rationale for Nwabunor's fears and obsessions.

Although throughout *The Victims* Okpewho emphasizes the part played by chance, accident or even mere coincidence in strengthening these fears and obsessions, Nwabunor's intuition of insecurity relates to the order of the traditional cosmological system. Her frequent recourse to divination by consultations with the village soothsayer should be seen as the appropriate traditional means of confirming, rather than ascertaining, what she thinks she already knows—the human cause of her life problems —before she can then set about restoring the cosmological balance. As the novelist further indicates by means of an episode illustrating the opposition shown by the goddess *Ushe*, through her worshippers, to the Catholic missionary enterprise, traditional belief in the supernatural has persisted in spite of the serious inroads made by Christianity

xiv

into the religious consciousness of the people concerned in this novel. As part of that religious consciousness herself, Nwabunor has acted independently and selfishly in her choice of the ultimate means with which to free herself, paradoxically, from the system.

Okpewho's novel *The Victims* rewards close study, particularly when its interpretation is carried to the level of the tragic significance of its title. Although the novelist deals with a specifically African situation and offers us a good insight into one of the most important and dynamic cultures of Africa, his principal concern is with the problem of suffering and the human condition in general. Viewed from this angle, the tragic universality of the theme becomes apparent. For individuals are victims not only of their cosmological system and of the beliefs they hold in common as members of a particular society, but they are victims also of their own private fears (particularly of their fears of not being able to live but merely exist), their own suspicions and distrust of others. But what should be most disturbing about this novel is that in his striving for the purely cathartic, Okpewho draws into his "sad profiles of a retreating menagerie" the death of the two half-brothers, Ubaka and Bomboy, who do not belong to the tortured and "polluted" world of their parents. The reason may as well be, as the fortune-teller has warned his consultant, that the gods "do not accept any half measures."

SUNDAY O. ANOZIE
Department of English
The University of Texas at Austin

THE VICTIMS

shook her head, mumbling, 'Poor woman. Poor woman.'

Another sharp cry came, and the first old woman squirmed. She clutched her little cat closer to herself, slunk gently down between her bedclothes, unmindful of the quiet-burning oil-lamp inside or the angry wind outside, and listened.

When Obanua and his first wife Nwabunor grew tired of hitting and tearing at each other they fell back each to some kind of support, panting furiously like fallen lizards and blowing their noses and glancing at each other from time to time with caution and hatred and shame. He had come home drunk and weak, but not too drunk tonight to offer some fight to a woman. She had been waiting for him all through the day and now far into the night, and the longer he stayed away at the drinking place the more bitterly she reflected how much she needed the money that he was consciously throwing away. Anger and bitterness had nurtured her strength. Now thoroughly spent and holding off from each other of their own accord they looked like two perpetual enemies merely acting out a painful routine, waiting for a next chance. Even Ubaka, Nwabunor's only son and child, seemed to be tired of his crying and now stood by, watching and sobbing in fear of every next moment.

'You will—you will have to kill me,' Nwabunor panted and spat as she cried, 'but you must pay—you must pay your son's fees.'

'Well, come and take the money then,' Obanua replied, spitting and panting too. 'Did you not think—you could force—force the money out of me? I have told you before and—and I tell you once again. I have no money.'

She rubbed her eyes and blew her nose.

'You don't know what you are saying.'

'Alright. Come and do what you like then.' The fight seemed to have activated his drunken inertia. 'Is your son the only one in this house who goes to school? And how many of them do I pay for?'

3

'What is my business with somebody else's children? If you call Ubaka your son you must be prepared to show it. Otherwise you will have to kill me in this house.'

He hissed, then tried to walk towards his bed.

'You are deceiving yourself,' she sprang after him. 'There is not going to be any sleep for either of us tonight.'

She gripped him smartly by the waist. He swung round quickly and caught her by the neck. Together they crashed to the floor and struggled on.

In the next room Ndidi and Ogo, the two daughters of Ogugua, the second wife, who had been listening keenly and with some amount of stifled joy, sprang up from their mat and made to go over and watch the fight. But their mother cut them short.

'Come back at once, you little beasts!' she shouted at them. 'Who called you? Or do you want to join mad people in their madness? Come on, lie back on that floor before I cut off your ears this night!'

The two girls slunk back disappointed.

Back in the other room the fight raged on with renewed fierceness. It had all the unguided bitterness and frustration that comes to a family when love has long since died, when the one has discovered that there is nothing to look forward to, particularly as she has little to offer, and the other wonders what use it has all been and decides that he loses nothing now by hating.

Obanua Ozoma had decided that he wanted a second wife.

He was a driver by trade, and had met his first wife, Nwabunor, in Aje, one of the villages on his route where he stopped to pick passengers or refuel or buy food. He had been consistently nagged by his mother, who was worried that her only son was almost in his middle age and had still not given her a grandchild, until he met a woman who made an unavoidable impression on him.

Nwabunor proved herself a very dutiful wife. While her husband went off to work, plying the roads to Benin and

4

Warri, she traded in small articles and tried to supplement their living. But good luck hardly seemed to come her way. For some time she had been feeling her strength steadily reduced by some kind of internal weakness that taxed her breath at times and gave her pain around the heart and lungs. She had taken it as largely due to over-exertion of her energies at the trade. But then she could not be very sure, and that was not her major worry.

For three years she lived with her husband and never had a child for him. She began to wonder what was wrong with her. Could somebody else be wishing me ill? Besides, her husband was not very sympathetic.

'I . . . . I don't know—' she stammered as they slept together one night. 'It seems to me . . . I can hardly explain it. But God will certainly answer my prayers.'

Obanua merely turned his back at her and sighed. She was very worried.

'Are you annoyed with me?' she asked, perplexed.

'Don't worry me,' he grunted. 'I want to sleep.'

She continued to suppress her tears until sleep finally came to her rescue.

For those three years sadness and anxiety tormented her life. But at last she gave birth to a son.

That child brought joy and relief to Obanua and Nwabunor, relief from all the unhappiness that harassed three years of marriage and from all the scandal that hovered round them like bad breath. He was such a pleasant little thing. He hardly cried unless he was hungry or you tried to take away a play-thing from his hands. But even before you took that thing you had to battle with ten little fingers that gripped it as tightly as though they had been glued to it. And when you finally took it he cried and kicked his two tiny feet with all the infant fury at his disposal. Even in infancy he showed impressive quickness of mind. If you waved an object before him his eyes followed it with magnetic attentiveness until you stopped waving it, and then his eyes would turn to stare at you, glittering with a liquid glee of triumph.

But he was the only child. For nine more years husband

and wife lived without another. That time was scarcely a happy one. She cried and cried, and he sulked and left her in the house and stayed out long. Fear, suspicion and distrust tormented her mind and nothing seemed the same again. Gradually her faith in God began to give way to a conviction that something was behind her ill fortune. And one day he announced to her that he was going to take another wife. She was very sad, though she tried not to show it. She would not make him a reply until, in a mixed passion of fear and jealousy (because she had long been suspecting his movements with this other woman), she decided to talk to him.

'Do you love her?' she asked.

He did not reply. He was smoking nervously.

'Hm?' she asked again.

'I don't know,' he retorted impatiently, turning away from her. She fought to keep back her tears.

'When does she move in?'

'Any day now,' he said after some hesitation.

But she was not satisfied.

'What does "any day now" mean? If you two have made up your minds to get married'—she blinked to let a tear fall off—'would you not fix a date?'

'Well, we have fixed a date.'

'So when does she come in?'

'Next week.'

Nwabunor went away and cried. But with this frustration came a new determination. She was not going to be pushed out of her rightful place. She was the first to come into this house, and she was going to stay first. Anybody else could move in, but nobody was going to make her second best.

Shortly afterwards she commenced to translate this resolve into practical terms. One evening early in the following week, she began to pack her belongings into her husband's room. There were two bedrooms in the house, and a wife or wives would normally live apart from the husband, leaving it to him to 'call in' the woman, on whatever night he chose. But Nwabunor packed all her things out

6

of the second room and moved completely into her husband's room, making sure to take her son's things as well. He could sleep on a mat on the floor.

Obanua stood by and watched the act.

'What are you doing?' he asked.

Nwabunor made him no reply. She merely kept on moving in and out of the rooms, lugging boxes and bags, picking up clothes as they fell, and shouting orders at her perplexed son Ubaka.

'I say what are you doing, Nwabunor?' Obanua repeated.

'What else am I doing?' she confronted him. 'I am making room for your wife to move into.'

He could hardly believe her.

'Are you wanting to cause trouble here?'

'Me? Cause trouble? God forbid!' she snapped her fingers over her head. 'On the contrary I want to avoid it. Ubaka!' she shouted, ignoring her husband now, 'have you brought your school bag in?'

'I am coming, ma!'

Obanua looked on for a while, then swallowed and walked away. He pulled out a chair and sat outside, shaking his legs and looking into the distance. He saw nothing but houses and trees separated from one another, and birds flying home not in the usual groups but in different directions.

But he refused to let the picture bother him. He sighed, and lit a half-smoked cigarette.

When Ogugua moved in later that week, she was immediately struck by the strangeness of the atmosphere she had walked into. After all the rejoicing and other manifestations of welcome (from which Nwabunor had been conspicuously absent) she proceeded, with her two children from a previous life, to move her belongings into place. Then she noticed that she was going to be alone in one room. She turned round to her husband, who was standing around and anticipating the confrontation.

'Am I going to have all this space to myself?'

7

He could not fail to detect the sarcasm in her tone.

'Don't worry about anything yet,' he said, trying hard to conceal the tremor within him. 'Just take your things in and we can talk about it afterwards.'

A brief thought flashed through her mind and for that fleeting moment an entire picture presented itself. She didn't like what she saw or thought and wondered briefly to herself why she had so foolishly decided to saddle herself with a husband. But then she quickly dismissed the thought with a sigh and carried on with what she was doing.

'Ndidi!'

'Ma!'

'Ogo!'

'Ma!'

The twin girls had been talking with Ubaka outside. They didn't consider their mother's call very urgent yet.

'Where is your mother?' Ogo asked him.

'She is inside sleeping.'

'Does she always sleep in the afternoon?' Ndidi put in.

There was an instinctive squirm on Ubaka's brow. He was wondering what the question meant.

'No.'

'Our mother always does, unless she is doing something very important, or she is away to a function. Does your mother often go to functions?'

'No,' Ubaka said, more with distaste now.

The two girls chuckled.

'Our mother likes going out often.'

'I see.'

There was a brief pause.

'And where is your father?' Ubaka asked them.

The twins looked at each other, and frowned.

'We don't know.' The reply sounded rehearsed.

'Ndidi!'

'Ma!'

'Ogo!'

'Ma!'

The girls hurried inside. Ubaka sighed and blinked his

8

eyes with a touch of triumphant relief. But he felt rather happy to think that he had now got children like himself that he could feel close enough to, as a brother would to his sisters.

Not even Obanua could explain why he married Ogugua against even the protests from his own mother. They were both citizens of this town, Ozala, where she did not have a very good reputation. She had proved a very difficult daughter to her parents, very independent-minded and caring not the slightest bit for their word. At the age of seventeen she had got herself involved in a love affair with a Portuguese merchant, popularly known in the town as 'Potoki', who ran a goods transport between Warri and Ozala, and had borne him these twin girls.

A few months after Ogugua came in to Obanua's house she gave birth to a boy. Her own insufficiency was thus harshly brought home to Nwabunor, who had not known childbirth for more than nine years. But her frustration went further than that, for something happened to her that even more deeply aggravated her feeling of failure. About a year after Ogugua bore her child, Nwabunor had a miscarriage. She began to wonder. What could this mean? Is this an empty-handed event? Look what has happened, just when God was almost answering my prayers. I cannot understand this. There has to be something in it. There must be something. . .

So it turned out that Obanua had brought on something he could hardly control. Besides, he could scarcely conceal his partiality for his new and much younger wife. Thus arrogance, jealousy, fear and suspicion gnawed at the household as mice on a human sole.

And when he and his first wife fought tonight every blow carried with it all the abandon that defiance and despair could put into their hands.

The storm outside increased in its fury. There was no

9

other noise around, except for the helpless crying of Ubaka.

'You will—you will have to kill me tonight,' she gasped.

'I will do that,' he gasped back.

The struggle took them through the length and breadth of the room, under the bed, against the door, legs up, heads down, hands on the groin and against the throats, eyes wide open as death. When they felt tired again they retired, threatening, swearing, cursing, while the rain shot down its darts as though it meant to pierce the thatched roof.

2

Early in the morning Obanua got up to go to work. Nervously he tried to take care not to wake Nwabunor up and re-enact the previous night. So, though it was still a bit dark, he did not light the lamp, and tiptoed every movement he made. He went to the back of the house and threw a few handfuls of water across his face, then tiptoed back into the room. But when he got in she was up and waiting for him.

'You are not going anywhere without giving me the money, let me tell you,' she declared, determined as ever.

His heart melted and he relaxed in despair. He walked to the clothes-line above the bed and fumbled through the clothes. He took a long time doing this, and she became somewhat impatient.

'You can do whatever you like there,' she said, getting up from the bed, on which she had sat, and trussing the wrapper between her legs. 'If you like you can spend the whole of the morning there fooling yourself, but you are not leaving this house without putting your son's fees into my hands.'

'Look, Nwabunor,' Obanua turned to say, 'it is not every day that husband and wife wake up shouting.'

'Shouting?' she mocked. 'You can be sure that it is not going to stop at just shouting. Would it be the first time?'

'O-ho! So you want to beat me as well, do you?' There was a mischievous grin on his face.

'You can think what you like,' she replied, 'but you are not stepping out there until I have your son's fees in my hands.'

11

'I told you last night and I am telling you again this morning. I have no money.'

'You lie!'

'Well, come and strip me then and take the money, since you think I'm lying.'

'To tell you the truth,' she said, 'rather than that I should continue to bear alone the burden of bringing up a child that you call your own, I am going to strip you naked this morning whatever that will cost.'

'Well, do what you like then.'

'You can be sure about that.'

He put on his work clothes with nervous haste and lost a fly-button in the process. When he was ready he made to go out, but she posted herself firmly at the door, eyes alert and lips screwed to a petulant pout.

'Look, Nwabunor,' he said, 'I don't want any trouble today, do you hear what I'm telling you?'

'I don't want any trouble myself. Just give the money to me.'

Outside, men and women were exchanging greetings and wishing each other good health and peace. The crier Nwanze was on his regular rounds with his gong, summoning the youths to assemble and clean up the chief's compound. Hard by, chickens pecked and clucked and goats knocked their horns in friendly display. Day had broken and all life was on its course.

'Nwabunor, get out of the way and let me go to work.'

She made no reply and instead began to shake one leg in uneasy reflex, looking defiantly away. He scanned her and thought what an ugly bitch she was, skin folded like a maggot's and biceps dangling like the dewlap of a cow. He felt his manhood insulted and angrily made to force his way through the door. She lost her stance and was startled into fury, and in anger grabbed his shorts tightly, breathing hard, eyes aglare. He tried to force her hands away and in the process two buttons snapped off, and his bristles showed. At this moment a neighbour greeted, and in anger and shame he pushed madly back into the room and they both landed with a thud. The shorts were down to the knees and he was almost naked.

'You see what you have done?' he fumed.

'What have *you* done?' she countered. 'Shame on you if you don't—' she spat the blood from her mouth, '—if you don't kill me today! The fight has—only just begun.'

Amid all the tearing and blowing, blood began to stream down from her nose too.

The fight attracted considerable attention. Ubaka had woken and was about to pick up his bucket and pad to go to the stream when he caught sight of the fighting. He ran to the scene of the struggle, watching helplessly as the familiar fury took its course. In fright he burst into tears and ran this way and that for help. He ran into the room of Ogugua, Obanua's younger wife, but she warned him not to bother her, saying that the trouble had nothing to do with her.

The fight dragged on. Their clothes were practically in shreds and there was shame on their bodies. The blows came in much slower now and the gasping much harder. Ubaka cried painfully and helplessly in one corner. Close by him Ogugua's four-year old son Bomboy cried in sympathy. Neither of them was looking at the scene. But Ndidi and Ogo, the twin mulatto daughters of Ogugua, stared at the fighting couple with some measure of sadistic delight, nodding in approval whenever a blow fell on Nwabunor.

Suddenly footsteps were heard from the main entrance, and a mad struggle ensued between the combatants. Obanua fought towards the room. Household children were alright—they saw this all the time—but how could he face outsiders in his nakedness? And while he fought to abandon the fight and get himself covered up, Nwabunor, regardless of the shame, fought with equal enthusiasm to make them stay where they were. And so they tugged, back and forth, back and forth, like cattle in stampede, in and out of the room. But this time there was greater spirit, nurtured by anguished shame, on his side. As she tore after him in mad gasps he gave her a hard push and

13

sent her reeling out of the room till she fell hard on the floor. He quickly seized the nearest wrapper and wound it round his loins. Nwanze, the crier, hobbled up to the scene. He quickly saw the familiar exercise and grabbed Nwabunor as she made furiously towards the door that had been slammed against her.

'Leave me at once! Leave me—o! Leave me!' she wailed as she tore and kicked. 'He either kills me today or we shall both set this house on fire!'

'Don't say a thing like that,' Nwanze exhorted. 'If you set fire to the house, are you not going to destroy all that belongs to you, including your own son?'

'I don't care,' she said, 'but this will be the end of all my troubles in this house—mine and my son's.'

Nwanze's grip was fast. Considerably calmed now, she panted to regain strength.

'Nwabunor, what is the reason for—'

'The reason for what? Don't ask me anything!' she snapped.

'What is the matter again this morning?'

'Go and ask him. Leave me! Do you hear that? Leave me!'

At this point Obanua's mother, Ma Nwojide, also came in. She had just come from a prayer meeting.

'Come, my daughter,' she said, 'what is the trouble?'

'Let nobody ask me any questions,' Nwabunor hotly retorted, throwing up her hands, though Nwanze's grip was secure around the shoulder-joints.

'What is happening again today between you and your husband? Will I never call at this house without meeting some kind of uproar? What is the trouble this time?'

Nwabunor made no reply.

'What is the matter, I say?'

'Ask your son,' was the curt reply.

Inside the room Obanua was putting on another pair of shorts and shirt. But there was a deep worry now on his mind. The clothes which his wife had ripped to pieces off his back were his work clothes, a khaki-upon-khaki uniform for a driver of the company for which he worked.

14

He took a good long look at the shreds he had left on the floor. How was he going to report this to his boss? And considering all the warning he had been given already about several misdemeanours, mostly of drunken driving and a number of accidents resulting from this, how was he going to face his boss with this fresh case? He thought, or rather stared blankly for a long time, and put on a fresh set of clothes, his own personal clothes. Then he looked out of the window, and the day was fast growing old. He made to hurry out. Suddenly he remembered cigarettes, and rescued a pair of crumpled sticks from the pocket of the shredded shirt on the floor. He stuffed these into his shirt and quickly opened the door.

Ogugua passed by the scene and curtly exchanged greetings with the callers. She fixed a stern look on her twin daughters who were standing by, and withdrew them forcibly from the scene. In the process she exchanged an eyeful of spite with her husband's wife.

As Obanua passed through the door his aged mother accosted him.

'Oba, my child,' she said, 'what is the trouble between you and your wife again this morning?'

She got no reply.

'Am I not asking you?'

'Please leave me alone,' he replied. 'Let no one trouble me any more this morning. I am already late for work and I don't wish to be held back any further.'

'You are deceiving yourself,' Nwabunor threw at him. 'You are not leaving this house today. We shall both be buried under this earth this morning,' and she slapped the floor with her palm to stress the point.

'Keep quiet, and let's hear,' Nwanze cautioned her at once.

'Oba,' Ma Nwojide said again, 'will I never meet this house in peace? Enh? Is it not a thing of shame that I should call at my son's house every morning only to meet him fighting with his wives while the whole town passes by and sneers? Come, tell me, what is the matter this time? Come, my son—'

She raised her hands appealingly to catch hold of him. But Obanua slipped off and walked on.

His wife made one desperate dash at him but was held back by the tight grip of the crippled crier. She kicked and shrieked and cried to be left alone. She felt her shreds loosening again, so she held back a little to cover up.

Obanua had now gained some distance. Nwabunor still struggled, wept, cursed and swore. But soon her husband had gone far away, out of reach of her and out of sight of the household and of all the inquisitive persons who had gathered round the regular scene.

Inside, Ma Nwojide could still not get a word.

'Won't anybody tell me what is going on in this house?' she shouted. 'What kind of shameful thing is this? Every morning all respectable families wake up in peace and go about their businesses without any word of abuse from anyone to the other. But in my son's house it is always different. Not a single day has passed in this house without one kind of trouble or another—with this saying this to that and that saying that to this, endlessly. It is always quarrelling—quarrelling, fighting, cursing, slapping, scratching. I wonder that you are not all living in the forest with the rest of the beasts. That would have been much better than that you should expose yourself to a town of reasonable human beings. Now look at the shame you are bringing upon yourselves! Just take a look at yourself now, Nwabunor. Are you happy that the whole of Ozala is looking at you in your nakedness? How much different do you think you look from the mad woman in the streets? And consider the amount of fear and scandal you are exposing these little children to. Do they not mean anything to you and your husband? I am asking you. Are you happy that they wake up every morning to look at their mother and father in their nakedness, tearing at each other like wild animals? How do you expect to raise them to be good children?'

She paused briefly and hissed.

'Come,' Ma Nwojide continued, 'where is Ogugua? Ogugua!'

16

'Ma!' came the reply from the kitchen.

The old woman walked up to the kitchen.

'Where are you?' she enquired.

'I am here, ma.'

'Do you not see all that is happening here this morning! Enh? Do you want to pretend you don't know what is going on? I ask you.'

'Ma, I don't know,' Ogugua replied with cool malignance. 'I just woke up this morning myself to find them fighting. I don't know anything about it at all. And even if I knew what could I do to stop a fight between two giants? I don't want anybody to knock my eyes out.'

Smoke was getting into her eyes, so she blew the fire with a fan until the flame rose and drove the smoke away.

'Why can't you people live in peace in this house like everybody else? It is always fight, fight, fight. Why?'

'But what do you expect me to do, ma?' Ogugua asked. The old woman knew she had no answer to the question. She knew it was useless to try to get Ogugua to explain. So she hissed emphatically in despair.

Elsewhere the crier Nwanze was trying to console his friend's wife. For she was now crying in pained lament and blowing her streaming nose and wiping her tear-soaked eyes with one of the shreds of her cloth, wailing, 'What kind of life is this? Is it any fault of mine that I have only one child for my husband? There are families in this town that have no children at all but still live happily. Why must it be different in my case? What have I done to have fallen into the hands of such a husband as this? Enh, what have I done? He has no regard either for me or for my son, do you hear? For over one year now I have borne alone the burden of his upbringing in spite of the suffering that this has brought upon me. Why should I be subjected to all this torture just because of the presence of some other woman in this house?'

From far off in the kitchen Ogugua dropped her utensils and snapped.

'Let no one mention my name this morning, or else she will have her fill of all the trouble she has been asking for.

17

Do you hear me? I don't want my name brought into this matter, otherwise we shall all see fire with our eyes this morning.'

Then she settled back into the kitchen. The challenge would probably have been answered. But Nwanze interposed his wit and didn't give either of them a chance.

'You see, that's what I've been saying. I came into Obanua's house this morning hoping to get a chip of kola or at least rinse my gums with a tiny drop of the good liquid. After all a working man must get his reward sometimes —was I born to grab my gong and scream round the whole town every day before little chickens have passed their morning droppings? But what do I find on getting at the door? A cluster of children who cannot clean their anuses properly. And instead of going about their parents' errands they begin to pry into the homes of people minding their own business. I asked one to let me pass and the little ant opened her mouth to ask me if I alone had the right to look! You see that? Frankly, the little rats of these days have no respect for their elders. Was it not only two days ago that I stumbled into the house of Nwalie Okubulu *who-cries-for-other-people's-property* and met his wife and children eating—and what was the first thing that greeted me? Even before I stepped my foot over the threshold his tiny four-year-old son reminded me that I was in the habit of coming at mealtimes, and when I told him "shut up" he snapped back "shut up yourself". I warned him that if he didn't shut up I would pick a broomstick and beat his butt till it looked like that of a baboon, and his elder brother replied that if I touched his brother he would knock my mouth dry of the okro-seeds! Have you ever seen a thing like that? That's why I was telling Obanua the other day, Look my dear friend, I said, what's wrong with you? You cannot continue to come home every night to your house smelling as if you have been pissed upon by a goat. What's the matter with you? Grown-up as you are you do not appear to know that a man sleeps on his mat according as he has spread it on the floor . . .'

And so he babbled on until nobody minded him any more. Ma Nwojide had lost confidence in her ability to get any sense out of either of her two daughters-in-law. So she had adjusted her cloth and left in anger, murmuring in disappointment. Nwabunor had also stopped crying and had now left Nwanze and retired into the bedroom to think, hand on chin, watery eyes to the floor.

Ndidi and Ogo were performing their household chores. Ogo was sweeping the floor of their mother's bedroom while her twin sister was picking out the clothes for washing. Their mother was out of earshot and they were gossiping, all aflutter, like two little butterflies.

'Did you notice the way her neck was being twisted and she was screaming—'

'Yes—like a cock when the knife has been brought near its throat.'

'And the way he almost throttled her and her eyes were gleaming wide—'

'Like a scuttling rat when the cat has grabbed him in his claws. Frankly, I wish he had killed that evil woman.'

'Don't mind her. Hardly a day passes but she looks for one kind of trouble or the other and will never allow the poor man to go about his work.'

'One mind told me to go and help him tear the rest of her clothing to pieces and leave her there completely naked.'

'God saved you! She would have skinned you as soon as she recovered from the fight.'

'She could never have caught me, ugly and clumsy as she is like a pot—'

A few yards away their mother was coming towards the room. Their topic changed.

'You remember when that little boy set that masquerade on fire yesterday?'

'O-ho . . . yes! He would probably have been burnt to death. But two or three of his followers pushed him on the ground and started pouring sand on him. People said the two masquerade groups had never agreed with one another and each time they met there was always some fighting—'

'Keep quiet you two,' their mother blared out, 'and let me hear something reasonable. Useless children! It takes you hours every morning to perform any small duty assigned to you. You, Ndidi, you have been picking those clothes since the cock crew this morning. Let me remind you that if you don't get them washed you are not going to school today. . . . Give way and let me pass, you tiny little broomstick, sweeping like an old woman! Look, drop that broom there. Go to the kitchen and give Bomboy his food. And let me not hear a single word from either of you again this morning or else I'll cut your ears off.'

The girls scuttled away, giggling and hitting one another in childish frolic.

Inside, their mother was tidying her bed and sweeping the rest of the floor. From the next room came a groan, hard gasping and a thud on the floor. Ogugua listened hard, and when the gasping came thicker she dropped her broom and hurried towards the scene. Nwabunor was sprawling on the floor and squeezing hard at her sides. She was breathing hard and sweating profusely, like one subjected to a malarial cure. Ogugua was not too sure what would be the reaction of Nwabunor if she offered to help. But she stood over her and tried to steady her frantic hands.

'Nwabunor! Nwabunor!' she shouted in confusion, 'What is wrong with you? What is happening to you? Say something! Nwabunor! Nwabunor! Nwabunor!'

This was beyond her. It had happened to Nwabunor before, but that was some time ago. Again Ogugua shouted and tried to stop her. But the other writhed and clawed in suffering and pain. Ogugua ran out and screamed for help. Their immediate neighbours were the first to assemble. Before long there was a fresh crowd in front of the house, some of them mischievous little boys delightedly expecting nothing different from what they had already been treated to—only this time the details might be a little more view-worthy.

People thronged and pressed into the house. They started asking what was wrong. Soon they would begin to ask who was responsible for the event. The fight had ended a long time ago. So something else must have taken place. The thought came into Ogugua's mind amid all her confusion: how could this be?

'E-hen' she said. 'I've been saying it in this house, I have been shouting it every day, and the whole town will bear me witness in this. I have long been saying that the daily quarrelling in this house would result in something serious one day. Now look at what has happened. I have always advised Nwabunor that fighting is not the best way to open a day. Look what happened this morning. Ask the children. Our husband had made preparations to go to work this morning and was on his way out when she suddenly sprang on him, grabbed his shirt and told him that they still hadn't settled last night's score. Have you ever seen a thing like that? Before he could open his mouth to utter a word she had ripped his shirt apart and landed him a slap on the face and dragged him down on the floor. You understand what I'm telling you? Ehn, you understand? Now the fight she brought about has ended and the poor man has gone to work. She still wasn't satisfied with the trouble and she went into the room to cry. See what she has brought upon herself now—'

'Ogugua!' shouted one of the patient's attendants, as all eyes turned towards the raving woman. 'Ogugua! Stop shouting there and run for Nwosisi—your husband's wife has fainted.'

'Ehn? What did you say?'

'I said your husband's wife has fainted.'

'Did I not tell you? Have I not always—'

'Shut up and run for Nwosisi.'

The early morning smoke had now gone off the eyes of the day. Trees and houses were still wet from last night's rain, but a cool breeze caressed the world like a gentle hand.

21

Ubaka had picked up his bucket and pad for the stream and had left the house, after his father had gone, in the belief that the trouble was over. Bomboy had wanted to follow him, but Ubaka had refused to take him along because they would waste too much time and he would be late for school.

There were three other boys, his age- as well as schoolmates, with whom Ubaka was perpetually at war. The contest was playing *koso*. They all carried their *koso* wherever they went and it had become an agreed ritual that almost wherever and whenever they met they should pull these *koso* out and settle for the occasion. The contest was largely a matter of pride. These other boys came from another street, and it seriously hurt their sense of belonging that this tiny rat should prove superior to everybody else each time. One of the opposing three, a fatheaded boy, was particularly stubborn about the matter.

The procedure was spinning and balancing the *koso*—the shell of a small snail, carved into a conical shape—in a variety of styles. The penalty for defeat was losing one's *koso*. The last loser had to have his knuckles rapped in addition—probably because he was the most stubborn. The prize of victory was inflicting these rappings and claiming the forfeited *koso*.

So Ubaka was now settled in the game with his three friends on the way to the stream, they all having decided to steal a few moments before school hour for the game. Two of the boys, including the fathead, had been eliminated and Ubaka was now faced with the third. This one proved truly obstinate and refused to lose. He got a good deal of encouragement from the other two, who now menacingly crowded around Ubaka and thought to make him lose his self-control. They tugged his shirt and jogged his elbow to throw his spinnings out of order, and were annoyed when he merely smiled and spun on. If he looked up at them and protested they warned him to shut up and go on spinning or they would beat him when they got to the stream. But Ubaka went on with relative ease and

22

confidence while the other boy laboured in despair as the game drew to a close.

In the end Ubaka had outspun and outbalanced the last opponent. The loser now spread the fingers of one hand on the ground, with the knuckles close together, for Ubaka to rap. The other two tried to persuade him to refuse to be rapped, but he knew that Ubaka would beat him if it came to a fight between the two of them. So he submitted meekly and asked Ubaka to go ahead and rap. Ten strokes, and each time he snatched his hand from the ground in pain, two more.

One!

Two!

Three! The victim squirmed silently.

Four!

Five!

Six!

Seven!

'Take time, my friend!' the fathead warned Ubaka. 'Do you want to kill him? Look, remember that if you hit above the fingers you will be liable to two raps yourself.'

'I know,' Ubaka replied calmly, then 'steady your fingers!' to the victim as he spread and closed his fingers alternately to ease the pain.

'No wonder his father almost throttled his mother just now,' the fathead taunted.

'Don't mind him,' the other eliminated boy said in support. 'If he does not take his time we will do the same thing to him here now.'

Eight!

The victim winced in pain and spread his fingers. Ubaka glowered at him. As he set his hand to take the next shot the fathead jogged his arm and the *koso* fell on the ground. Ubaka spun round at him in anger.

'Be careful!' he warned.

'What have I done?' the fathead glowered back.

'Don't push my arm again!'

'Did you see me do it? Be careful yourself!'

They stared menacingly at each other for some time, until Ubaka settled back to work.

Nine!

Across the road some labourers were clearing weeds. A lean and dwarfish palmwine tapper was riding by on a rusty old bicycle whose creaking made a bell unnecessary. He was whistling merrily and familiarly.

'*Diochi!*' one of the labourers called at him.

'Eh? Eh? Eh?' the tapper clowned.

'What do they say is happening in Obanua's house?'

'He was fighting with one of his wives and she has fainted. Nwosisi has been called in to attend to her.'

Ubaka abandoned his victim and looked up when he heard this. He thought it had been all over. What was this again about fainting and Nwosisi? The *koso* dropped from his hand. The veins of his neck swelled out, and his face became painfully distorted, as tears rose and issued from his eyes. His friends had also heard the tapper's words and felt sorry for him. His victim had now snatched his hand from the ground in relief and was condoling with him profusely.

With tears streaming down his face Ubaka picked up his *koso* from the ground. His friends helped him take up the bucket and pad and hooked the bucket on his arm. They had all fought and played before and would do it over again many times. This, as well as sharing their joys and pains, was what their friendship involved.

Slowly and crying still Ubaka left them. There was no room for envy now. They all stood and stared pitifully at him as he departed with the bucket on his arm and sorrow in his heart.

The crowd outside the door had thinned down considerably. Standing around the scene now were barely the essential people. Relatively essential, that is. Neighbours still feel the call to know what is happening in one another's houses, and the faintest scream is sure to attract a number of people drawn together partly by an ungovernable curios-

24

ity and partly (probably more so) by an ancient mutual commitment. So now there were three neighbours, each with almost his entire household, and then a few more outsiders for whom the day had not fully broken. They came to about thirteen to fourteen spectators.

The 'doctor' Nwosisi felt crowded. He rubbed his eyes constantly, partly to rid them of the rheum of sleep (he had been woken out of bed) and partly to achieve enough visibility for the work he had on hand. He alternately squinted and ducked this side and that to discern how his patient reacted or to establish just where to apply the liniment. He was a goodnatured old man, but he could no longer stand the discomfort.

'Please leave the doorway and let me have some light,' he exhorted, half-angrily.

Two naked children shuffled and struggled to save enough room to go on looking.

'What is all this crowd? Do these children not have something to do at home? What kind of irresponsibility is this? Ehn? Instead of going to school or washing plates you stand around here waiting to pick some subject for gossip. Please, I want everyone to leave the doorway and let me have some light.'

Two men took it upon themselves to clear the crowd and ask the people to be about their day's work, trying to give the 'doctor' the impression that they had got the situation under control and would remain to help him if he needed them. The 'doctor' blinked unimpressed and settled down to his work, applying some liniment on the stomach of his patient.

He was not actually a doctor. He had worked as an un-skilled attendant at the local dispensary, doing such jobs as cleaning sores or washing emptied medicine-bottles or counting the tablets that came to the dispensary in regular consignments from the hospital at Benin. Sometimes he rubbed the methylated spirit on about thirty to forty upper arms before they received the vaccination cut from the sanitary inspector. As the only hand at that tiny unit who assisted the local dispenser he came very close to all aspects of the work there and came to be familiar with most of the medicines and operational outfit. But he barely knew the applications or effects of most of them. His knowledge was largely restricted to the administration of aspirin or codeine for headaches and pains, quinine for malaria, Sloans' liniment on bruised limbs, or such other details as attended the most elementary experience. So when, five years before, he had retired from active service at the age of sixty, he had smuggled away scores and scores of bandages and bottles of all sorts of pills and liquids, along with scissors, plasters and plates and such other minor items as might represent a sizeable gratuity for what he considered thirty-five long years of true service. After all, a working man must have his rewards. He could probably have smuggled a syringe as well, but he didn't know how to use it. Besides, he avoided syringes religiously. A needle had broken in his thigh in the course of an injection, and he had undergone the mortifying experience of an operation. Thereafter his contact with the instrument at the dispensary had been restricted to washing it and putting it safely away after the dispenser had used it. So now in retirement he was possessed only of the smaller items of medication and cure which he managed to buy regularly after his illegal store had been exhausted. Serious ailments were treated with medicines that were not often the most appropriate. If the patient's condition worsened he was referred to the doctor but warned—secretly and almost under a curse—*not* to reveal where he had his first treatment. But if he felt any more comfortable after Nwosisi's treatment it could probably be that the symptom was not meant to kill him anyway. . . .

Nwabunor had now regained some consciousness. She still sweated and breathed heavily, but a good deal of the agony was gone. Her face still showed what great pain she felt and her head moved this way and that from the discomfort. But at least she summoned enough strength to mutter a few inaudible words.

'Get her a cup of cold water,' Nwosisi blared out his

familiar interpretation, putting down the little bottle he had in his hand.

He stood up and looked down on his patient, rubbing his hands with relief and feeling satisfied. He paced a few steps around the troubled woman and settled down to administer the cool water, fetched by her son from the cool clay drinking pot, to her mouth. The water dripped from her quivering lips but Nwosisi held the cup firmly with his old, practised hands.

'Gently, my good child,' he comforted, 'drink it gently. You'll be alright soon. There is no trouble now, you'll be alright. Drink all of it now. That's right, my good child . . . that's right now . . . that's right. Ubaka, come and keep the cup. Your mother will be alright soon, don't cry any more. Go on and make ready to go to school, so as not to be late.'

He scanned through his pharmacy—he had brought three bottles of pills and two of liquids—and picked out a bottle of white and another of yellow tablets.

'Listen, my daughter,' he counselled Nwabunor a short while later, 'you should take two of each of these tablets first thing every morning and last thing before you go to bed at night. Don't drink too much water after them. Take just two gulps with each set of tablets. This should keep your stomach down. There is not much wrong, actually. You have a number of bad worms in your stomach and they are responsible for these convulsive pains you have been having. These tablets will see to it that the pain stops. Also, you should rub this liniment after bath every morning on your stomach. It should keep your stomach cool for the rest of the day and prevent any discomfort after some strong action. Which reminds me, you must avoid all this quarrelling and fighting that you and your husband do every day. If you think that it is alright for you to be fainting like this every time and risking your life, you can ignore my advice and do what you like. If you and your husband have any senses you had better stop all this foolishness and live like reasonable people. We don't apply an ear-pick on the eye. I have said all I want

27

to say. Goodbye. Ogugua, come and clean up all this rubbish and let your husband's wife breathe some good fresh air. Buy some *akara* and prepare her some pap—that's all she should be taking every morning until she gets well. Bomboy, my son, are you up from bed? You seem to be growing every day. What! Look at your stomach—I think you are eating too much these days! You two girls make haste and go to school . . . I am going home. Goodbye.'

'I don't know how we can thank you for all this,' said Ogugua.

'Thank me for what?' asked the old man. 'If she had died we would have been saying a different thing now. Please don't say anything about thanking me. Take care of the children, and you people should learn to be reasonable and live in peace. Goodbye.'

He had given his advice. Ogugua swallowed it with indifference, and even the sick Nwabunor knew it didn't mean much to them. Quarrelling had become a routine and it looked as if that was the only context within which a peculiar kind of peace would be maintained in the house.

Ogugua picked the pieces of cloth from the ground and set the room in relative order. She threw a token word of sympathy at the woman on the bed and went out of the room. She had expected no reply and none came to her. She went into the kitchen and served out the food to her children. But she left none for Nwabunor's son.

From far away the first school bell rang for assembly and the children hurried over their food. Outside they could hear the noise of slates and satchels as their mates ran by, and the sound of crying from the little ones left behind by their faster, impatient elders or grieved that they had not been given their penny-for-*akara*.

3

For about one year now, having given up plying the roads in the passenger transport business, Obanua had taken up a job as a driver for Umukoro & Sons Transport Ltd., a small company (the only one in the town) that handled conveyances for persons and agencies. His duties consisted largely in conveying from the quays huge loads that had been ferried across from the other side of the Niger. There were always things to convey, particularly with the early morning arrivals of stuff going as far as Agbor or Benin. He was one of about three drivers, and he was responsible for the early morning conveyances. Every one of them had to come to the yard early, register his attendance at the gate, and clean up his truck for the day's work.

Obanua's lateness was therefore easily noticeable, and as he walked the two to three miles from his house downtown to the commercial side of Ozala he had a lot of worries on his mind. He had lost a uniform once in a fight with Ogugua the younger wife, and he had explained it away to his boss as having been lost. Now he had lost a second one in another fight, and how was he to explain it? Also, he was now arriving in the yard over two hours later than he was due to be there. He had received many warnings before for countless other offences, and what would happen now?

Then he thought about his house. How much longer would this kind of thing last, to come back at night only to be challenged and fought? He could hardly even open his mouth to talk to his wives without receiving abuse in return. And he thought, why did I have to put myself into all this? Suppose I sent one of those women away? Would it not lessen my troubles?

He walked on towards the garage till he got to his truck. He had forgotten to stop at the gate to put his name down in the attendance book, but that hardly mattered now. As he tried to climb into the truck and start cleaning it he saw the boss leaning by the side with the attendance notebook in his hand and a meaningful stare in his eyes.

'Good morning, sir,' he hastened to greet, jumping down at once.

'Come into my office,' said the boss. 'I want to talk to you.'

'. . . and the principal of that school has reported that about ten of the chairs you took to the school had their legs badly broken, and—'

'But, *oga*, that was how—'

'*Sharrap!*'

'Yes sir.'

'You damage people's property that you are supposed to take to them safely, and when a report is made you open your dirty mouth to tell me that was how you found them. Were they delivered to you like that?'

'*Oga*, you can ask—'

'*Sharrap!*'

Obanua kept quiet.

'You realise this is not the first time I have had to warn you for these acts of irresponsibility? You have damaged that truck a number of times out of drunkenness and concealed the damage, and when it was later discovered you tried to deny it.'

'But, *oga*—'

'I say *sharrap!* And this morning you were trying to sneak into your truck long after you were due to report for duty. Let me warn you for the last time. If I have cause to talk to you like this again—just one more time—I am going to terminate your job. Is that clear to you?'

'Yes, sir.'

'Now take these papers. Go at once to the ferry as usual and collect thirty bales of stock-fish. They are for Mr. Oliha, the schools contractor at Agbor. Give the papers to the clerk at the ferry and he will hand over the fish to you. As soon as you collect them, drive right down to Agbor and hand everything to Mr. Oliha in perfect condition. I don't want to get any report of damage. He expects the fish before noon and make sure he gets them by then. Do you hear what I'm saying?'

'Yes, sir.'

The boss waved him off. But as he turned to go the boss called him back abruptly, and took a long look at him.

'Where is your uniform?' he asked.

Obanua was afraid.

'I said where is your uniform?'

'I forgot it, sir. I was in a hurry.'

The boss stared at him again for some time.

'Make sure it is on you when you come back this afternoon,' then more sternly, 'and you had better not fail.'

Obanua's stomach had been rumbling with hunger. He had eaten nothing since day broke, and having trekked all that distance to work there was hardly any energy left in him. The boss has said his mind, he thought, but I must find something for this stomach first. What if I die of hunger on the way? Then he hissed. And instead of driving straight to the ferry, he swung the truck towards the town, his hand quaking with hunger as sweat spotted his strained face.

For some time now he had scarcely eaten in his own house. There had been a standing system in the family whereby the two wives took weekly turns of cooking for the entire household. But this had now dwindled into meaningless theory until it finally collapsed under the weight of the jealousy between the two women. He had been unable to resolve the conflict of pride between them and now deepened it by consciously staying away in the vague belief that someday they would get over their mad-

31

ness and settle back into what reasonable housewives should be expected to do in their husband's house. Thus he thought to punish them by not giving them the monthly food allowance, expecting each instead to make an effort to support the household from the proceeds of her trade. But far from being able in this way to turn their jealousies to advantage, he only succeeded in shifting a sizeable sum of the animosities against himself while the fire of jealousy still burned between the two women. And so each of them left him completely out of account and instead laboured for the upkeep of her own side of the family, including feeding and the children's school fees.

The resultant loss of respect and authority frustrated Obanua and drove him practically out of doors. What he earned from his job was hardly enough to clothe a beggar, but even with that he now felt he could take care of himself outside while his household suffered. When he got his money at the end of the month he went to the drinking bar. He drank and gambled, playing mostly at draughts with a handful of other tramps like himself. This was where he now spent practically all his days. When his money was exhausted in this kind of indulgence he operated on credit. The woman who owned the bar, a lusty matron of unenviable morals herself, generally treated her customers with an understanding as lax as her favours and often allowed Obanua these credits, particularly as he made some effort to pay up at the end of every month. Thus he thought the drinking bar a good, safe escape from the uproar of his home. Closing his eyes seemed to give him such a good feeling, and even if the drinking bar made him, a householder of about forty-six, a drunkard and a tramp, at least it gave him some measure of security he would never have got at home. Also, even if sometimes, by accumulating so much debt, he became a nuisance to the woman of the bar, at least from her he enjoyed a much greater sympathy and understanding than he would ever get from his wives.

He braked to a halt outside the bar and got out of the truck wearily, forgetting to remove the key. The sun by now was labouring up its tiresome arch and life below moved like an old woman.

At the entrance Obanua was accosted by the little barmaid, who was sweeping the floor of her bar and shifting the tables and chairs into position. She was noted for her sharp tongue.

'What do you want again this morning?'

'Shut up,' he said. 'Where is your mistress?'

'Who is that?" the woman enquired from within.

'It is Obanua giving you greetings,' he returned.

The woman came out slowly and sighed in distaste when she saw him.

'Good morning,' she said cheerlessly. 'Are you not working today?'

He pointed wearily outside.

'Can't you see the truck?' he replied, cleaning the sweat off his brow.

Then he raised his eyes slowly up at her, craving understanding.

'What is it again?' she quickly asked.

'Have you not got something for a hungry stomach?' he made an effort to say.

'Come, what have you got wives for? How can a big bull like you be scrounging food every time? I have never seen a shameful thing like this.'

She sat down on a chair and yawned away listlessly.

'Please let us not talk about that now,' Obanua pleaded. 'Can't you give me something to bite?'

'I doubt that there is anything left. We have had our breakfast and you can hardly find anything. Aliam!' she called to the barmaid, who had disappeared into the room. 'Ma!'

'Is there any food left?'

'No, ma,' the girl hastened to reply. 'There is only one small slice of yam, but there is no soup.'

The woman looked at Obanua to bring the message home.

'You can bring that here,' he called to the girl. 'Bring the yam here with a little oil and salt. It is better than

33

nothing.' He turned to the woman, 'At least I can follow that up with some bottles. Please.' Seeing the woman's look, he sighed, 'You women will never understand.'

'Understand what?' she retorted. 'When are you going to pay up all the debt? One of these days I am going to stop you drinking anything here.'

'Alright. Alright. I've heard,' he agreed jocularly.

The barmaid brought the food. Obanua devoured it hurriedly and chased it down with the drinks. At the end he had emptied three full bottles of palmwine.

'Are you going to work today drunk?' the woman enquired.

'Is that not better than that I should die hungry?'

He cleaned his mouth hurriedly and stood up, considerably activated. He felt his pockets for the key of the truck and remembered that he had not taken it out with him. He rushed out and waved her goodbye.

'I will see you later today,' he called back.

'Don't come here without all the money you are owing,' she reminded him.

'We shall settle that when I come.'

He drove off at once towards the ferry.

The ferry officer, a thin, dwarfish Bini man of about fifty, was prancing about busily and issuing frantic directions to a lorry backing out of the newly arrived ferry-boat at the shore.

'. . . dress come here—here, here, *here!* You fool! You no sabi drive? I say *here!* Das right . . . das right. Take time—o! *Take time!* Look, you go kill people—o! Hey! You foolish woman, you no go carry your load commot for dere? Abi you de wait make motor kill you first? . . . Driver, turn your hand come dis way . . . *dis* way! Oh, God! Dis way, you fool! I no know how una de manage get licence self. I say dis way! Das right . . . sof'ly, sof'ly . . . das right . . . das right—'

'*Oga,*' Obanua interrupted him, 'I come collect something—o!'

34

'Clear out dere!' the officer shouted back. 'Make you no wahala me. Driver, turn your hand come dis way . . . das right . . . sof'ly—o! Oya, straight' am come dis way . . . das right. *Oto!* Stop for dere!'

The officer took a deep sigh and cleaned his streaming brow. The sun was hot and there was a bit of a crowd at the ferry. He turned round to confront the host of drivers and other people waving their papers at him. But he ignored them and walked straight into the little booth of an office which he shared with a couple of attendants.

Obanua hurried up to him and demanded attention.

'*Oga*, I beg you answer me first. I dey for hurry well well. I beg.'

'Wetin you want?'

'I come carry stockfish for—'

'Who sen' you?' the officer demanded.

'I come from Umukoro Transport. Look my paper.'

He stank heavily of alcohol, and the officer looked at him with disgust.

'Wetin you de do since? No be for early morning you for come carry una stockfish?'

'I know, but I beg make you—'

'Wait first for yonder. 'E get many people wey first you come. Instead wey you for come here since you dey dere de drink tombo. Make you wait yonder.'

Obanua tried further to explain, but the officer ignored him and paid attention to the drivers who wanted to cross with the next ferry.

Having failed to gain his way and discouraged at the long line of drivers that he had to wait on, he walked off to the shade of a nearby tree and sat down. And now considerably fatigued by the strains of a near-sleepless night, and with the alcohol working its effects on him, he fell into a deep slumber under the tree while the bustle went on around him . . .

Long afterwards, when the ferry had been cleared of the crowd, he was still snoring under the tree. The officer looked round and wondered.

'Wey dat man wey from Umukoro come carry stock-fish?' he asked.

'Look am de sleep yonder,' answered one of his attendants.

'De do wetin?'

''E de sleep.'

The officer shook his head and hissed.

'Come, Sule,' he called to the attendant. 'Make you run go tell 'im oga for Umukoro say dat driver wey 'e sen' here come carry stockfish de sleep. Dem go teach 'am sense today.'

It was nearly noon and would take about an hour to get to Agbor. The immediate reaction of the boss at Umukoro was to send another driver with another truck on the mission, leaving Obanua quietly to doze on awhile.

About this time schools were having their mid-day recess and the children played outside in their school grounds. It was time for the regular juvenile diversions.

There is today still the tradition among us that even though twins are born on the same occasion, the one who comes out first is the elder of the two. Triplets, quadruplets, quintuplets and the lot have not really been very common, and only God knows what private contests for seniority have been going on in all the four corners of this country. Perhaps an examination someday of this kind of situation would make interesting study of the psychologies thus generated in poor communities where inheritances have to be divided among children in the absence of a father's will.

The twins Ndidi and Ogo had stolen two tins of sardines from the stock of the sick Nwabunor. Now at recess time they had settled down to divide the loot between them. They had opened the tins with the keys.

Ndidi, the 'elder', raised her eyes rather nervously and saw the look of unyielding concentration that Ogo's face wore.

'Why are you staring like that?' she asked.

'How am I staring?' Ogo replied.

36

'You are staring as if you have never seen sardines before.'

'Alright.'

For Ogo that was not the most important issue. Ndidi looked down again at the tins, fumbling around them, knowing what challenge she was sure to meet with if she tried anything unacceptable to the other. Then she began to divide the sardines, removing some from one tin and placing them into the other.

'What are you doing?' Ogo challenged her.

'What do you mean what am I doing?'

'Why are you removing those pieces from their tin?'

'Do you expect me to divide them equally?'

'Why not?'

'Why? Am I not senior to you?'

'And then? Did we not take the two tins at the same time? If it comes to that, was I not the one who took them alone by myself while you just waited and looked?'

'What does that matter?'

'It matters a great deal,' Ogo insisted.

'You don't know what you are talking about,' Ndidi said, and tried to snatch the overloaded tin.

But Ogo was quickly at her. She grabbed Ndidi by the hand and a few sardines fell out of the tin and dropped on the sand.

'You see what you have done?' Ndidi stared menacingly at Ogo.

'I have done nothing. It's your fault.'

A struggle ensued. Ndidi tried to fill up her tin from the other one she had left for her sister, but Ogo held her again by the hand. In the scuffle one tin was overturned and all the sardines poured out onto the sand. In anger Ndidi overturned the other tin and all the sardines were wasted. They were about to resort to their fists when the noon angelus announced the end of the recess.

At the end of the working day, about five o'clock in the evening, the boss called Obanua into his office. He wore a

37

solemn look on his face, while Obanua stood with tremulous feet in front of his table and took all the message.

'It was only this morning I warned you,' the boss said, 'and it seems to me that my words did not get into your ears. Well, I do not think it will serve any purpose—'

'I beg you, sir, it was because—'

'Let me finish,' the boss cut back sharply, looking sternly up at the driver. 'I have given you too many warnings and I don't think I am prepared to give you another.' He tapped his pencil on his desk a number of times and stared at Obanua. 'Is there any reason why I should send you down to do some work and you go off to sleep while the business suffers? And the officer at the ferry reported that you were stinking of alcohol, this morning', emphasising the point, 'this morning, as early as that, when you were supposed to be doing some work, and knowing full well you were running late? Is there any reason?'

'Myself? I never took a drop of wine, sir.'

The boss squinted at him.

'Can you swear to that?'

'I swear to God, sir, I—'

'Alright. I am sorry there is nothing I can do about that. You have been caught several times drinking while at work, and on more than two occasions you have been involved in accidents arising from drunkenness. In any case you have no reason to go sleeping when you were supposed to be on your way to Agbor.'

'There were so many—'

'Alright,' the boss waved him off. 'It's all over. Go over there and let the cashier pay you your money. From today on you have ceased to be a driver for the company.'

As Obanua walked away from the premises with the three pounds ten shillings in his hands there were a lot of uncertainties in his mind. He was walking homewards though he wasn't sure if that was the best way to go, thinking, Had I not better go away somewhere, rather than meet more trouble at home? He wondered how he was going to spend this money, knowing that even if he forebore to take it to the bar to pay his debts or spend it the best way he now knew how and decided to take it home he

38

was going to run into the problem of how he was going to share it between his wives. Besides, even the latter came last in his considerations of what was to be done with the money. He knew he had to be very careful with it, now that he had lost his job and there was hardly any other way of coming across money but by theft.

Twilight was now slowly and imperceptibly stealing in. This was about the time that birds sing their last songs, and mothers start chasing their adventurous little ones back to their nests, and the palm trees again assume a kind of enforced quiet.

'Papa is back! Papa is back!' chanted Bomboy innocently, jumping for joy as he did and running up to meet his father. 'Papa is back! Papa is back!'

'Let us hear something else,' his mother shouted at him from the back of the house. 'Is it such a great thing?' settling down again to peeling the yams and murmuring, thinking aloud, I wonder what is so encouraging about that.

Obanua stepped into the house grunting reluctant and effortful responses to his son's words of welcome while the little boy tugged at his hand in filial joy.

'Papa, where are my sweets?'

'Didn't you see it rained today? I asked the little girl selling the sweets and she said the rain fell and spoiled them.'

Bomboy sulked in disappointment.

'Alright, what about the shoes you promised me,' he said.

'Shoes? Oh, shoes. I went to the shop and they said they didn't have your size. So you will have to wait for some time longer. Stop worrying about shoes.'

'I won't agree. I won't agree,' Bomboy sobbed.

'I said stop worrying about shoes. Will the world end if you don't have any shoes?' Then he looked sternly at the little boy and asked, 'Who tore your jumper?'

Bomboy looked down in embarrassment, fumbling with a corner of his jumper.

'I am asking you, who tore it?' Obanua repeated.

He was nibbling at his lower lip and some amount of tautness played upon his brow. A bit of indignation crept into him, not so much because the little boy's rascality deserved such ready showdown as out of general disappointment with the fortunes of today and particularly because he was being required to give away now when the need to preserve had never been greater.

'Won't you tell me?' he shook the boy's arm.

'Okuchi—Okuchi—Okuchi wanted to make trouble with me, and it was he who pushed me first, and I—and I told him, Okuchi leave me alone, but he refused to leave me alone, and—and he pushed me, he pushed me again, and I did not touch him, and he kept pushing—pushing me, and I fell down, and he dirtied my jumper, and he tore it, and—and—'

'Who is Okuchi?' Obanua threw in.

'Okuchi—Okuchi is a certain boy, and he has been wanting to make trouble with me for a long time, and I did not—I did not—'

'Alright,' his father cut him short, an unkind stare in his eyes. 'If all you are going to be doing is fighting and getting your clothes torn, then carry on. But don't come asking me to buy anything more for you. Do you hear that?'

He gave the boy a push on the head towards the backyard where his mother was, and walked away. He hardly felt the need to acquit himself pleasantly with the boy. On the contrary, he did not wish to bother himself with this little problem when he had more serious things to worry about.

Bomboy was overwhelmed with sadness and began to cry. He got no comfort from his mother, who merely mocked him and said, 'I told you there was nothing to be happy about.'

Obanua walked into his room and took off his cap. Then he pulled off his shirt and flung it over the line of clothes

40

above his bed. Under the grudging and disappearing light of dusk he briefly surveyed his body and found that he was very dirty. He was very hungry also, but he knew he dared not ask for food. He sat down wearily on the edge of the bed to pull off his shoes and looking briefly at the floor he saw a number of articles scattered about on it with disturbing carelessness: an overturned plate, a rubber ball, an empty sardine-can apparently used in mock cooking, and an old adult shoe, laceless and with its leather instep yawning away from the sole, that had probably been used in playing 'parent'. He shook his head. Then he pushed his shoes under the bed and rose. As he was about to leave the room his eyes caught some movement on the other bed, and he stopped and fixed his gaze on the object that had looked like a mere heap of cloth when he had entered the room.

The bed was at a corner of the room dimly concealed by the darkness that was now creeping in slowly and furtively amid the odours of the evening and the cries of the insects and the geckos. He drew closer and looked down. He saw that it was his first wife Nwabunor, but he could not understand what she would be doing in bed so early. He turned away with a mere grunt, swallowing the spittle that now blocked his throat, thinking, Better let her lie on. I've had enough already. But before he got to the door his mind told him he should make her explain, though he knew he had to be very careful about this if he didn't want the day to end the way it had begun.

'Nwabunor. Nwabunor,' he called.

But there was no reply, and all she did was turn on the other side. By the side of the bed was a small stool and on top of it were a plate with a spoon in it and a half-empty cup of water.

'Nwabunor!'

She merely coughed and drew the cloth properly over her. Some cold ran through his hands and feet and his nerves were a little disturbed. He knew he could not do much even if he wanted to because he was very hungry and very tired. Besides, he had had enough trouble already.

So he gave up asking and turned to go. Just then he heard the voice of Ubaka, standing by the door.

'She is not well.'

Ubaka's voice was soft and reluctant, for he was afraid to say anything that might bring down his father's wrath once more upon his mother.

'Not well?' Obanua asked. 'What is wrong with her?'

Ubaka did not reply, and his heart beat a little faster as his hands sketched invisible figures on the door-post.

'What do you say is wrong with your mother? Are you not the one I am asking?'

'She has been lying down since morning,' Ubaka replied.

'Since morning?'

Ubaka looked up, but quickly avoided his father's menacing glare and continued his sketching. It dawned on him that further explanation would involve putting a blame on somebody, and he dreaded the prospect of a re-enactment of the terrors of this morning when every blow that fell on his mother seemed directed at his own heart. So he ventured no further explanation, and amid the shiver of his nerves and the plunk-plunk of his heart he prayed that it would all be over and his mother be left alone.

A few yards away a hurricane lamp, with part of the globe broken off, was standing on a bench. There was a mild breeze blowing but the thin flame shook fervidly describing elusive shadows on the boy's face, placid and unresponsive but saying much more in its placid unresponse than any verbal explanation could have done.

Obanua looked at the boy again, then at his mother, and shook his head, thinking, Was it for this I set up a home, to mean so little in it? But before he left the room he told the boy 'Go and get me some bathing water, quick.'

Right from behind in the room came another voice, much more insistent.

'Ubaka!'

'Ma!' shook the boy.

'What are you doing there?'

Obanua stopped in his steps, surprised.

'I asked him to get me water for a bath,' he said, looking back into the room with the wonder still in his eyes. 'What is the matter? Was it not you I was talking to just a while ago and you wouldn't say a word?'

She ignored him completely.

'Ubaka!' she insisted. 'Is it not you I am asking?'

'Ma! What is it?'

'Come here at once, you accursed child! Hear him asking me what is it. I say what are you doing there?'

'Papa said I should get—'

'Have you brought in the clothes you hung outside?'

'Yes, ma.'

'What have you done about your food for tonight?'

'Nothing, ma.'

'Alright, go on quickly and put some yam on the fire.'

'Alright. But let me finish—'

'Listen to me, you wretch! I say go and put some yam on the fire at once—and don't you open your rotten mouth to tell me you are doing anything else. Do you hear what I am telling you?'

'Yes, ma,' Ubaka replied, reluctantly and after a brief interval during which he tried to weigh which voice represented the more serious threat and which laid more pressing claims to his loyalty. At least for the moment.

For ever since he came back from school today there had been a worry on his mind. His fees had still not been paid and the headmaster had threatened to expel him from school. Telling this to his father was enough of a problem, and it was now being made more serious by his mother's continued intransigence. But he imagined he could still improve matters for himself. So dodging his mother's order he ran stealthily to the backyard, grabbed a bucket and set down the water for his father.

He then came back and confronted his father, who was still not undressed for a bath but was pacing this way and that, as if trying to make up his mind on something. Before his movements took him back to his room Ubaka informed him that the water was ready.

Obanua went into the room and came out again, still

43

not undressed. Outside Ubaka waited for him, trying to work out the best way to put his request.

'Papa,' he finally ventured.

'Hm? What is it?' Obanua replied. He suspected he was not being waylaid for nothing.

'I—we—I—the headmaster told me about my fees today.'

'And what about your fees?'

'He said he would send me out of school if I didn't pay up.'

'Is he the owner of the school? Don't trouble me with yet another problem, do you hear me?'

'Papa, everybody has paid but me.'

'Tell him you can't pay yet!' Obanua said emphatically. 'He doesn't eat people. But why don't you ask your mother? I thought she owned you.'

'She says she has no money.'

'And you think I have? Please don't trouble me—I don't want to go to bed tonight thinking about your fees.'

He left the boy distressed.

Obanua still hadn't had his bath. But to him that was not the most important thing now. He thought he should go across to his second wife, Ogugua, to seek an explanation why Nwabunor had been lying in bed since morning. He did not seriously believe that he would be able to extract it. It was merely a way of making a few last weary attempts to reassert an authority he knew was now slipping completely away from him.

When he got to her in the kitchen he found her eating with her three children, and a feeling of cold, gutless anger flashed across his brow.

'What's wrong with Nwabunor?' he asked her.

She merely took her time with the food.

'Ogugua, I'm asking you a question.'

'Hm-m?' she drawled. 'What did you say?'

'I said what's wrong with Nwabunor?'

There was a brief silence. She still took her time answering him.

'Am I really the best person to answer that question?' she said at last, not even looking at him.

'I am asking you.'

'About your wife?'

'I'm asking you all the same. Hasn't that got into your head yet?'

'But she is your wife? Why don't you ask her? Why ask me?'

He stared at her. That was all he could do. The air was motionless between them.

'I think you are very selfish and very wicked,' he said weakly at last.

'And I think you are a very shameless man,' she retorted, springing up smartly before him.

'Very selfish and very wicked,' his voice sounded subdued in comparison.

'And I say you are a very shameless man. You almost beat your wife to death and leave her fainting behind you, and you have the mouth to ask me to tell you what is wrong with her. I am quite satisfied taking care of myself and my own children, and God bring fire upon whoever wants me to put my head into what does not concern me. I say you should be ashamed of yourself.'

When she got no further reply she settled down again to eating with her children.

He had no energy for the encounter. So he carefully withdrew and took a chair and sat outside in the full darkness, thinking, And they still have to learn that I have lost my job, and then I won't even have to open my mouth to be shouted down. He thought of the several things he was now liable to suffer with the loss of a job. But what came uppermost in his mind was not really his complete loss of respect in his own house. Somehow that did not seem to matter to him all that seriously. It was, instead, the danger that he would at last lose his credit at the drinking bar, which after all supplied a valid change and exchange for a domestic situation he could hardly bear.

He still hadn't had his bath. But now he was sure he wouldn't be needing it, for he was making up his mind to go where he wouldn't be needing it. He rose from the chair and went into his room and put on some fresh clothing, making sure to transfer the money as well. At least this is one thing I can hold on to, he thought.

Outside, the night was silent with an uncommunicative darkness that was belied and at the same time emphasised by the screeching of little creatures, the lurking of snakes, the smell of dewdamp leaves and of clay drinking-pots smoked by burning palm tinder, and all the countless other things that constitute the delights and the terrors of the night. This was the night that he was now preparing to go into, confident that at least he would not have to be beaten on the head before he went to sleep, or worry which wife cursed the other last or which was to blame for letting the other's clothes hang outside long enough to be prize for the midnight thief.

'And I think that one day you will have to tell me what put you onto painting your nails,' Obanua ventured as he left.

'And I think too that one day you will have to tell me when you became man enough to worry about my looks,' Ogugua spat back at him instantly, slamming the door with all vehemence behind his back.

4

It was so very dark this night that if you listened hard enough you would probably not hear anything beyond the pained shrieking of insects and the dismal cry of the vagabond cat as the adder gripped his leg in her jaws. Maybe if you listened harder still you would even catch the sound as two owls nodded and knocked their skulls in agreement over what home should be the next victim of their visitation, or moaned in disappointment over the operations of the night before. You would know that it was very late in the night and certainly not the best time for a sensible human being to be about, even if he thought that by whistling or singing aloud he could scare off the spirits and all other agents that thrive in the dark.

The two old women were still outside their hut. The night was very cold. The first woman had made a fire outside the hut and was seated before it with her arms folded across her shoulders while two cobs of corn and four pears roasted in the heat. The little black she-cat was also taking advantage of the warmth and now indulged her characteristic feline euphoria by rubbing the length and breadth of her body many times against the leg of the old woman, until the spot felt too warm and she instinctively pushed the cat away. The other cat, the one-eyed male, was huddled up in his compact and diminutive size away on top of a mud dais in the foreroom of the hut. When he saw the plight of his companion he blinked coldly away as though in an unsympathetic notice that that was what she got from flirting too much with humans.

The second woman was battling with some troublesome

47

problem. Her goat had apparently lost the only kid she had and was bleating disconsolately and running all over the neighbourhood looking for it. This worried the old woman too. She joined the goat in the search, complaining, 'I still cannot understand why a little kid who hasn't yet left his mother's teats should stray so far. And it worries me too what kind of goat it is that does not understand that she should keep her only baby at her side wherever she happens to be. This is one more mischief from the hands of Mgbushe, heaven knows she never lacks for one. When I went to buy a goat from her and she offered me this one I took one good look at it and told her this wasn't a good goat, but she said, Take my word for it, this is the best goat I have in the whole herd, and if you ever find her otherwise send her back to me and I will give you your money back. And now I know that this goat is no use and is worse than a bitch and my mind tells me to send her back to Mgbushe. Only she has been very kind, bleeding my back these last few days when death nearly made sport of me . . . E-hen! Here he comes! There's that devil of a kid! Come here . . . come here . . . accursed thing! Wish you had broken a leg straying thus far and bringing such agony on my aged bones. . .'

She waved both mother and baby, much less with anger now than characteristically with an owner's injured affection, into the little hut where human and beast shared shelter, feeling the satisfaction creep into her that their lonely little world had got over that momentary stress and all was well again within its confines.

'These animals are troublesome,' the first woman said in sympathy. 'One could break one's bones trying to chase after them. And then the question wouldn't be asked what brought about the misfortune, but how it came about that such aged limbs went romping about like a baby antelope. But God be praised.'

The fire was warm and welcome and the corn was sweet. But the night was dark and mysterious in its near-starless gloom. Presently the one-eyed cat sprang lithely down from his roost and took his place near the fire also, but making sure not to bother anyone. All other human activity was now retired and silent, and the two old women were alone, crouching before a fire on a cold night, dank and dark, with their corn and their cats, exchanging reminiscences and fears. A fair distance away in a grassless expanse stood a towering iroko tree and from it issued the long wail of an owl.

'I don't like that sound,' said the first woman, stopping between chews to hear the diminuendo. 'It usually comes well after midnight when all that has to be done has been done, but it's scarce midnight yet and I'm worried to hear it.'

'I'm worried too,' the second woman agreed. 'It makes me think there's been a rush, but otherwise I should have thought the day has been as it has always been.'

'You're right. I'd like to know where these birds are going though.'

They resumed their chewing. A grain fell down near the she-cat and she turned her head and smelled it over but left it alone. The first woman looked at her with a kind of doting understanding, stroking her a number of times until she was stirred up by the voice of her sister.

'I see our neighbours have just lighted a lamp. Can he have come back?'

'Come back! How could you ask a question like that, when you and I have constantly watched his movements and know he hardly gets home but the whole neighbourhood knows about it? No, I think it could only be that the sick one needs a drink of water or somebody wants to go out and urinate. I think he is a long way from even thinking about coming home. Did you notice the way he left the house early tonight?'

'Yes, I did,' said the second woman.

'I think too that you and I are going to be wanting to stretch our weary bones in sleep sooner than he is likely to be coming home. I think he'll be away a good while yet.'

'So, indeed. Who would blame him? It looks to me as if he has come to prefer it outside, seeing how every bit of his floor is strewn with thorns.'

49

'Who put them there but he? I would have thought that if a fisherman aims to go out to the middle of the river hoping to cast his net and control his canoe at the same time he should have fed well and made the cloth fast about his loins. I think he will have a good deal of trouble yet. And it looks to me as if there is something he hasn't had a good look at yet.'

'And what would that be?'

'Have you noticed anything about his second wife lately?'

'I have always doubted that she is a good woman and from stories I hear in the market she seems to have taken after her mother.'

'But have you noticed anything lately yet on your own?'

'Not particularly.'

'Sister, sister,' the first woman said, 'how you amaze me! But you and I have been under this roof for God knows how long now and been watching the sport of these younger things—that's all our aging minds can feed on now. The young woman has taken to doing herself up elegantly and seeking attention outside. I am quite sure I am not deceived by the look of things. I have not been too happy on a number of occasions that I have seen her coming home late in the evening and looking like a spinster who has had a good day at the market. Sister, sister, these women are surely something! Let us both keep a close watch yet, but I think the feeling has got into her that she has got to reap her crops now before the floods come and the whole harvest is carried away, and then it will be too late to try.'

'True. True. Very true indeed.'

They had long finished their corn and their pears. The cats were dozing away hunched up like live dolls near the fire. Even the fire was now dying out gradually as the sticks burnt away leaving crumbling skeletal contours of ash on blinking red coals. The first woman packed in fresh sticks and stoked the fire a number of times until lively flames burst up in the wake of a thin skyward sheet of smoke. Then she picked up her snuff bottle from her lap and stuffed three generous fingerfuls of the powder into her gums, grimacing under the effect. Her sister fell into a meditative posture, head downwards, hands clasped between outstretched legs, like an aged priestess deep in prayer.

'And you saw what happened to the elder wife today?' the first woman asked.

'Mm.'

'Poor woman. All that beating, even were she a toad. What could she have told her spirit had Nwosisi not run to her rescue! To think that—Sister! Sister!'

'Mm? . . . mm?!' the second woman stirred frantically.

'Wake up, wake up! Can't you feel your cloth burning? Or have you lost all feeling too?'

'Forgive me, dear,' lying, 'but I heard the last thing you said. I must have just been carried off.'

'I think running after that wretched kid has taken the strength off you.'

'That is true. Very true.'

The fire was dying out again. But this time neither of them cared to bring it alive any more. The last bits of dry wood crackled heroically out and a creeping languor settled over the scene.

'I think we had better go to sleep,' the first woman said. 'But I've been longing all night to do one thing and before I retire I would very much like to see it through.'

'And what would that be?' asked her sister.

'I still want to see which way these owls are flying tonight.'

The policeman stamped into the bar and, at the doorstep, knocked the sand off his boots. He was wearing very heavy rain boots and also had across his back his thick black policeman's raincoat. He was a huge man. When he walked his body was all friction and his limbs described a wide area of control, and his voice compelled attention. He had thick, rough lips bulging out ahead of a set of heavy, sooty grinders, a big nose with large nostrils and bristles sticking

51

out of them, and reddish, weary eyes with heavy brows standing over them in a grisly hood. He was the kind that mothers threaten to invite when their children will not stop crying.

This night he was returning from a special duty that had taken him to a village a few miles away from Ozala. The night was very cold, very deep and dark, and as he came to town and rode towards home on his bicycle he thought he should stop over at the bar and refresh himself briefly, though it was very far in the night and the bar was likely to be shut or at least empty of company.

And now coming into the bar he found it was indeed empty except for two people. On one of the benches was a man sprawled in all his length, and but for the regular rise and fall of his breast he could be taken for dead. At a corner of the room the barmaid was busy gathering empty bottles and cups and cleaning up the tables and chairs that were now in a mess. There was a peculiar kind of atmosphere about the place. Peculiar because even in spite of its quiet there was a certain air of peacelessness, for the room looked like the scene of a pelting match with a number of broken items lying here and there and one of the benches bearing what looked like a casualty. And it looked as if the rest of the contestants had just left the scene.

As he pulled off his raincoat the policeman revealed his uniform. Looking up the barmaid saw this and, frightened, dropped and broke one of the glasses she had in her hand. She was still quavering between the impulse to scream and the compulsion to explain when the policeman addressed her.

'Be careful, *titi*,' he said. 'Don't let those things cut your feet. What's the matter?'

The girl's heart was beating fast. There was hardly any sound around. The night was dark and deep, too dark and deep for her to even want to scream or attempt a ready explanation.

'Why are you so afraid?' the policeman spoke again. 'Have you never seen me here before?'

He threw his raincoat upon one of the chairs, and ground towards the figure spread out on the bench. He shook its head a couple of times, then tugged at its collar with professional gruffness. Obanua grunted coarsely in response and laboured up on his haunches with dull, wondering eyes. He looked up, gazed hazily and briefly at the two figures that stood in what looked to him like a crowded wrestling ground with hostile spectators. Then he dropped his head again, as though daunted by what he saw. A kind of confused thought harried his brain as from palm-nuts or pebbles raining ceaselessly down on a roof or a crowd of sticks rattling a mad dance, and when the two figures talked the conversation laced through his confused mind with only a few occasional phrases registering.

'What happened to him?' asked the policeman. 'Why is he like this? Has there been a fight?'

The girl was still very much afraid.

'Won't you answer me? I said what happened?'

'It was all his fault,' the girl hurried to explain, breathless. 'He caused it all. He started the fight.'

'What fight?' the policeman insisted.

'He comes in here every day, and every day he gets into trouble with people,' the girl swallowed quickly, still breathing hard from fear. 'He had been owing us for a long time, and this night he walked into the bar and demanded drinks but would not pay his debt, and my mistress told him to pay up his debt, that otherwise there would be no drinks for him in this bar tonight, and he wanted to force us to let him, and he went forward and grabbed a bottle of palmwine to himself, but my mistress refused firmly, and told him—' she swallowed again '—and told him he would certainly not take anything until he had paid his debt first, and when he saw that my misstress meant it, he put his hand in his pocket and brought out some money, but that was not enough, and my mistress still refused to let him take anything, so he put his hand in his pocket again and brought out the rest of the money, so my mistress took the money and let him sit down and be served, but she warned him that he would have to pay

53

for all that he was intending to drink tonight, so he sat down and started drinking, and he drank very many bottles and kept asking for more, and my mistress was afraid he was drinking more than he could pay for, and warned him that he was not going to leave the bar tonight without paying for all he was drinking, but he would not listen and kept on drinking, and shortly after some men came in with whom he usually plays draughts, and he had been owing them for past games that he had lost, and they asked him to pay up, and he asked them to hold on, that he would pay later, but the men insisted and forced him to pay his debt, but he said he was going to recover the money in no time, so they settled down and started playing, and when he noticed that he was losing too many games he started to make trouble, and when they began to argue he overturned the draughts-board, and the man with whom he was playing became very angry, and they began to fight—' she blew her nose and cleaned it with the edge of her cloth '—they began to fight and to destroy many things, until people came up and separated them, and my mistress asked them to leave her bar, and those other men left and went home, but he would not go home, so my mistress threatened to send for the police, but other people begged her to leave him alone, and he sat down and started to drink again, until he got drunk and began to make a lot of noise, and to say that he owned this bar, and that if my mistress talked any nonsense he was going to buy up the bar, and after buying it set fire to it, and burn it down with everything in it, including me and my mistress, and that we would then have no more wine to sell, but would go about the streets begging, but my mistress did not pay him any attention, and nobody—' she swallowed again '—nobody paid him any attention, and he was very drunk and was going from this place to that, until he started to molest the wife of one of the other people, he went up to her and put his hand around her neck, and began to kiss her on the cheeks and to call her his wife, and the husband of the woman told him, Look here you drunkard leave that woman alone before I lay you on the floor, and he replied,

Shut up who asked you to speak for this woman don't you know that she is my wife, and he asked the woman, Is that not so, and the woman said yes, just to humour him, and he was happy, but he would not leave the woman alone, and he started to rub her body, and to rub her breasts, and the husband of the woman grew annoyed and got up and pushed him away, and he grabbed a tumbler and hit the man on the head with it, and the man grew very angry and turning round grabbed a stool and knocked him hard on the head with it, and he fell down and fainted—'

'Do you know who these people are?' the policeman interrupted.

'No, I don't know them, but they have been here before, this was not their first time, they have been here before, but he was the one who caused the fight, you can ask anybody.'

She stopped and stared at him, still afraid. The policeman took a look at the figure sitting on the bench with his head dropping down and occasionally bobbing up again in a belch or a hiccup.

'Let me have a bottle of palmwine,' he said, looking away casually from Obanua. 'I hope there is still some left.'

The girl immediately hurried in and brought forth a bottle of palmwine, and set it down before the policeman. She was still not sure what he wanted, coming in so late in the night, and she was too frightened to do anything but watch and wonder. She was thinking, He has probably heard of it, and that will be the end of mama and me. She stood cautiously away from the policeman, staring tremulously at him and wondering what he was likely to do now. She had even forgotten that she was cleaning the place up.

The policeman took a long, full draught and swallowed, waiting for the drink to reach down well. Then he belched heavily and nodded a couple of times, feeling satisfied with the results. He looked again at the figure on the bench. But he did not think that the man deserved any serious

attention. He merely looked at him in a kind of blank concentration, more now with the policeman's intuitive
indifference at the sight of a drunkard than with any faint
desire to take official action on a tramp who was merely
one of too many.

So he merely looked away from Obanua, unperturbed
and more interested in the cup before him.

'And are you going to let him stay here all night, here
in your bar?' he asked, rising from his chair and putting
his hand in his pocket, making to bring out something
that in the frightened imagination of the girl was as likely
to be a whistle or note and pencil as money for the drink.

'I don't know . . . no. He always rises to go when he
has come to his senses and his eyes are clear. And my mistress—I heard her saying that if he didn't leave this place
and find his way home before long she was going to send
for the police, but that was before she—'

She stopped abruptly, uncertain and afraid, as if her
stream of thought had been drained in one quick, magical
draught by the policeman's quizzical stare or as if the instinct that prompted the explanation had been frozen in
one sudden stroke of self-reproach. Perhaps she thought
she was talking too much. The prospect of her mistress
forcing her to sleep outside, as often, because she was
'chattering volubly like a fowl whose rump had been
sprinkled with pepper' frightened her as much as that of
them both getting into trouble with the police. So she kept
suddenly quiet, though still afraid.

'Before she did what?' asked the constable. 'Where is
your mistress?'

The girl made no reply.

'You said that she threatened to call the police for him
before she did something. What was it she did after she
said that? Hm? Where is she?'

The girl still didn't say anything. And now she watched
as the officer took his hand from his pocket and paced
slowly towards the door leading into the room. The door
was left half-open, and only a dark, worn curtain concealed
what little privacy there was inside. The officer drew this

aside and looked in, but before he stepped in he looked back at the girl.

'Go ahead and do what you are doing. But look outside first and make sure that my bicycle is still there.'

Then he went in.

The night was dark and cold. There was hardly any noise within earshot except that of a tribe of toads exchanging endless love-calls and a few other creatures that seemed to enjoy saying whatever it was they were saying . . .

Why don't you take your time, dear?

I am taking my time, dear.

The girl took a peep outside and carried on with her work. She now did it with a new spirit, inspired by a feeling of relief. She knew there was nothing to be afraid of now, nothing to fear from the policeman any longer.

'Obanua! Obanua!' she shook the stooping figure on the bench. 'Obanua! Wake up and go home. Do you hear me? I say wake up and go home.'

'Leave me alone, you—you foolish girl,' he babbled. 'Of course I hear you. Why should I not—hear you. Don't —bother me, you—foolish girl.'

He spat squalidly on the ground. Then he rose unsteadily and ran the back of his hand across his slimy mouth, his legs shaking like those of an unbalanced doll and nearby figures making multiple images before his eyes. He was giddy and insensible, and had lost the power to decide whether or not to go home, wherever home might be. It was as if he stood, half-awake and half-asleep, unfeeling yet alive, insensible of all that was taking place around him and more or less waiting for his mind to be made up for him, like a sheep that had been suddenly knocked up in mid-slumber and stands still in a stolid gaze, until chased into its pen with a broom. And before he knew what was happening he had lost his balance and fallen down, unsettling a nearby table from which two aluminium cups fell to the ground.

'Get up and go away from here, you foolish drunkard,' the barmaid screamed at him. 'Go home before I split your head with a bottle.'

57

'Aliam, what is the matter? What is wrong?' her mistress called from within.

'Ma?'

'I say what is happening?'

'It is Obanua. He still doesn't want to go home, and he is about to destroy everything here.'

'Leave the wretch there. He will soon come to his senses and go away. If he tries to be a nuisance any more pour some cold water upon him. You hear me? Pour some cold water upon him.'

'Yes, ma,' and turning to Obanua the maid threatened, 'Go home now. Go home before I drench you with a pail of cold water.'

Obanua scrambled stupidly up. Some amount of the daze and inaction had been shaken out of him.

'Touch—touch me—touch me and you will see,' he fumbled.

'All right,' said the girl, 'you stay there and watch.'

She scurried off in mock fury to a corner of the room, shuffling a bucket with the same mock intent and feeling quite sure that the trick would work with the drunken man as it had done many a time before. And it did. For Obanua scrambled for his cap from nearby and staggered out of the room in a kind of panic, spitting and cursing everybody that had anything to do with the bar and still swearing that one day he was going to tear the place down.

So he began to head homewards. This was not because he thought that home was the logical place to go after a man was through with whatever it was that kept him outside so late. He could not reason now. More than anything else he was being pushed home by the natural instinct that an animal has for its habitat. If he could bring himself to think, he would not want to go home. But now no place of escape could well be contemplated under such giddy circumstances.

Everywhere was quiet and dark with terror. But he was hardly afraid. The instinct of fear was as lost to him as terror itself. He staggered on and sang and fell and laughed. And when he finally got home, there was cursing

58

and commotion enough to rouse even the most stony
sleeper.

> . . . *Open the door before I tear your jaws apart!*
> *Go ahead and do that!*
> *Do you hear me, you beast!*
> *You will still find your drink if you go back!*
> *Open the do-o-o-r!* . . .

5

After one of those eternal conflicts between parent and child (this time after he had refused to take his morning bath), Bomboy sat sulking at the foot of the main door. Close by also sat their neighbours' black she-cat, purring demurely and peacefully and with the unruffled confidence of a creature that belonged where it lay. On the floor right in front of her lay a tiny broomstick that a few moments earlier had offered no possibilities of harassment. Bomboy's eyes fell casually on the stick and, for lack of anything else to engage his attention, tried to pick it up. As he did so the stick twirled briskly on the floor and drew the attention of the cat who, probably unaware of the human agency behind the action, tried to rap the nuisance down before it could grow out of control. Bomboy frowned at the opposition but smiled at the sudden reflection that this could be a fine thing for a game and to tease the cat with. So he twirled the stick on the floor again, and again the cat rapped it back. This time he smiled at his intelligent discovery that what really excited the cat was the flickering movement of the stick. So he picked it up and flashed it a few times before the eyes of the cat. Again the animal stared and rapped, and again the boy grinned with joy and satisfaction. He thus continued his joyful experiment, until the cat became quite worried and could do nothing but lean slightly back with one hand at the ready while she let her eyes follow the movement of the stick with magnetic alertness, occasionally jabbing at it.

This went on until the cat grew sick of it all and gave up trying, dismissing it as one more piece of human fancy that represented no serious threat to her well-being. But the boy was not through yet. He tried to tease the cat into another spell of the tournament by pricking her sides with the broomstick. The animal endured this for a little while until it became more than a joke. This was no longer a dance you could afford to do with the pipe in your mouth. She became aggressive, turned swiftly round and engaged the stick in a furious and desperate struggle to end all struggles. To the boy this was something good. He kept indulging his innocent mischief until the cat could do no more than growl wildly in pain, yet refusing to shift her ground as though firmly convinced that she had every right to stay where she was.

Just back from the stream, Ubaka had emptied the water in his bucket into the drum at the backyard and, on getting to the door, was gripped with awed pity as he saw the poor creature subjected to this bit of sadism. Behind him their little dog stared with speechless indifference.

'Bomboy!' shouted Ubaka.

The little boy shook with fright.

'What are you doing to that cat?'

'She is refusing to play.'

'But she doesn't want to play with you. Why don't you stop hurting the poor thing?'

'I am not hurting her.'

'Well leave her alone. She doesn't want to play with you. Someday you will have to say what you have seen in the body of this cat. Give me that stick.'

Ubaka snatched the stick away and the little boy began to cry. From somewhere in the back of the house came the stern voice of Bomboy's mother warning Ubaka to leave her child alone and not molest the poor thing this morning. This rather hurt Ubaka who, used though he was to the domestic warfare, endeavoured with all juvenile purity to keep his fraternal love above the storm. God knows I meant no harm, he thought. And bending down over his weeping brother he tried to clean his eyes and cuddle his head against his breast.

'I am sorry. I am sorry' he consoled. 'I only wanted you

to leave the cat. Don't you know she belongs to those two women? Papa says they are witches and fly about at night looking for people who have wronged them. If you hurt the cat they will fly in here in the middle of the night and scratch out your eyes. Do you want your eyes scratched out by witches?'

Bomboy shook his head.

'So leave this cat alone. She is a witch-cat, you hear?'

The other nodded.

'Come, take this pear. Do you want to accompany me to the work place?'

Bomboy nodded as he fondled the pear in his hand.

'Alright. After food we shall go together, you hear?'

That did it. Together they left the place. All this while the cat had resumed her peaceable pose, but still kept on the alert just in case all that human dialogue was being used in planning new strategy. When her enemy finally departed some kind of peace, however transient this might turn out to be, settled around her. The little dog, with whom she had a never-ending score, sniffed jealously and shuffled menacingly around her but departed anyway. This time the cat felt truly free. She stretched her limbs full-length, licked herself neatly over, drew a wide, toothy yawn, then carefully adjusted her sitting posture as though thoroughly satisfied with this vindication of her civil rights. . .

Slowly, reluctantly, the raw freshness of the early morning was giving way to a kind of creamy wanness, as of a stray and much-weakened aura of light setting furtively in where smoke had all but cleared. Even the calmness looked uncanny and unreal. Out in the distance an iroko tree rose tall, superior and awesomely alone, like a raped priestess. Around her at a reverent radius a few houses stood, stolid and sombre, as though watching the desecration in dumb horror. In the immediate vicinity there was not much living brightness. Much of the space had been taken up by sand or by very low and scanty border grass or weeds, and a solitary allamanda swayed barely noticeably in the grudging wind, a smiling solitude, like a painted wooden doll. An impertinent beetle engaged it in a taunting romance, alternately perching and backing out, as though the flower had to it something inviting that came off bitter and forbidding each time he landed a kiss on it. But he finally gave up the game and flew off to more distant parts in search of something a little more rewarding.

Away in the distance the morning sun peered effortfully and weakly through a thin but obstinate sheet of cloud. It never really prevailed with a golden fullness, and threw down on the world below a meagre measure of dawnlight.

Nwabunor had recovered, so it seemed, from her physical torment. But each passing fit of pain seemed further to increase the great psychological distance between her and Ogugua. When she thought about how narrowly she had escaped death she did so not so much with any sense of thankfulness to whatever it was that was responsible for her rescue as with an unbending conviction that she had once again beaten a determined conspiracy, thinking, My spirit was too strong for them. Otherwise they would have done it. She felt it deeply, often muttered it, sometimes even said it aloud, letting it all out with that instinctive thrust which one applies to an overwhelming burden.

She was unpacking her wares in the front yard where she set them up for sale, and she was fumbling and stumbling as she turned the thoughts over and over in her worried mind. I have always said it, she thought. I have always felt it deep within me. This could hardly be an ordinary thing. There has to be something behind it. Would it be a woman's fault that God has given her only one child?

She was taking a small table and a stool through the main door, but muttering thus pensively she did not notice as one leg of the table hit the doorpost and the table fell down and hit her foot. She flinched, but took the table up again and moved on, thinking, And the more I think about it the more I am convinced that this is not an ordi-

63

nary thing. But God was determined that I should never walk around with shame on my head, a laughing stock and a thing for talk before the whole town. And that was why He listened at long last to my prayers and gave me a child. Otherwise they would have chopped my head in this town! And then *she* came into this house. And all this time, think of the attention he has given to her, leaving me aside as a rag. *Heu!*

The morning sun was still working uncertain changes of light and shade overhead, and she was not sure whether or not to spread a mat above the articles. But she kept thinking, And think of all I have had to bear, all I have had to suffer just to overcome the envy of two people who have decided there is no comfort till I am out of the way. All these years I have felt my powers steadily drained, have steadily lost the power to experience that which is the joy of all womanhood. Many times I have felt the pool well up within me, but almost at once I have seen my entire hope, my entire strength, flushed out in one sudden flow of waste. . .

Someone passed by and gave his greetings and she replied to him faintly, spiritlessly, almost as if she was involuntarily muttering a casual thought. A little child came up and asked for a brand of cigarettes and she said it had finished, without thinking; for she was thinking, And were my spirit not too strong for them they would readily have got me out of the way—me and my son, the only thing I can truly call my own in this house. Yes. I know that very well. They want me and my son out of the way. But my spirit is too strong for them. And they cannot do it.

In her room Ogugua was busy setting out her sewing machine and the dress that she was going to be busy with that morning. There was a lot to do on that, and there was some urgency. If she worked hard enough and with sufficient concentration she would be able to dispose of all she had to do before the day went very far. She was anxious to finish off all the work in time to get away from the house and go out. For she was now increasingly spending most of her time outside. Her house could no longer contain her and she had discovered that she could very well obtain her happiness elsewhere. So now she was hurrying out her stuff with determined urgency, thinking, I told him I would come this afternoon. I hope I can finish off all this in time and be able to get off.

The sun was gradually gaining control above. Whenever it reappeared from behind a passing screen of cloud the light chased off the shadows below on the ground before it in a routine sweep, as when a masquerade turns round and describes a formidable arc with his whisk while the crowd falls back with awe in the same formation.

Nwabunor had now brought out all the things she generally put out for sale—petty articles like cigarettes, matches, candles, sugar, biscuits, sardines, corned beef, and other varieties of tinned food. But after she had taken count of all the stock she became worried. Something seemed to be missing. It was becoming fairly regular now that one of the casualties of her illness was her trade. She counted again. Certainly something was missing. The sardines. Two tins were gone, and there was little doubt in her mind how they could have been lost, for she thought, They have come again! They are at it again!

'Ogugua,' she called anxiously to the other, 'you don't happen to have seen two tins of sardines anywhere?'

'No,' replied Ogugua. Then after some hesitation, 'Why, what has happened?'

'Hm,' Nwabunor sighed meaningfully. 'There were twelve tins last week. Now I can only see ten.'

'Have you looked all over the house? Are you sure—'

'Why should I look over the house? Did I keep them all over the house? Or is our house such a big one that something would get so lost as to escape the notice of seven people?'

Her mind was already made up.

'O-ho,' Ogugua said, 'I'm sorry I made the mistake of asking you to look harder for what you have lost. But please, whatever you do—I beg you sincerely not to scatter my belongings or that of any of my children or look end-

65

lessly around me as if I had your sardines tied up under my loins.'

She turned to what she was doing, with much less desire now to cooperate than her question may have carelessly betrayed, thinking, No she wouldn't. She dare not. She knows what it would mean. Her machine ran with a little more speed and the pleats came a little too pronounced. She drew the cloth quickly from under the needle and loosened all the threads.

Nwabunor finally looked all over the house, and around it too. Those two tins of sardines had been used, she thought, and whoever did that was likely to have left a trace around the house. Yes, they could afford to leave a trace. It does not matter to them that I could find out if I looked hard enough. . .

Among the rubbish around the house she found two empty cans of sardines that some amount of wetness from the weather had made to appear fresh from use. She examined these. Here they are, she thought aloud, almost voicing, hardly even stopping to reflect that those cans could well have been kicked into the premises from afar by boys at play.

She picked up one can at the screwed end and smelt it. It smelled fresh, as fresh as it looked.

She picked up the other one. The same thing, only reinforcing her conviction.

She held the second can long in her hand, looking sullenly out over it as though taking a silent oath or as if through the sheer touch of it she could reconstruct the experience that the can might have gone through.

She thought deeply about it, trying earnestly to arrest in her mind what she considered to be convincing possibilities. She had lain in bed roughly one week, and with sufficient strain she could cast her mind back and reconstruct whatever comings-in and goings-out of members of the household looked suspicious, and who appeared to be doing what, under normal circumstances, he or she would have been expected to stay away from. There was no doubt what persons appeared to her likely to have done the mischief. Ubaka was certainly out of that consideration. No, not my son, she thought. It couldn't be my own son. Her husband too. He doesn't really live in this house, she reasoned, and whenever he happens to come in here he goes through all his foolishness without laying a finger on anything that happens to be mine. And he wouldn't steal my sardines. No, not him. I know he is a drunkard, a villain, a wretched and accursed creature. But it couldn't be him.

And Ogugua herself? Whoever wants to ruin you would go any length to do so and would certainly not stop at stealing your sardines. How often did she do any cooking all that time that I was tied to the bed? I cannot think of more than three occasions. Even then she strove to appear not to be doing it at all, because she would not be seen doing any cooking in a week when, dead or alive, I was supposed to be feeding the family. Yes, she would do anything to run away from the responsibility of feeding me and my child. So what could she be doing for food all that time she was not cooking? Her children too. Whatever obtains with the yam must also obtain with the cocoyam. This would not be the first time. . .

'I have no other prayer for whoever is responsible for this than that that person should continue in the same path,' Nwabunor said aloud as she threw the can away.

Ogugua kept quiet, thinking, She dare not. She knows what it would mean.

'No, that person should not stop, but should continue until she gets a crown for her very kind deeds. Since we have come to the stage where the fowl scarcely looks away without losing a chicken to the hawk, that fowl should count herself lucky that can, at the fall of light, find a single chicken to hide under her wings. God sees everything.'

Ogugua still didn't say a word. There was no direct reference yet to her or any of her children. So long as this did not happen, she would not mind if her husband's wife exhausted her store of saws. She thought it better to seem unconcerned, mechanically humming a song to herself while she ran the cloth under the machine with anything but clear-headed care.

Nwabunor had settled down to her articles, but hardly so her mind. A customer had bought two cigarettes and left the stand, and while she put the money into the cup she still felt she hadn't said what she had to say.

'All days are for the thief, but one day is for the owner of the house. Will all this trouble not get settled the day I see this mischief-maker with my own eyes? We shall see. God knows that my son will never be found doing a thing of this nature, and who—'

'Nwabunor,' the other sprang up with theatrical agility, 'let me make this clear to you this morning. You have been trying to make all kinds of subtle references to me and my children and trying in your usual way to drag us into guilt over your sardines. Let me—'

'Did you hear your name?' retorted Nwabunor. 'Did you hear your name? All this time I have been talking about sardines, did you hear your name?'

'Let me make it clear to you—'

'I say did you hear your name? Why drag yourself into this with your own mouth when nobody mentioned your name?'

'So what do you think is in your mind when you count your son out of the matter?'

'O-ho! So apart from my son you are the only person in this house?'

'Who else is left but me and my children—unless you are with your own mouth accusing your husband of having stolen your sardines?'

'Would you accuse him yourself? How long does he stay in this house to have the opportunity of doing such a thing?'

'I see. So the only people likely to have done it are my children and myself. Is that not so?'

There was an endless exchange of pouted abuses, wrappers readjusted, hands clapped too dangerously close to each other's faces.

'Are you asking *me*?'

'Yes, I am asking *you*—'

'Why don't you ask *yourself* why you are so consciously

68

dragging yourself into the matter when nobody mentioned your name?'

'—and if you are not bold enough to say it I will tear it out of your mouth. If a shameless woman like yourself does not have sense enough to be taking care of her belongings, you will tell me what reason you have for taking other people to task over their loss.'

'Taking care of my belongings! Are you not ashamed to be saying a thing like that? How many people are there that live in this house? Do sardine cans grow legs overnight and start running away from where they are? Why don't you count your teeth with your tongue?'

'Look at her! Which of us should be counting her teeth —you or I?'

'Is that question meant for me? Please don't let me unfold my tongue on you today.'

'Heh-heh!' Ogugua clapped. 'Don't you see what your wickedness keeps doing to you? What are you going to unfold your tongue about? To tell the whole world that you are not being continually visited by all the vice that you are planning for other people? What are you going to unfold your tongue about?'

'Are you telling me *that?*' the other lighted up. 'Are you saying that to hide yourself? Do you think the whole town does not see how you go about putting yourself on hire because your husband's house is not big enough for you? Please don't let me unfold my tongue on you—I don't want to say anything.'

'Hear her! I suppose one day you will have to show me whom I have hired myself to, won't you?'

'Me? You think I have the time to waste watching you while you go about your journeys? Not me!'

'Envy and jealousy! That is what has left you in the state you are in today. Just because you have nothing to adorn yourself with and you see me put upon myself what I have earned with the sweat of my brow, you accuse me of putting myself out on hire! At least nobody would stoop low enough to hire you, should you ever put yourself out.'

'Who wants to be hired?'

By this time they were dangerously close to blows. They were already jabbing fingers towards each other's faces more as though pressing the points home depended on that than out of a desire by one to get the other angry enough to give the first blow. But it looked as if nothing could stop a fight now. And if anyone was going to start it, it was likely to be Ogugua. She was younger and thus felt more confident of having the upper hand, and in any case she had more reason to want to fight because apart from her knowledge of the physical disposition of the other she felt she didn't come off too well in the verbal duel. So she jabbed her finger much more frequently and doubled her current of abuse even when it was evident that the other was slowing down.

'I say you should be ashamed of yourself. You hear me? You should be ashamed of yourself. Are you tired of unfolding your tongue? Tell me! Are you tired? Shameless thing! I say you should be ashamed of yourself! I thought you would never grow tired of running your mouth . . .'

At this point their mother-in-law stepped into the house.

'Has the day broken again for you two shameless women? Ehn?' she fired in her fierce, disciplinary tone.

The two contending women drew slightly apart under the impact of the rebuke, staring harshly at each other as if unwilling to disengage completely. Now again a small group of people had gathered a short distance away and was watching the drama, as it built gradually up towards the familiar climax.

'Take a look round the whole neighbourhood,' Ma Nwojide said, 'and see if you can find any two people exchanging spittle or poking at each other's eyeballs. Wretched things! Every wife in Ozala who respects herself is now about her responsibilities, trying to see what she could do for the good of her household. But when you come to my son's house you will find two vultures trying to make carrion of one another. Shameless things! I say take a look round the neighbourhood and tell me what two people you will find trying to strip each other naked for a public spectacle.'

She took a brief breath, during which she gave each of them an eyeful of contempt. She was a large, imposing woman who liked to make her wishes clear and to exhaust all she wanted to say. The two women were now settling to their places.

'Look here, you—' she pointed to Ogugua, 'you who feel so confident about your strength that you are always the first to give fight—what would you tell the world you were doing in her shed? Even if you think you have all the right on your side, do you think you can convince anyone you have any reason going to meet her where she is selling her things? What is wrong? What could be the matter between you two this morning? Ehn?'

'You can ask her,' replied Ogugua. 'Since she is senior I imagine she should have the first chance to do the explaining to you.'

'I am asking you!' blared her mother-in-law. 'And don't you open your mouth to talk to me like that again. I say what is the matter between both of you.'

There was a brief silence, Ogugua not wanting it to appear that she was being too easily subdued. Then she clapped in the air as she sprang up under a sudden impulse and began to rant off her explanation, her voice soaked and unsteady with anger.

'Where on earth shall I run to from this wicked woman? What have I done that she should not allow me to drink a cup of water in this house? Is it my fault that somebody brought both of us together under one roof—'

'Gently,' Ma Nwojide motioned. 'That is not what I ask you. I say what is the matter between you and your husband's wife. There is no need for you to recite to me all the wherefores of your living together and this and that. What is the matter between you two this morning that you should be wanting to tear each other apart?'

'The children and everyone had just left the house, and I was packing the clothes out, getting ready to do my sewing job, when she sprang upon me and started accusing

71

me and my children of stealing her sardines, without
even—'

'Liar!' shouted Nwabunor. 'Liar! Can't you see how
true your story sounds? Do you—'

'Shut up!' Ma Nwojide intercepted. 'Who asked you?
I haven't yet asked you to open your mouth, so wait until
it is your turn to put forward your own case . . . .
Continue.'

'It was only one word I said, thinking I was doing my
best to help her. I asked her if she—I saw her going about
here and there, turning the whole house upside down, and
I asked her if she did not think it better to settle down
properly and look carefully for those tins of sardines, and
she let out all her mouth on me saying Ehn! This, this,
this; that, that, that;—that God knows that her son does
not steal anything, that my children have—'

'Shame on you, Ogugua, shame on you!' Nwabunor
again interrupted, thinking that her opponent was at least
gaining a dramatic advantage. 'How can you open your
mouth to say such—'

'I say keep quiet until I ask you,' her mother-in-law
again ordered.

'I cannot bear to look on while she tells lies that even
her little child would be ashamed to utter.'

'Are you afraid that you are going to be proved guilty?'

'How can I be proved guilty?'

'Then keep your mouth shut until it is your turn to put
your case in the open . . . . Continue, my child—or is that
all?'

'What else is there to say?' Ogugua concluded, feeling
vindicated. 'I settled down to what I was doing, but she
would not let me rest. It was in the middle of the whole
thing that you came in—there is nothing more than that.
She has got it into her head that she is the owner of this
house and that everything—'

'Alright—alright, I do not ask you that. Nwabunor, now
what do you have to say to—'

'What else can I say after she has unfolded all the lies

72

she has tied up under her filthy tongue? Why don't you go ahead and judge the matter on that?'

'Are you asking me that question, you worthless animal?' Ma Nwojide felt challenged. 'I ask you to give your own side of the story and you open your mouth to tell me what to do. Did you accuse her children of stealing your sardines, or did you not?'

'If I ever opened my mouth to say that her children took my sardines may that iroko tree fall down and tear my bowels apart! If I ever said such a thing may the goddess of the river not let me see the end of this day . . .'

'Make sure what you say. Nobody takes oaths in vain. But did you at any time say that your son could not be guilty of the theft?'

'And what if I said it? Does that mean that I was accusing any other person? I know my own child and what he is capable of doing. And whoever takes offence because I say my son is not capable of theft must be worried by some sense of guilt.'

'Who would be so foolish as not to catch the purport of your remark?' Ma Nwojide asked, with Ogugua gesturing and humming her approval of what she considered sound judgment. 'Is it you and your son alone who live in his house? I cannot understand why grown-up women like you should not learn to stay in peace. Shall your husband put a rope around his neck and hang himself because he married two women? Ehn?'

She looked at the women, one after the other. None looked back. She readjusted her wrapper, then hissed and left the house.

The day was fast growing old. The inquisitive crowd had thinned gradually out and now disappeared completely.

6

The amber-coloured sun, with a mischievous grin now and then on its face, was gradually burning the youth out of the day. For schoolchildren the mid-year vacation is often a refreshing spell, coming as a welcome climax to a week or two of manual labour whose unpleasantness is emphasised by the immediate prospect of long fishing mornings at the river-bank or roasted yams at the farm. For the lucky ones it affords the chance to spend smart vacations in far-away cities, then come home at the end of it all to indulge their urban delights, displaying their duckling feet and silken backs on lily-white Sundays.

For Ubaka, holiday time had to be worktime. Probably his juvenile sense of good cheer strove by some kind of internal, subconscious effort to minimise the pain that need involved. But no doubt at this stage his domestic experience had brought him to accept that what he had to do to earn his money was not to be made the subject of unchecked sport. Thus at least in this one respect he was wiser than a good many children of his kind, that he recognised that however deeply he indulged his youth outside in the company of his mates he had to have an answer for the stern realities that would be waiting for him whenever he got back home.

He was one of a number of children who fetched sand for hire. A big man in the vicinity had come home with plans to put up a house, and had reckoned that he could get cheap labour by gathering the young boys of the neighbourhood and engaging them in what he convinced them was a fine holiday treat. He made them collect sand

74

from the river-bank for use in moulding blocks, and promising to pay each of them what indeed had never got into their tiny hands before but which under a more upright reckoning would certainly amount to a travesty of compensation. Payment would come to them at the end of the vacation, when a good deal of the sand needed to do the block-moulding would have been gathered.

For the children that was a most delightful prospect anyhow, and they literally fell over one another to turn in their bucketfuls. To a good many of them it meant new shoes, new dresses and a greater buying capacity for the delicacies that would be sold on the school premises when schooldays rolled back again. But to Ubaka it meant much less these than the possibility that when school resumed he would be able to help his mother pay his school fees and avoid the threatened ejection. He had seen enough of the fearful drama that often resulted when his mother asked money of his father and he was glad now that there was a chance to avert this. Mother will be happy, he thought. She will have no more need to cry.

'Shall we stay very long at the work-place?' asked Bomboy, who was untiring in asking all kinds of questions.

'No, we shall not stay too long,' answered his brother good-naturedly.

'How long shall we stay there?'

'Until they ask us to go for today. Are you getting hungry?'

The little boy shook his head.

In the thoroughfare bicycle bells rattled confusion amid the pedestrian traffic and old women gave way to avoid being knocked down, load and all. Morning was slowly unfolding into afternoon.

'Uba, will they pay you a lot of money today?' asked Bomboy.

'No, not today. But they will pay us a lot of money.'

'How much money will they pay you?'

'I don't know yet.'

'Will you buy a new shirt with the money? Will you buy a new shirt?'

'No.'

'What will you do with the money?'

'I will . . . I don't know. I will give it to mama.'

'Will you give her all of it?'

'Yes.'

'Will you not take some of it?'

'She will probably give me some.'

'But why must you give her all of it?'

'She will . . . oh! Stop asking me—I don't know,' then, noticing some disappointment on the little child's face, 'she will pay my school fees with it.'

'Will papa not pay your school fees?'

'Papa says he has no money.'

'But papa buys many clothes.'

'I don't know.'

There was a brief pause. They were nearly at the work place now. Some of the boys had already arrived with buckets in their hands and hopeful smiles on their faces.

'If I help you fetch some sand will they give me any money?'

'They won't let you fetch any sand.'

'I want to fetch some sand so that I can get some money.'

'What will you do with the money?'

'I will use it in buying a tennis ball, and then I will use some of it in buying breadfruit from those old women living near us. Their breadfruit is very sweet, but I will still beat their cat if she comes around again to our house.'

At this point his brother squinted down at him and tugged his little hand.

'I have told you to keep away from those old women. They are witches. If you eat their breadfruit you will turn into a witch. And if you beat their cat they will fly into our house at night and pluck out your eyes. Do you want your eyes plucked out at night by witches?'

Bomboy shook his head in unspoken fright, a finger in his mouth.

'Then keep away from them.'

They joined the hopeful assembly.

76

Odafe Gwam came out of his late father's little thatch-topped cottage and stood briefly with his arms akimbo. The sun was now bearing down on the earth with a sharp golden splendour, but so far the heat only warmed the skin. Gwam looked out at the waiting crowd in front and his face formed into a narrow-eyed grin, though one could hardly attribute this with certainty either to the sunlight or to a feeling of satisfaction. With a measured sweep he moved his head from left to right over the expanse of land that lay ahead of him, surveying the area of the proposed building with something of that distant eye that a cattle-rearer exercises over the grazing animals when he envisages a doubled herd. He swallowed, then drew the old straw-hat a bit closer over his brow. His heavy, baggy shorts were slipping slowly down underneath his worn leather belt. He folded the waist-line twice over the belt to hold the shorts in a convenient grip, then strode towards the children with a gait that carried a lot less sense of justice than purpose, thinking, I am doing the best I can. I'm trying. I have to have my share.

He had come home from Lagos, where he had been working for as long as he could remember as a store-keeper in a large expatriate manufacturing company. Over in that big faceless city he could hardly be reckoned with, but he was one of the leading lights in this little town and his presence was felt in any big events that took place. At this time there was a good deal of politics around as the town warmed slowly up towards the forth-coming regional elections. He belonged to the *Great Future Party*. Not really because he identified himself so much with the principles (whatever of these there was) or the manifesto of the party—that would demand a lot more sincerity and conviction than he could afford. Anybody in the town with even the least political foresight could see that the *GFP* was the underdog party and had a rough, rugged climb ahead to achieve even the most negligible support. This was largely because two years after the British had left and many more after the tribes had been accustomed to living with one another, somebody was still telling the people that the party could not truly represent the aspirations of the sons and daughters of the land because its leaders did not come 'from among us'. And when the organisers of the parties came to address the chiefs and elders too many people spoke in the native language on behalf of the other party, the *Quick Progress Party* led by Enyinabo, to leave any doubts at all in the minds of these people that this was 'our own thing'. But to Gwam the GFP was the great party.

He *was* the GFP here. He could not boast anything that might be called a following, though it lay upon him to make sure the party made an impression. He had some money placed at his disposal towards this end, and the party headquarters had made sure that additions were made to this whenever Gwam made the request. The money was meant to woo the support of the chiefs and elders of the town and of the little villages around and was also to be used in purchasing bicycles for the use of assistants in these places who could foster the interests of the party. But the money hardly got into the hands of anybody else, and somehow headquarters managed to overlook the slow progress made. Whenever representatives came down Gwam would always convince them that the best time really to assess the strength of support was one month or so before elections, and there was no need to worry yet when even the opponent was resting on his back. He was already erecting houses in Warri and Sapele, and was now planning to put up a big one in his home town. But headquarters was beginning to get a little bit reluctant whenever he asked for money these days. Indeed, the last couple of trips that he made up there to make his requests turned out to be useless. He was thus gradually beginning to find himself incapable of living up to the big plans he had laid.

He had made an unwritten contract with certain labourers, strangers who lived on the banks of the river, for the collection and conveyance of sand from the sandbanks in the middle of the river to the shore. And he had kept making them promises of payment until one day their patience ran out and they all trooped to him—all three of them, with their oars in their hands and their loin rags knotted tightly round their waists—and made it unmistakably clear to him that if he did not make them any payment before sunset they were going to throw all the sand back into the water. So he had paid them something that came to about a third of what they were due for so far, and they had resumed the job once more.

Thus a sprawling heap of golden sand was awaiting collection at the banks of the river, and it clearly gave Gwam a feeling of joy to think how nice it would all look in this large expanse of land on which one day a mighty house would be standing. He could already imagine himself stretched out on an easy-chair in the front yard in the evening, smoking a pipe and shaking his crossed feet, with children playing all around him and him telling them to pack up their wares and go in for supper and after to go to sleep. He could imagine younger men, and even older men less fortunate than he, paying their morning respects and him telling little schoolboys how useful it was to be industrious and all that, or a labourer cutting the lawn clean, or a housemaid saving enough corn from the meal to feed the chickens.

Recently also he had been taking interest in Obanua's younger wife, goaded on no less by her lewd attractions than by his own feeling of importance. He was sufficiently aware of the marital discomfort in Obanua's household, and he was taking advantage of this. Engaging Nwabunor's son, Ubaka, was for him a good way of seeking acceptance with the family. He was having his own secret meetings with Ogugua, but then anybody who saw them together had a chance of thinking of him merely as a friend of the family. He thus took the opportunity to make his desires known to Ogugua, supporting his arguments with good money—who then was he to say no when a pretty woman came dancing up to him and telling him she felt better by his side? He was even trying to persuade her to leave her husband's house and be his wife (he was a widower), and could now already picture himself settled comfortably into the new house with a pretty, new wife . . .

79

As he came up to the children he clapped for attention and they all left their games and gathered round him with bright, expectant eyes.

'I have explained to you and your mothers what you are all required to do during this vacation.'

There were still a few subdued shuffles as each child struggled to come closest to Gwam.

'And I want you all to make sure that you put your heads down and make it a worthwhile exercise. I have also told you what you shall be getting for pay when your vacation is over and you have gathered what will be considered sufficient for the work. Do you all hear me?'

'Yes, sir' they chorused. In the continued struggle for position one child was nudged forward rather hard and Gwam managed to catch his sand-filled head (on which he had been doing a head-standing exercise) before it could hit his stomach.

'Look here, you little louse,' and they all giggled, 'looking like a cherry-seed fallen into a pad of excrement—' the children laughed again, '—are you quite sure you have enough energy for this work? If you don't you'd better go home because I don't want any child to collapse under the weight of a mere bucket of sand.' Then addressing all the children once more, 'And I want to warn all of you that this is no place for playing. Anybody found playing with the work will be sent home at once to his mother and he will not be paid a single penny—do you hear what I am saying?'

They again again chorused their consent.

'Okoh!' he called towards the house.

No reply came.

'Okoh!' he blared, before he heard his cousin roar back. 'Sir!'

His two cheeks bulged with food and he was desperately trying to fasten the loin-cloth as he hurried out to the response.

'What were you doing in there?' Gwam asked.

'There was . . . I was cleaning up the pots—they were all—'

'Will the day ever come when you won't be found scooping up this plate or that pot? Look at his stomach—no wonder there is hardly anything up in your head!'

The children giggled again.

'Starting from today you are going to be sitting out here to make sure that these children fetch ten buckets of sand each every day until their holiday ends—*every* day, ten buckets each one of them, do you understand what I am saying?'

'I understand.'

'How many buckets did I say?'

'Ten buckets.'

'How many days?'

'Ten days, eh—'

'*Taa!* Shut up! I said "until their holiday ends".'

'I am sorry. I made a mistake.'

'How wouldn't you, potbelly!'

The children giggled again, and Okoh eyed them with menacing intent.

'And how do you intend to keep count of the number of times each boy fetches the sand? Hm? If you had any brains in your head I would have asked you to take their names down and mark it against them accordingly. But you can neither read nor write and would sooner take your hand to your mouth than set it down on paper. How do you intend to keep count?'

'I will remember.'

'You will remember! How will you remember?'

'I will note each child down with my eyes each time he comes up with his bucket of sand.'

'No. I don't think I can afford to be fool enough to rely on your memory, because you have none. Look. Let each boy put down his shirt before you—line them up at intervals. Then let them pick ten pebbles each. As each comes up with his bucket of sand, he surrenders a pebble to you and you put it down on his shirt until he has all ten pebbles placed upon his shirt. Do you understand what I am saying?'

81

Okoh nodded somewhat half-consciously, and Gwam was sure that he had replied before he understood.

'How did I say you should keep count?'

Okoh pulled up his slipping loin-cloth.

'You said that each child should place ten pebbles on his shirt, and that as he fetches a bucket of sand he should pick up one pebble and give it—'

'You fool!' Gwam rebuked him, the children knowingly amused. 'I didn't say they should place the pebbles on their shirts before they have fetched the sand. Have you no sense in your head? Hm?' He shook his head, and hissed. 'God knows I am merely throwing away my money by entrusting this job to such a nit as you,' musing. 'If I ask those greedy labourers to take care of the work they are going to be asking for their money even before the work is through, and before I can open my mouth to say a word they will be threatening to split my head with their paddles. And now that I am asking one of my own blood to do it I find that he cannot even so much as keep count of how much work is done.'

He went over the instructions once again, and at the end of it he roared at his foreman, 'Now is it clear to you?'

'It is clear to me,' Okoh shook, falling backwards.

'Now get to work. At the end of these boys' holiday I want to be satisfied I did the right thing by keeping the job out of the hands of those labourers.'

No sooner had he left than Okoh, clearly humiliated, tightened his loin-cloth, put on new manner and took full control.

'Now come on, put down your shirts, you rats. I'll see what chance you have of laughing this time. . . . Here, you fathead, you were the most eager to laugh, ehn? Weren't you?'

'Put your hand on me and see if I won't report you,' the boy threatened.

'Report me, you tiny ant, hoping to earn money. I suppose you will earn so much it will all come out through your nose.'

'Is that why you cannot keep ordinary count?'

The others laughed.

'Are you talking to me like that? Ehn? Are you talking to me like that?'

He pulled the boy towards him by the head, tousling the hair. The boy stumbled and gripped his loin-cloth, tugging at it until he almost stripped Okoh naked. The others hooted at him and surrounded him to complete the disgrace. Thus harassed, Okoh let go of the fathead, grabbed the vanishing cloth with one hand, and with the other tried to beat off the naughty little boys.

'Okoh!!' Gwam roared, noticing the tussle from afar.

'We are getting ready to work, sir. Come on, you ants—'

The boys disengaged, then quickly pulled off their shirts and set about looking for pebbles.

Ubaka was the first to get his ten pebbles. As soon as he was ready, he picked up his bucket, took his little brother by the hand, and made towards the river-bank.

'Uba, will they give you any money today?' asked Bomboy.

'No' Ubaka replied, 'but they will give us a lot at the end of the holiday.'

'Uba, how much money will they give you?'

'I don't know. . . . I told you I didn't know.'

But then, penitent, he drew the little boy closer to him as they went.

Far short of its midday intensity the sun was till playing its sport of bright and dim, at one time chasing the shadows ahead like rapid bushfire licking neatly through dry elephant-grass, and at the next falling quickly back under the determined counterchase.

Long after midday the twenty little boys were still trotting between the half-mile that separated the river-bank from the site of Gwam's projected palace, past women coming home from the stream and families of goats resting here and there under the shade. Even the lizards seemed to have settled to rest.

Okoh was lying spreadeagled, in deep and insensible

slumber, a drowsy trail of saliva running down one corner of his gaping mouth and the bristles showing clearly above the waistline of his loin-cloth.

'Uba, how many times more are you going to fetch the sand,' asked Bomboy, the tedium now taxing his fraternal loyalty.

'Four times. Are you tired?'

The other nodded.

'Are you hungry?'

Bomboy hesitated, but nodded just the same, looking up. Ubaka understood.

'Do you want to go home? Shall I take you home so that you can have your food?'

'No, I will stay with you.'

'But you are tired and hungry. And I am not ready yet.' He was confused, and sympathetic. 'Alright, you can stay. But you will not go down to the stream with me. Sit here under the trees and wait for me. I will try to finish up soon. You hear?'

Bomboy nodded. As soon as he had settled down Ubaka gave him his *koso* to play with while he went off again to the stream.

Shortly after the fatheaded boy came round with his bucket of sand and stood briefly over the snoring mass of their foreman, a vengeful and irreverent look in his eyes. He would probably have emptied the sand over him but then he changed his mind when he realised there was some other way. He threw the sand on the heap, then dipped his hand into his pocket and cast two pebbles down upon his shirt. When he looked at Bomboy he caught the boy looking at him too.

'I will tell him.'

'Tell him what?'

'I will tell him that you cheated.'

'Shut up!'

'I won't.'

'How did I cheat?'

'I caught you putting down two pebbles instead of one.'

'Alright. I will give you a berry. But don't tell him.'

'No. I will tell him.'

The fathead stared at him with menace.

'Alright, tell him if you like. If you tell him I will beat you to death,' and he flung his finger to emphasise the threat.

'If you beat me Ubaka will beat you.'

'I will beat you and Ubaka.'

'Ubaka can kill you.'

'Shut up!'

'I won't shut up.'

'I say shut up.'

The fathead walked up and gave him a knock on the head. Bomboy cried and gripped his shorts and the noise of the struggle roused the sleeping Okoh. He shuffled up clumsily on his haunches and saw the two little boys tousling up one another. Clearing his throat he warned them to be quiet, but recognising his old enemy he rose up and pulled them apart, applying greater vehemence on the side of the fathead.

'Are you not ashamed of yourself?' he asked the boy as he thrust him aside.

'Are you not ashamed of yourself too?'

'Shut up!'

'Shut up!'

Turning to Bomboy, Okoh enquired the cause of the dispute. Bomboy told him.

'You rogue!' Okoh turned on the fathead. 'Was that what you were up to? I always knew you would be up to something. Come here—'

With a random sense of justice he roughed up the person of the fathead and after thrusting one pebble back on the rascal he pushed him off towards the stream. He then went back to the shade, readjusted his loin-cloth and settled down again to his rest, like a tired cow. The fathead was still cursing from a distance and threatening to take it all back on the mocking Bomboy . . .

An hour later Ubaka had settled down to *koso* with his usual opponents, their sand trips now over. Their faces wore the concentrated look of people playing for honour.

Not long after the issue was settled and the winner was taking his prize.

'If you shake your hand again I am going to claim two more raps,' Ubaka warned his victim.

'Try that and you will see all the *koso* go to pieces,' said the fathead in gratuitous defence of the victim.

'Alright, continue and stop making such a noise,' said the third opponent. 'We hope you will like it when the day comes for you to get your own raps.'

Five!

Six!

Seven!

'Put your hand back!' screamed Ubaka as the other snatched his hand away under the biting pain.

Six!

Seven!

Before Ubaka could rap again the fathead nudged his elbow and they both stared each other out like two glaring dolls.

'Be careful!'

'Be careful!'

Eight!

Away at the door of the cottage Gwam stood looking broadly out over the land. He raised his straw hat and scratched his head that itched under the scorch of the dazzling sun. But when he looked closer and saw his foreman-cousin sprawled uselessly out in a corpse-like spread, his grin narrowed, his brow furrowed above an unbelieving squint, and he let the hat drop back on his head.

'Okoh!' he called out, with not much more clarity than was needed to make sure. When he got no reply from his cousin he set briskly out towards the scene with a set face and steps that could scarcely keep pace with his passion.

'Keep your hand!' warned Ubaka, in a subdued scream.

'Don't you see . . .'

'Keep your hand!'

Nine!

Ten!

Then he collected the four *koso* and put them quickly into his pocket as they all feigned calm . . .

With one furious and determined thrust Gwam heaved the foreman up by the neck and tried to force him on his feet. But Okoh's knees gave and his eyes glared as a body rescued from drowning. When he half came to he scratched and gawked quizzically round as though wondering where everybody else had gone. Still scratching he finally fixed his gaze on the fathead and blinked a few times while all the boys had a good laugh.

'Come, blockhead, how old do you really think you are?'

When Gwam reflected that his cousin was meant to secure an economic advantage he was truly worried . . .

Shortly after he reassured the children, and Ubaka was on his way home with his little brother.

7

'Ogo,' said the elder twin sister, with a touch of displeasure, 'I have often told you that if you keep spending your money this way and showing it you will have to explain one day how you got it all—and what will you tell them?'

'How am I showing it?' said the other. 'What do you want me to do?'

'Must you really put on this new belt. Can you not loosen it and conceal it as soon as we are near home?'

'Do you think they will not finally know that we have new things? Please leave me alone. On Sunday you put your earrings on to go to church and nobody asks you how you got them. But when I put on my own things you immediately want me to keep them out of sight.'

'Are we equals?'

'What difference does that make?'

'If you don't check your swollen head I am going to take away all these things from you, do you hear that?'

'Do they belong to you?'

'That doesn't matter—I'll take them from you all the same.'

'Come and take them!'

But they were now too dangerously close to home to continue accusing each other, and even though they tried to talk in subdued tones they realised that conspiratorial silence was as incriminating as open defiance. And they had practised this conspiracy long enough to achieve an adult capacity to change their expressions at brief notice and pretend nothing had happened, each with a face clean as a leaf.

Away in the yard their mother was still busy with the machine and the clothes. The two girls had to sneak furtively into the house more in order to conceal the direction of their entrance than out of fear that their mother would be angry that they had not all this while been usefully employed.

'Good afternoon, ma.'

'Good afternoon, ma.'

They were afraid and uncertain.

Their mother stopped and looked up at them, and there could have been a whip in those eyes.

'Where have you two been?'

The girls stood silent and guilty, each looking at the other as though waiting for her to drop the cue for a lie, and occasionally looking at the ground.

'Will neither of you answer me? Will neither of you open her mouth, you vagabonds? The cock will hardly crow before you wretched gnats set foot on the streets and roam the whole town like children without a home. And it is only when hunger starts turning your bowels that you will remember that you have a home to return to. I am asking you, where have you been since morning?'

'We went to our school compound,' said Ndidi.

'Your school compound? You went to your school compound, on a Saturday—and during your holiday? What could you be doing in your school compound when school is not in session?'

'We were asked to report for choir practice. Our teacher—'

'Does your teacher not have any children in her house? And even if there are no children in her house does she not understand that children have a duty to perform in the house before they can run off to work for charity? No— my children will always be the first to leave this house because they are needed more at school! Well why don't you stay out there and let hunger bite the devil out of your stomachs—why come home? I suppose you expect to find the food all laid out on the table ready for you to rally to! Well come on then, worthless children . . . whatever you decide to do with yourselves I want you to set about fixing Bomboy something to eat before I raise my eyes a second time from this machine. Do you hear what I am saying?'

'Yes ma,' replied Ndidi. 'But where has—'

'Shut up there and don't ask me any questions, if you don't want me to lay my hands on you this afternoon. Now I don't wish to open my mouth again.' She settled down again to her work.

The two girls hurried out of her sight and into the house.

'You still haven't told me what has become of the one shilling that was left,' Ndidi said.

'I told you there was nothing left—I don't know what shilling you mean,' replied Ogo.

'Have you forgotten that it was seven shillings I counted out to you on the day I gave you the money to keep? When we came to divide it you brought out six shillings and put them into my hands. Later that afternoon as we were going back from school I caught you buying *chin-chin*, and when I asked you you said it was part of your own money, even though you still had three shillings in your hand. Have you forgotten?'

'I told you there was nothing left. You are always finding fault with me when I use my money.'

'But it was seven shillings I gave you—I counted it very carefully and it was seven shillings.'

'You are always—'

Just then Nwabunor came upon them from her shed and made as though she was looking for something. They would probably have changed their topic, but the surprise was a bit too sudden. Thus confused, they were trying to make for two different directions when Nwabunor called their attention.

'Tell me, you children,' she said, 'you have been sweeping parts of this house and you may have noticed one or two things—'

90

'I did not pick up anything at all!' snapped Ndidi.

'I did not pick up anything either!' chorused Ogo.

'I see you are already answering my question even before I have asked it,' Nwabunor noticed. 'Are you quite sure you did not find some tins of sardines lying carelessly somewhere around?'

'Not me,' Ogo said.

'God forbid!' swore Ndidi. 'What will I be doing with tins of sardines?'

'Shall we then put a curse on the head of whoever stole the sardines?'

'You can put a curse if you like,' said Ndidi. 'What will I be doing with your sardines? Am I supposed to be looking after them for you?'

'You have got a nasty tongue in your head! All I asked was a simple question.'

'Why are you always asking us questions whenever any of your things are missing in this house? Can't you ask your son too?'

'If you don't talk to me with respect I am going to bare your buttocks and give you a good flogging.'

'Touch me today and see if there won't be anybody to pay you back. Do you think—'

'Ndidi!!' Ogugua called from the yard.

'Ma!'

Briefly regarding Nwabunor with irreverence and scorn Ndidi ran out to answer her mother's call.

'Have you done what I asked you to do?' Ogugua asked.

'I was getting ready to put water on the fire when Ubaka's mother started accusing us of stealing her sardines.'

'Now don't let me see you again wasting your time on a useless argument when you should be doing what I asked you to do. If anybody calls you a thief you should call that person a thief also and do what you are doing, and let the person direct her attention to me. Now go ahead and do what I asked you and don't let me hear your voice again—both of you.'

91

The two girls exchanged glances, feeling more vindicated than reproached.

Nwabunor retired to her stall, not because she lacked an appropriate response but from a feeling that energy spent on *that* response was wasted, thinking, Everyday is for the thief. Just one is for the owner of the house.

At this point Obanua shuffled into the premises. He stopped and looked round at their faces and no one paid him attention. Silence, more assumed than spontaneous, had settled upon the scene, and the deference that prevailed was more like the distance observed when a cat settles down in the midst of a number of dogs . . .

In the advancing afternoon the thatched eaves described rough-edged, bumpy shadows on the corrugated surface of the sand. From the nearby shrubbery foraging finches hustled for roost and chirped querulously as though proclaiming *Keep off my stalk, curse you curse you! Keep off my stalk, curse you curse you!* But very soon they departed just as they came, flapping feverishly to some other destination, swearing maybe to continue the fight out there while their twittering curses faded fitfully out in the ominous calm.

The entire family was in the house, but the two units paid not the slightest attention to what one or the other did. Or rather they regarded one another with an inner eye, tense, purposeful and as deeply furtive as it was forbidding, like two hostile families of beasts enclosed in a pen. Hardly much was said, even when each unit talked within itself. And like animals it was the mothers who more than the children felt the threat to survival and the vital need to ensure it in this charged enclosure where the slightest infringement was sure to cause a determined fight.

The children were eating what food their mothers had managed separately to organise for them. But the two women were busy each with her trade. Ogugua chugged defiantly away at the sewing machine while Nwabunor waited silently for customers that hardly came, slowly chewing something inside her mouth like a disgruntled cow under the shade. Occasionally one glanced briefly at the other but quickly withdrew the gaze as though it hurt or sickened. None had taken any food. Food could wait— there was enough 'inside' to fill the space.

The two sisters ate, but silently accused and abused each other.

'I have always known you for a thief.'

'Are you not a thief yourself?'

'You will have to tell me what happened to that shilling.'

'You will have to tell me yourself what happened to that shilling.'

'If you don't I will tear your mouth open and bring it out.'

'And I will tear your own mouth open too.'

'It is at home you have the strength to talk.'

When their mother stopped her machine and looked towards them they held their peace and concentrated on the food.

Ubaka and Bomboy ate separately but glanced cordially across at one another. If the soup escaped Ubaka's palm and trailed down the arm and he struggled to lick it quickly from the elbow up, Bomboy would giggle amiably at him. If a morsel fell off Bomboy's hand onto the ground Ubaka would screw his face at him in playful mockery. But then he would seek to relieve the little boy's frustration by offering him a morsel from his own plate. Before Bomboy stood up to accept he would first look towards his mother and she would merely return a brief and unhelpful glance that seemed to say, *I won't ask you not to, but whatever happens to you will be your own problem.* Yet Bomboy would be unable to resist the temptation, and after a brief hesitation would walk up to his brother and accept the kindness.

Obanua was in the house also, but he got no attention from anybody and that made him angry and uneasy, as he thought, In my own house too?

93

The afternoon heat pierced through the roof and he found it as uncomfortable inside as it was outside. He was lying on his bed, thinking. Looking towards a corner of the ceiling where a pencil of sunlight had splintered upon a leaf of the thatch into numerous shafts that illuminated the immediate nearness, he saw an ant kicking feverishly in a web while the spider gave it a watchful distance. He looked away from that onto the wall and here again he briefly watched a gecko stealing slowly but determinedly towards a frolicking fly. He rose from bed and went to where Ogugua was busy with her machine. He called her and asked her to follow him into the house. Reluctantly, she complied.

He sat on the bed. She stood by the door, looking away.

'Ogugua,' he began. The other merely listened. 'Starting from today, I want you to resume cooking for the whole house for the rest of this week. After that Nwabunor takes up. Let it all be as before. Do you hear that?'

She waited for him to finish, and then she turned her head slowly towards him.

'Have you finished? If you have, tell me because I'm busy.'

'But has what I said got into your head?'

'I don't listen to such talk, do you hear me?' she said. 'In the first place you haven't even put any money into my hands. In the second place, why should the whole thing start with me? Please don't worry me this evening.' She walked away.

Obanua rose angrily after her.

'Do you think this house can contain you and me?' he fretted.

'I have never given a thought to that question. I have never bothered to think about it.'

He merely looked at her. Even within himself he was sure there was nothing he could do, for he was not in the least confident that force would get the better of a wife's determined petulance. The scene had attracted the curiosity of the children, who now drew close and looked help-

94

lessly up at a scare they knew they could not prevent but only prayed would pass.

But he sighed and swallowed and left her triumphant presence, going back into the room. The children looked at one another with that frightened question in their eyes and then dispersed with some feeling of relief. Nwabunor was still staring into the distant emptiness with the same indifference that she would have felt is something alarming had happened between the two people. And Ogugua chugged away at her machine, after that brief interlude.

Shortly after, Obanua came out of the room. He stood knocking the dust out of his cap before he put it on his head. Then he walked away from the house without saying a word to anybody.

Scarcely had he left the doorway when Nwanze emerged from a corner of the yard and greeted.

'Kpom! Kpom! Kpom! Kpom! My greetings to every single thing in this house, soup-pots inclusive,' he clowned. 'Oba, my man, how fares the python in the sun, or have I come in at the wrong time?'

'Greetings, my friend,' Obanua endeavoured half-heartedly, 'but I am going to some important errand and I cannot wait.'

'Can't you even sit down for one blink of the eyelid and let us break a kolanut to the good spirits?'

Nwanze got no reply from his departing friend, but one look round at the rest of the household was enough to tell him that all was not well. He scratched his head understandingly, then brushed the ground under him and sat down. He felt rather disappointed, because he had thought that with luck he would meet the family in a mood in which they would not be unwilling to part with some food. But he hadn't given up hope yet, and scratched his buttocks somewhat.

'The things that happen to a man can be really funny sometimes. When I woke up from bed this morning some wonderful feeling got into me and I thought and said to myself, "Nwanze", I said, "You have no wife, nobody to care for and none to care for you. No farm, no fish traps

95

or animal traps and no palm-trees to tap. So what are you going to tell your spirit when right before your eyes every single human being is going about some business and striving to make a decent living and even the poor dog is smelling around for some excreta to clean up—and here you are scratching under your scrotum and quarrelling with every single bug that bothers your skin, so early in the day. Can you not do anything to help yourself, and would you rather wait on like the tramp you are till your grandfather's house collapses over your head?" I have grown tired of beating the gong every single morning for our old chief because at the end of it all the blind man does not even compliment me with a gumful of the good liquid and all he tells me is "go and find something to help yourself with, you idler". So I get up and proceed to the farm of Akpukwu, thinking that if I help him do some clearing he will be good enough to rub my palm. But all I hear from the scruffy miser is that I am no good for any job, and that if he makes the mistake of looking away for one second I will be throwing some yams aside. Can you imagine that, *me* stealing anything from anybody? Does a poor man automatically become a devil as well? So I left the wretched fool to his troubles—God knows he got half of all the farmland by theft—and went my own way. That is why a man should thank his creator if he has a good friend to look to when all the world drives him away from their doorsteps. My thoughts immediately went to my good and unforgettable friend Obanua. He and I have known each other even as far back as when we were still pissing on our mother's beds and he alone understands that I am always ready to help myself if only I can find the opportunity to do so. And if everything fails me I know that—I am quite confident that—no matter how it is, no matter what happens to me, I can never come to his house to ask for anything and he tells me he can't help me. This is something I can always say for Obanua, and I know very well—'

'There is no food in the house,' one of the girls cut him short.

'Shut up and let me finish! Since when have you learnt

to show your face when adults are discussing more serious matters, you little brat that have scarcely even learnt to clean your nose yet?'

'There is no food in the house,' she insisted.

'Are you going to speak for your mother? You are always pretending to know better than anybody else. Why don't you wait for reasonable people to talk?'

But neither of the two women paid any attention or showed any signs of heeding his appeal. So when he saw that he was not making any impression he rose and brushed his buttocks.

'I am on my way. I just called in here to see how you people are doing, and now that I see that everybody is in good health I am satisfied. As for you, needle-tongue,' he pointed, 'you must learn to curb your sharpness and not open your mouth when important matters are on the ground. I am on my way. Goodbye to you all.'

As he limped away the children trotted mockingly round him part of the way. He looked like a discomfited scrounger with jiggers in his feet . . .

Later that day, when the sun was closing its eyes on the world under, a light air hung between the glowering hood and the earth. One one side of the sky the sun had taken all away but a diminishing brillance. On the other side massive crests of white cloud were photocast against the blue beyond like giant billows petrified on the rise. And the birds were flying home.

Not long after she had arrived at the soothsayer's house Nwabunor was still finding it hard to explain.

'I beg you in the name of everything that appeals to you,' she said, 'can't you bear with me for just a little longer? My sales are poor and my husband cannot help me, and you know I have nobody else to ask. Or do you want me to go naked and beg through the whole town? If it will suit the spirits to have me in that condition, it is well—'

'But what do you want me to do?' asked the soothsayer. 'I have told you what the spirits demanded this time: ten goats and ten white cocks, or the price of them; five sheets of white cloth, each two arm-spreads in length—or the price of them; four bottles of gin and ten kegs of palm-wine, or the price of them; ten bowls of kolanuts and ten of alligator pepper, or the price of them. And if after one month or two the source of your adversity is not removed from the roots, and the spirits still consider that a little more needs to be done, you will be duly informed and you will have to seek about for whatever is asked. These are not words that come out of my mouth. I am only an agent of those that know and see better than we blind fools.'

'But would the spirits not have mercy on my condition? The little I make from my sales I spend on food to keep my son and myself alive. My son also goes to school and if I don't pay his fees he will be sent out of school. His father is a helpless drunkard and he cannot help me. My son is the only thing I have, the only thing keeping me alive today and free of total shame. Do the spirits not understand? Can they not bear with me a little longer? Do they not feel?' she asked now in frustration, ignorant of the dangers there are said to be of impiety.

The soothsayer looked slowly up at her from the seeds spread on the ground, then opened his eyes a bit wider.

'My daughter,' he said in a warning tone, low but steady and full-throated, 'do you ask me *that*? If you feel any doubts about the power of the things I tell you, I will draw a circle of chalk here and let you stand in it—then say once again what you have just said and you will see for yourself whether or not the spirits can feel.'

He gently relaxed his brows and waited for the oracular threat to go down, letting his eyes run down the perplexed figure of the woman. Then he looked up again and asked, 'Did you not come of your own will to ask my help?'

'But surely you—the spirits—can bear with me a little longer,' she replied.

'My daughter, the dangers threatening your life and that of your son are too great. I have told you more than once before and I won't hesitate to tell you again: the threat is right at your doorstep—*right at your doorstep*—but I am not mentioning any names. That is not what you have asked me. You have merely asked me to remove the danger from you, and this is the only help I am trying to give you. You are asking a big favour of the spirits. Now they have named their price, and do *not* accept any half-measures. And when I tell you the price they have named you reply that you have to pay the fees of your son. Will you think of sending your son to school tomorrow if he is dead?'

'That will not happen!' she snapped instinctively, then asked, hands bared and face drawn in an anguished plea, 'What else will be left of me?'

'So then, which is more important to you—your son's schooling or his life and yours and the chances of bearing another child and beating the shame?'

She merely looked down and sighed, disarmed. And feeling reasonably justified the soothsayer used the interval to repeat his catalogue of terms while the woman gathered her cloth.

'I have heard all you said and now I know there is no other way. Here is some of the money. That is all I have made in my sales and all I have today. I will not stand in the way of your work. I know it is for my own good. I will give you the rest when I can.'

The soothsayer took the money in his right palm and contemplated it for three blinks of the eyelid, making a show of leniency.

'The spirits do not accept any half-measures,' he slowly intoned, 'but I have seen your plight and they can sometimes make exceptions after the right things have been said and done. But that is very rare—', he raised his eyes half-way to emphasise, 'that is very rare. You can go home now, but do not forget the rest of the payment. And remember that they will listen only if you appease them in season. Stay well, and be careful.' He waved her off.

Nwabunor said goodbye. The soothsayer gathered his seeds, then stood up from his mat, stretched his arms full and wide, and bared his kola-tanned teeth in a contented yawn.

Shortly afterwards Nwabunor was sitting on a very low, three-legged stool (the fourth leg had been knocked off) outside the door, contemplating the grey emptiness before her, her hand on her cheek and her face hollow and drawn, like a mournful widow, thinking, They will keep trying. But they will always fail! She was unaware of the chickens retiring past her to their roost. This was about the time when the last lights of day were disappearing, and the houses were lighting up their hurricane lamps, and the geckos and the insects were shrieking in their numbers, and child-worn mothers, too tired to run after their stubborn children, were warning them that no matter how far they ran they would not smell their supper unless they took their baths.

This was also the time when Ogugua thought she should be going home. Not by any means because there was anything binding to do at home or because she feared her husband might be suspicious, but because she just felt like going home. She had thus stood up and declared she was going, and though Gwam begged her to stay a little longer she had convinced him, more by her practised irresistibility than by appealing, that she really must go.

'Are you going to let me go away again this time without anything,' she had said, tying her cloth and eyeing him.

'But you know I need all this money now,' he appealed, 'with all the work on hand. Think of the houses I am putting up, all the people working on them. And you know the election campaigns are approaching, and people will—'

'Yes, but do you think I do not need any money myself?'

'Why not wait until next time?'

'No—that's what you have kept telling me. I won't agree this time.'

'Oh, you women!' shaking his head.

So he had dug into one of his pockets and counted her some ten pounds . . .

He was seeing her off, and they were exchanging recollections and discussing plans and holding hands part of the way, like two youngsters in love. But scarcely had they gone forty paces from the house when they spied a figure staggering towards them. Without waiting to say more than goodnight they parted from each other and Ogugua quickened her steps as though there were a lot to do at home that needed her attention.

Obanua staggered to an unsteady halt. On his right hand was a half-full bottle of palmwine and from one of his side pockets a torch pointed its full light upwards into the dark void. Through the wine and the dying light of day he had dimly seen a woman and a man and for that brief moment the scene had tickled his drunken fancy. He had spread his hands, smiling under the impulse, and tried to embrace the woman, but she slipped past him disdainfully. And suddenly the smile vanished from his face while the mouth was left drooping open, for he had been touched by the familiarity of the reaction from a woman whom he now almost instinctively recognised to be his wife.

'Ogugua!' he shouted. 'Ogugua!'

But she ignored him completely and marched towards home with unrelaxed urgency.

Still through a drunken reflex, he turned his head towards the direction of the man. But he too had gone out of sight and all that met his clouded gaze was the punctuated twinkle-twinkle of the fire-flies. He looked again towards her, but far from feeling any impulse for action he dimly imagined what he was likely to meet at home if he tried to follow her and seek an explanation. Thus stunned, drunken and powerless he resumed his unsteady trek towards the mission.

He had finally got himself a job, or rather picked up a job that had been lying around. Nobody wanted that job, nobody would touch it or come near it. But he had to grab it because it gave him a place to be in and paid his way.

The Catholic Mission had for a long time wanted a

nightwatchman for the premises of the new church. But there was too much taboo around that job and everybody was scared. Rocks and sand for concrete blocks used for the construction of the church were fetched—the rocks being hewn into convenient sizes—from the banks of the river some distance away. The spot from which the rocks were collected was part of a long stonescape interlaced with a murky thicket, the whole scenery presenting a dark, sinister picture as fearsome by day as it would surely be by night to those bold enough to pry. The whole stretch was an extension of the shrine of the river-goddess *Ushe* and, though no gong ever told it, was supposed to come within her pale, approachable to none but her priestess.

The parish priest had been warned of this, but he had dismissed the reverence as superstition and had told the labourers who brought the rocks that there was nothing in it at all, and sought to convince them of a much greater power by sprinkling 'holy water' on them each day before they set out to work. So in the day the men went down to the river and brought in the sand and the rocks. But by the following morning all the rocks were gone, and the nightwatchman who had been engaged had run out on the job on the frightened explanation that, holy water or no holy water, he could no longer stand the sight of the white-robed figures who came in the dead of dark to carry away the rocks one after another on their heads in a funerary file. Probably the labourers were just as ignorant as the priest of how this all came about, but even if they knew anything they would not tell. The labourers who brought the rocks by day were paid and so earned a living. Also they rested partly on the power they believed the holy water had and partly on their hope that any terrors could be conveniently escaped in the light of day. But every one of them had a deep religious fear of what the night might bring and no one wanted to come near the church at that time. No one, certainly, who knew that his life meant a good deal to him and felt that he had a responsibility to those who looked up to him for care and protection.

But Obanua needed a job, and he got the nightwatch

that paid relatively more. Besides, he could not get the day job because the priest had said there was no more, not because he had got enough day hands but because he thought to divert interest to the night work among the many jobless people in the town. Not only did Obanua need the money. But with him such fear had lost much of its sharp edge, less because he abounded in courage than because he was now used to a mood that made him insensible of the terrors of the night. The only fear that meant much was at home, and now he felt reasonably relieved that he had somewhere to stay away from it all. He was still running . . .

He hadn't done more than a few nights in the job, and tonight was like most other nights. Having ostensibly settled down he would saunter around the rising walls of the church for some time, cane and torch in hand, mumbling a tune to himself and occasionally stumbling against the rocks and rising up again. When the priest came round and saw him moving he would feel encouraged that work was going on.

'Well done,' the priest would say.

'Good evening, Father,' he would reply, unsteady in his pose and a drunken grin on his face.

'You are doing well. Keep it up.'

'Leave it to me, Father.'

Even the priest was afraid to visit the night scene of the church, though he wore a respectable disguise and made every possible show of courage. And it was largely because he saw someone who seemed not in the least moved by fear that he felt encouraged and appreciative. With someone around he could hazard a brief stroll, and go back satisfied that the stones would be protected. But he was a bit worried about his nightwatchman's drunken habits. He knew that nightwatchmen often did all sorts of things to beguile the nocturnal solitude, like smoking and singing and knocking their sticks about even with nothing in sight. But this one was always getting drunk—always—and passing out into heavy sleep. On one or two occasions he had had to knock him up himself and rebuke him. But a few nights had now passed with him as nightwatch over the stones when fetching had been resumed by the day labourers, and no thefts had been revealed. So there was still hope . . .

The priest talked briefly with him but left soon after, when he couldn't get any sense out of this man, intoning *In nomine Domini Jesu Christi* . . .

At midnight the Reverend Brother—a short, stocky, devout man who, people said, would have made the priesthood but for the deterioration of his eyesight—came to ring the midnight bell. He tried to bid Obanua good cheer but found the latter wretchedly asleep. After ringing the bell (in the old church) and on his way back, he still found the nightwatch in the same pose, looking pitilessly clubbed, his torch lying near him and pointing its light into the undefined darkness. The Brother shook his head and passed by.

Not long past midnight Obanua was still lying in unguarded sleep. Occasionally he was stirred up by some sudden impulse, either when some hot wind gushed up his system or an insect-sting overcame his insensible person. He would then wake up briefly to bellow an involuntary song and just as casually slip back into his doze while the smile thinned away from his lips.

Shortly after he fell back, the mysterious visitors came. For the past few nights they had failed to come to the scene—whether because the presence of a nightwatchman exerted a desecrating influence or a check on their visitation was not easy to tell. But now it seemed they had grown used to his presence and it no longer bothered them much. Maybe they saw through him—an ever-drunk guard was as good as no guard at all. So they came in their usual file (formidable figures in white, and they seemed painted white too), lifted stones onto their heads, and filed back again in the direction of the river whence they had come in a silence that seemed more furtive than the darkness of the night. They did this about six times and never seemed to tire, but maintained that same formation with the stubborn tenacity of soldier ants. Six times they came and went, six times the white figures coloured the dark scene of the church with still greater mystery.

At the end of their mission all the rocks had gone. But the more disturbing discovery that the labourers made in the day was that the rocks had not been carried back to the place from which they had originally been collected. They had either been cast into the river and thus settled at the deep bed, or they had been taken to some other place, or they had been left somewhere . . .

Thus the next morning the nightwatchman stared at the mysterious emptiness before him in wonder. The priest paced excitedly about the whole place, each hand struggling to crush the other behind his back, and he casting his eyes now on the scene and now on the man while he cursed in a passion of mixed indignation and fear.

'You beast, you idiot! I warned you. You fool, would you say I didn't tell you? Sleeping heavily away while these bastards made comfortably away with what the mission is paying through her nose for. And you say you are a night-watchman. Do you call yourself a responsible person? Hm?'

'Father, I am sorry—'

'Shut up, you drunkard! What could you do, when you were not in your senses? Now I am warning you seriously. You are either a nightwatchman on this place or you are not. If this theft is repeated you are not to be found on these premises any more. And I won't mind in the least closing up all work on the new church—I don't see the point in building a church for bastards who do nothing but steal away the stones that are being collected for the purpose.'

He took his handkerchief from his cassock and wiped his foaming mouth and his wet brow.

'Go—go away now, you fool!' he waved furiously, 'Remember, this is the last time I warn you. You either do your work or you get out!'

The last two words were said as if they were the only ones that mattered.

Obanua picked up his torch and his cap. He was mov-

105

ing towards his house, though he had not really decided that that was where he should go. A good many thoughts were fleeting through his head but none had prevailed sufficiently to form itself into a definite plan or decision. And then it suddenly occurred to him as he dimly caught sight of his house that there was no point in going there. There is sure not to be food for me, he thought, and so why not go off somewhere where there won't be so much shame if I am refused a bite? As the thought went through his mind he fumbled the switch of his torch, pushing it up and down, only to discover that the light would not show any more. He instinctively held his steps, then turned off and made towards the bar.

8

Ubaka walked briskly up to the sleeping foreman and called: 'Okoh! Okoh!'

A fly was playing around the gaping, dripping mouth of the figure whose only sign of life was the rise-and-fall of the big, irregular trunk. He did not hear the boy calling. Even when the fly settled on the upper lip and crawled over the skin he was too 'dead' to stir. Occasionally he snored, and then the fly would back away.

'Okoh!'

He still wouldn't stir. The three other boys hoped he wouldn't.

But Ubaka was determined upon his mission. So he stooped quickly and shook the man. But he had to shake a few times more before Okoh came to and struggled up, grunting stupidly.

'Hm! Hm! What is it? What do you want?'

'I want to make a report to you. These boys—'

'What is it again?' Okoh asked, as he rubbed his mouth and gathered his garment together.

'These boys have been cheating.'

'He is lying. We didn't cheat.'

The fathead led the defence.

Okoh glared at him with a heavy face and stabbed a finger at his head.

'Have you started again, you mischievous little rat? I always knew you wouldn't miss out on any mischief. I think you need some beating.' And turning to Ubaka, 'What has he done this time?'

Ubaka began, 'When we came here this morning, he

and these two others decided that they were going to 'find some way', but they wouldn't let anybody know what they were planning to do. On our way to the stream the three of them suddenly disappeared into the bush—'

'It's a lie! We didn't do any such thing!' interrupted the fathead.

'Shut up!' warned the foreman, 'or I'll split that calabash head of yours.'

'They disappeared into the bush with their buckets and stayed there for some time. When they came out they were carrying their buckets high above their heads. Seeing that I was watching them they avoided me and wouldn't let me see what they had in the buckets. Occasionally they ran, when they noticed that I was moving closer to them. When we got to the stream they stayed apart from everyone else and filled their buckets with the sand. But on our way back this one (*pointing*) stumbled on a root and fell with his bucket of sand. We all ran to him, and I found his bucket stuffed more than half-full with dry leaves and grass. And when the rest of us got here I also found that these two other boys' buckets contained the same thing.'

Ubaka finished his story and looked round, half-panting, at his opponents, as if challenging them to refute his story.

'How many times have they fetched?' Okoh asked.

'Five times, when everyone else has gone only three,' Ubaka replied.

The fathead knew what would be coming to them.

'He is just lying. He is jealous of us because we are faster than the rest of them,' he claimed.

The foreman looked menacingly at him.

'I know you,' he said. 'I know this is the kind of thing you are capable of, you clever rat. I am going to cancel all that you have done and you are going to start all over again—all three of you. And as for you in particular—you potheaded ant—if I catch you doing this kind of thing again I will throw you out of this work and you won't receive a single penny. Do you hear that? Now take back those pebbles and start fetching all over again.'

The fathead and his friends took back their pebbles, and as they set off towards the stream they eyed Ubaka menacingly and swore that they were going to take it all back on him some other way . . .

Bomboy had been regarding all this adult scene with considerable disquiet. He felt relieved when his brother took him by the hand and they made off again to the stream.

'Uba,' he asked, 'why did Okoh not beat that boy?'

'I don't know,' his brother replied, 'I think he did not want to.'

'But he beat him yesterday.'

'Yes. He beats him every day. I think he is getting tired of beating him every day.'

There was a pause.

'Uba, can Okoh beat you?'

'Don't you see he is much bigger than me? But I have done nothing to him.'

'If you do something, will he beat you?'

'I don't know!' But he looked down sympathetically and added, 'I won't do anything bad, so he won't beat me.'

They fetched on in the burning sun. Lizards lashed at one another's tails. Cicadas chirped and birds twitted. Leaves and grass rustled in the occasional stray breeze, but otherwise let the sunlight explore their naked forms. People passed back and forth along the path, but their necks were drooping somewhat now and they were getting a little too tired to greet one another.

Half-way back on the next trip Bomboy felt the strain on his knees and the discomfort showed on his face. He stopped and whimpered a couple of times. Ubaka stopped too and felt sorry.

'Are you tired?' he asked Bomboy.

The other nodded.

'Are you hungry?'

The little boy nodded again.

'Do you want to go home?'

Bomboy looked down, then shook his head.

'Alright. It will soon be over for today, you hear? Then

we will go home and . . . and eat, you hear? You hear?'

Bomboy nodded, sufficiently reassured. They rested a little while under the shade of a mango tree, then set off again. Sometimes Bomboy ran ahead to kick this orange or chase after that butterfly. When he rejoined his brother there was still no end to his questioning and comment.

'Uba, after you have given your mother some of the money, what will you do with the remainder?'

'I don't know,' replied Ubaka. 'I have told you I would give her all of it. But she may give some back to me.'

'What will you do with that?'

'With what?'

'With the money that she gives back to you?'

'I will use it in buying something.'

Bomboy paused a little, but was irrepressible.

'Uba, what will you buy with it?'

'I don't know. I haven't thought about that yet.'

'Why don't you use it in buying a catapult, and a tennis ball, and a whistle, and a *blow-blow*, and a whistle, and shoes, and a catapult, and a tennis ball—'

'I will buy them,' Ubaka cut him short.

Another slight pause.

'Uba, will they give you a lot of money?'

'Not very much.'

'Will you give me some of it?'

'Yes.'

It went on and on.

Under the shade the foreman gasped and snored. Along the route the fathead and his friends, feeling considerably subdued, laboured on, scowling at Ubaka and calling him names every time they met him. But very soon the animosity was lost in the pain of work and the joy of play.

The sun blazed on.

9

In the palmwine bar there were a good many idle men, talking about many things among themselves. The owners of the place, the woman and her maid, kept the atmosphere alive by replenishing each table's supply and sometimes giving it the benefit of their company. Those who drank and laughed and talked probably had a very good time, but in one corner of the bar, where the attention was not so much on cup or company, a group of men brooded and blamed, smiled and scowled, grumbled and teased. It was draughts, and they were playing for money.

'Play on,' Sinkea said, after a long brooding silence. 'You have waited too long.'

Obanua scratched his head uneasily.

'Hold on,' he replied. 'Hold on. We don't have to rush now.'

'Yes, but you are wasting my time.'

'Hold on. Hold on yet.'

They all kept quiet again. There were two players, with four spectators who should say nothing though each knew where his sympathy lay and could almost give telepathic advice. Their faces were all set, either with fear of discomfiture or joy of triumph moderated though by a slight fear that the opponent might thwart the winning move. Their faces were all set, motionless, and even almost expressionless—you could only read their words if you knew the mood of the game at the moment. *What would he do now, what move next?* Faces now like masks, smooth or unkempt, only showing an occasional sign of life when the eyes rolled or the throat squirmed in a gulp or the nostrils twitched in reflex. A tense, cautious atmosphere where if you stared at anyone he thought you were threatening him. Even the air there seemed motionless.

Obanua took his left hand off from under his chin and substituted his right hand, shifting in his seat somewhat. And for a moment the other also fell back in relief. They sighed and hummed, then stared on at the still inexplicable structure on the draughts-board.

'Play on, now. Play on,' Sinkea said. 'The day is passing,' as he looked outside awhile.

His opponent's eyes lighted up, and he took the right hand quickly from off his chin. Nwanze, who sat close to him, looked aside at his face as though to catch any message of triumph.

Obanua lifted his hand, poised it over the board as his eyes scanned the entire structure in a final safeguard, then put it down and moved a seed with measured certitude. After he had done that and been reasonably sure of the excellence of that move, he looked up at Sinkea, who seemed to have caught the meaning.

'Eat that,' Obanua announced.

The spectators screamed and whistled—three of them out of utter alarm at the danger in which Sinkea stood, and only Nwanze in sympathy with Obanua.

'Eat that,' Obanua repeated.

Sinkea sighed heavily, then shook his head slowly and hopelessly from one side to the other, like a man watching the blocks crash down from a house he had raised to a reasonable level.

'The day is passing, my friend,' Obanua retaliated. 'Eat that and let's be going.'

'Don't rush now,' the other said, slightly irritated. 'We have just come out of a long delay you put us in. Don't rush me now.'

At the other corner of the bar the people drank and talked and laughed. They were mostly people who wove palm-leaves into roof thatches for sale, or fetched firewood for sale, or were just plainly unemployed, and often met at the bar at all times of the day and exchanged gossip.

They spent the little money they made or else drank on credit. Either because she never aimed to get very rich on selling drinks or out of a naturally accommodating disposition, the woman of the bar bore all the debts hopefully and gave each company of customers unstinted benefit of her company and grace.

'Go on, eat!' Obanua reminded his opponent.

He felt carelessly triumphant, rubbing his neck in a mood of abandon and confident ease. He and Nwanze exchanged a few derisive glances and felt sure the game was theirs.

Sinkea's eyes had been scanning endlessly. Suddenly he jerked up his head, rapped his fingers as though a smart idea had hit his mind, then tensed his brow in a determination none of the others could yet explain.

'Alright,' he said.

Obanua looked to see what could have prompted such confidence.

Sinkea played and collected two seeds of Obanua's.

Obanua rounded five seeds of his opponent and collected them. As soon as he did that, Sinkea pushed one of his front line in a move that was bound to leave his opponent's side virtually cleaned up.

Obanua froze. His brow drew close in an unconscious frown. His fingers tightened somewhat, then relaxed just as brokenly. His neck stiffened and his eyes burned, and fear crept into him. No way out of this, he thought, no way out. And wherewith shall I pay the money? They had staked five shillings on each game and he had already lost four and won none. What luck, he thought. One pound, on top of everything else!

'Come on, now,' Sinkea said. 'Do you want us to spend the rest of the day here?'

Then he took a long, disdainful look at Obanua, his eyes fixed on the other's face as you would look at a child you thought deserved good beating.

'I thought you were very happy a while ago,' Sinkea taunted. 'Where has your joy gone?'

Then he looked at his supporters, and they all laughed

in agreement, and he felt encouraged to quip, 'When a hunter hits good luck he looks like a perfect shot! Come on, now.'

Obanua nibbled at his thumb and shook his head as disillusionment came upon him. His seat was already beginning to feel hot and the sweat shone on his face. A slight wind went through the bar but his mood beat the effect.

Suddenly there seemed a moment in which everybody else but he noticed an opening somewhere in the structure on the board. For a peculiar silence hit the scene once again and even Sinkea lost his euphoria. He stared intensely at the seeds and was convinced he shouldn't have made the move he did. Obanua didn't know this, and still stared blankly and in empty-headed concentration at the arrangement.

But Nwanze looked round roguishly at the others, including Sinkea, and, still looking, nudged Obanua at the elbow. Obanua turned inquisitively, and Nwanze became embarrassed. He had found a way to help his friend out of the tangle, but he knew he dared not let the others catch him doing such a thing. Yet none of them seemed to notice what was going on. Even Obanua thought that it was an accidental jolt, and turned back again to meditate the seeds on the board. Sinkea himself was no less distressed, feeling now considerably disappointed with the move he had made and hoped would win him all, thinking now, If he should see that! If he should see that.

Obanua was by now a perfect study in helplessness. He looked this way and that, grunted and sighed, shifted and scratched, but saw no possible way of escaping the artful tangle Sinkea had hooked him in. Sinkea himself, well aware of the delicate balance he had set up, no longer looked at Obanua with a superior eye. There was now a slight look of fear hanging on his brow as he glanced at his opponent and asked him to play. The moment was tense, and everyone had to be careful or something would go very wrong. A car hooted past and they all looked suddenly out.

'Play now,' Sinkea reminded his opponent. 'I gave you food to eat. Eat it,' looking stealthily now at the board, now at Obanua.

He had said it, but he knew he didn't mean the taunt.

Obanua finally sighed, then poised his hand over the board. He ignored the allowance and tried to push some other seed, which would have been in the best interests of Sinkea as it would have saved him from his terrible mistake. But Nwanze held Obanua's hand and warned him to claim the allowance that Sinkea gave.

'Eat it,' Nwanze said, almost screaming, to Obanua.

Sinkea's eyes glowed with anger.

'What's the matter with you, Nwanze?' he asked, furious. 'Have you forgotten the rule—that you shouldn't advise anyone? What's wrong with you?'

It was at this point that Obanau saw through the move that Sinkea had made, and understood that if he 'ate' his opponent would truly be in trouble. He lighted up briskly.

'Alright. Alright,' said Obanua. 'There's no trouble. I'll play.'

He then played and claimed his opponent's seed.

Sinkea was infuriated.

'That can't happen!' he declared. 'We have a rule, and we must all keep it. I will *not* allow this.' He stared round furiously at the other men for support in his protest and affirmed, 'You are all witnesses and have seen that. I will *not* allow it.'

'That's right,' said one of the other three. 'Nwanze, what you did was wrong. You should not have talked.'

'Everybody can see that very clearly. Nwanze shouldn't have mentioned it,' said another.

'What have I done?' asked Nwanze, with a look of innocence. 'Was it a crime that I pointed out what was so plain that even a one-eyed child could have detected it?'

With a villainous smile on his face, Obanua acted called-upon to arbitrate.

'What is all this?' he asked, in a relaxed sort of way. 'Do we need to quarrel over a mere game of draughts?

After all it is not Nwanze who teaches me all the moves I have been making.'

'Yes, but not this one!' Sinkea retorted in full measure. 'And is there a rule that no one should advise, or isn't there?'

'Do you call that advice?'

'O-oh! Well why didn't you play the seed all the time you had been brooding over the board? And you say it's not advice!'

'No, come, come, come,' said the peace-lover, still pleasantly amused. 'Come, my dear friend, you can't call that advice—'

'Who are you telling that?' Sinkea fumed. 'I call it advice, and I say I *won't* accept it!'

With that he toppled the board and the seeds clattered to the floor.

'Let us begin a new game,' he said as he rose to dare his opponent to challenge his action.

'Why did you do that?' asked Obanua.

Everyone felt uncomfortable, either with fear of possible results or with disgust at the absence of reason and restraint. But not surprise. Fights were so nearly a regular feature of such idlers' haunts that it was taken for granted as the most likely result of even the least dispute.

'Why did you do that?' Obanua repeated.

'Am I a fool, or a woman, that you should do all this foolishness and all I do is stand and stare at you? Let us begin a fresh game.'

The other people in the bar had by now noticed the tension and the imminence of a fight, and so came to exhort the two men to settle the dispute peacefully, like sensible adults.

'Nwanze, don't you know you didn't act properly?' one of them advised. 'You are a sensible man but I must tell you quite sincerely that you should not have done what you did.'

'True, Nwanze, you should never have interfered, seeing what the result was likely to be!' said another. 'Surely this is not the first time you have been here, and you yourself play too.'

Nwanze turned his head as each of these rebukes came to him, seeming to question with his eyes the sense of each remark.

'Someday somebody has to tell us what it is we are free to do when a game of draughts is going on,' he complained. 'When you scratch your neck somebody turns round to look at you as if scratching meant speaking. When you shift your buttocks to ease the strain of sitting and watching a game that never seems to end, they think you are doing something else. It is even an unspeakable crime to rise up and announce that you are going to the latrine. *Hiya!* One almost becomes careful not to let the breath escape one's nostrils! One would have thought that we were all playing to amuse ourselves.'

'Yes, but not in this game—'

'What is so unique about *this* game? Is it simply because I pointed out what any year-old could easily have detected that all this fire is raging over my head? So much that you have left the man with whom you are involved in the contest and transferred on to the head of the unfortunate he-goat the curse that was meant for the tortoise? I don't see what is so unique about this game.'

'You don't see what is so unique about this game?' Sinkea queried. 'Is it every time you play a game of draughts that you bet money on it—and you tell me you don't see what is so unique about this game? We bet five shillings on each game we play and you say you don't see what is so unique about this game? If by any chance you came upon five shillings would you be the wretch you are today?'

'You are quite right, my dear brother,' Nwanze replied in mock acquiescence. 'You can be sure I wouldn't be what I am today. More than that, I certainly wouldn't be where I am now, here in this place. Because I can't see how in these days of dearth I could light upon the sum of five shillings and be so foolish as to spend it playing draughts. *E-heh!* Fancy throwing so lavishly down to a goat when you haven't even had a bite yourself!'

The exchanges rolled and clattered on. Obanua made one or two ineffective gestures, but far from making serious and genuine efforts at arbitration he seemed rather relieved that the storm had shifted from him for a while.

But the others pleaded and reasoned. They did not make much progress and a few of them trickled out in despair, one of them saying to his companion, 'Come, my friend—I am tired of fights and fights. It was only a small matter like this that brought on a row between my wife and me and she greeted my brow *here* with the ladle. I don't want these jobless rascals to complete the disfiguration if I can avoid it.'

One by one all but one or two other idlers left the bar as the battle of words, now made somewhat more graphic with fists that didn't do more than threaten the face, raged on.

In the end it was the woman of the bar who prevailed.

'Are you two gorillas not ashamed of yourselves?' she clapped. 'Do you wish to turn my bar into a fighting ground? How could you make so much trouble over what infants could have settled peacefully among themselves? I say, you should be thoroughly ashamed.'

'I have told them—' Obanua began.

'Don't put yourself into it now!' she stopped him short. 'You lit up all this fire and when it started raging you withdrew your feet. Don't put yourself into it now.'

'Alright,' he resigned himself, 'you handle it the way you want to.'

'Yes,' she continued. 'I don't see what there is to break your heads about. If the game has been spoiled by Nwanze's remark it is only right that you should follow your rules and begin a fresh one, though I don't see that that is a reason for turning the board on everybody.'

'But you can bear me out,' Sinkea said.

'Alright. Alright,' she said. 'No need now to go over it again. Since this is your rule, you should all start a fresh game. I did not put a draughts-board in my bar so that adults would come here and lose their heads and threaten the whole place. I beg you all, play on in peace. Please.'

At last they all accepted the incident, with varying degrees of magnanimity, as a spell of folly, and played a fresh game. The usual rites of silence were duly observed, and each played as though not only money but also life and honour were at stake. This time no one rushed the other, no one taunted the other, no one menaced the other. It was a long, tiring game, but the watchers made sure not to give themselves away. In the end Obanua lost this game also. The fifth game lost. He was unwilling now to play any more.

'Alright,' Sinkea said as he rose and brushed his buttocks. 'You know how much it is. Twenty-five shillings.'

Obanua looked up at him, a cold appeal in his eyes. But Sinkea ignored this, unwilling even to have to repeat what he said. Certainly unwilling to come into any kind of compromise. He merely looked away. And he even emphasised the mood by commenting on the prospects of bad weather. Obanua sat uneasily trying to figure out how to make his case.

Most of the customers having left, the woman of the bar was reckoning up her proceeds while her maid cleaned the tables and collected the cups. A glass slipped from her hand but she caught it smartly up again before it could fall, and threw her mistress a glance, alarmed, quick, and roguish.

'Obanua,' reminded Sinkea, 'I have other things to do today, other places to go.'

'Look, Sinkea,' the other pleaded, 'this is not the first time you and I are playing, and playing for money for that matter—neither is it going to be the last. So I—'

'I don't want any of your preaching today. Just give me the money and let me be going away.'

'After all I am not running away from this town.'

'What good does your staying in it do me if you starve me and my family? Please let us not quarrel over that?'

Obanua sighed in despair.

'Sinkea' he raised his head up again, 'at the end of the month I'll—'

'There won't be any "end of the month" this time. I won't have any more of these postponements. I want the money today. Now.'

Obanua saw the resolution in his wide-staring eyes.

'But I don't have any money here with me,' half-pleading, half-asserting. 'So what do you want me to do?'

'Obanua,' the other spelled out with calm but ominous clarity, 'let me be honest with you. When I left my house this morning I reckoned on coming home with money, not without. If you do not give me my money now—one pound five shillings, and I am not going to insist on the fifteen shillings you have been owing for a long time now —if you don't hand me this money now both of us are going to be carried out of this place.'

There was a sudden silence. A cat miaowed and they all heard it. It was the woman of the bar who spoke.

'Sinkea. Please, I do not want this to happen here. Please don't bring—'

'Then tell him to give me the money!'

'I have promised—' Obanua started.

'What promise?'

As he spoke thus in angry distrust Sinkea shot his hand forward and grabbed Obanua by the shirt, his eyes glowing.

'Please! Please! I beg you two!'

'Leave my shirt,' Obanua exhorted in panic. The grip hurt.

'Are you giving me the money?' was the menacing question.

'Leave the shirt first!'

Sinkea read a threat in that demand and almost drew his hand forcibly down the other's trunk, to rip the shirt from the shoulders down. His eyes alone could have done that much. But before he could do anything so violent the others jumped in between them and pleaded for restraint.

'I beg you. I beg you,' said the woman. 'Leave him

alone. Please. I beg you,' and she rubbed her palms and made to genuflect in supplication.

'He has never paid me a penny of whatever he owes. How can I continue to be so kind—am I such a rich man?' Sinkea said.

'I know,' replied the woman, still pleading, 'but if you tear his shirt and both of you fight and break your heads is that going to make it any easier for him to pay? While there is life there is hope of making it all up. He has promised to pay you when the month ends. Please let us wait until then. If he doesn't do what he promised then we will know what to say. I beg you.'

Sinkea took one last contemptuous look at Obanua, who all the while had been making calm but spiritless efforts to disengage himself from Sinkea's grip, feigning restraint but in fact trying to hide his weakness.

After Sinkea and the rest had left, Obanua brushed his shirt, and turning to Nwanze, said, 'You know that two people cannot be mad at the same time.'

'That is true,' replied the other, then a bit in a whisper, 'but you did well to leave him alone. Besides, how would people receive the news that you have come to a drinking-house to court what you are running from your house for? Let him carry his trouble away with him.'

Obanua chuckled and shook his head . . .

Long after everybody else had left the two men were still at the bar. To Obanua at least this meant a great deal. They had even napped and woken up. But the woman of the bar was still somewhat angry with them for the irresponsibility that could have put her bar in danger. So though she let them stay on she didn't give them much attention, sulkily evading Obanua's every single solicitous glance. Finally he gave up the pretence and went across to her where she sat near the door.

'Come, come, my dear,' he coaxed, 'won't you—'

'M-m-m-m-m-m!' she shook her head and rose quickly

from her seat. 'Don't you come with your stuff today. I have had enough trouble from you already.'

Over in his seat Nwanze chuckled wittingly and scratched his neck as he reflected that this was mere feminine formality and that before long their table would be supporting a few bottles and cups.

'But you have seen what happened,' Obanua said. 'It was only a slight row started by a man who wanted to show he was smarter than everybody. And I merely left him because I didn't want to be found behaving like a little boy.' Then he looked down again at her, closely, and rubbed her shoulders. 'Come,' he said, 'you know what we want.'

'What?' she asked, looking up discouragingly.

'So what do you think we have been sitting down and waiting for all this time—to be asked to go away? Come on now.'

'Drinks? Isn't it drinks? You can let your throat climb down, because you are not going to have any drinks today unless you are ready to pay.'

And then she looked about the room with an expression of inflexible nonchalance.

'Come now, don't you understand when a man can and when he cannot do something? Why—'

'I don't know what you are talking about. When do you ever agree that you can? For over one month now you have owed more than three pounds here, and you come now to talk as if you will settle all your account when the money comes into your hands. You are not drinking a drop in this bar today.'

A little uneasy about the waiting, Nwanze stoked up the crisis and teased.

'You are quite right, my dear,' he mocked. 'A man who aims to keep his throat wet all the time must realise that there are a few tiny duties to perform in the bargain. Or does he think that these things are purchased with sand or cowries? I am entirely with you.' Then he and Obanua winked conspiratorially at each other.

'Don't mind that oaf,' Obanua said to the uninterested

woman, 'Look, I am making you a definite promise this time. As soon as I get paid at the end of this month this is the first place I will head for, and I will pay you everything I have been owing you for over—how long did you say?—over a month. By God, I promise to do that.'

'This is how you have always promised and I am tired of your promises.'

'This time I won't fail you. If I do, never let me set my foot in your bar any longer. Truly.'

The woman looked up at him, then down, contemptuously, then hissed, rising up and readjusting the wrapper round her waist.

'This is why I like you—' Obanua flattered.

'I don't want to be liked that way!'

'—you always know when a man is telling the truth.'

'Indeed!'

Obanua rejoined Nwanze, and they both smiled at what they knew to be the expected outcome. And before they could bat their eyelids two or three times the barmaid laid two bottles, each capped by the white froth, and two cups on their table. She giggled at the two idle men, then ran off inside.

From this point the dialogue was a more meaningful one—with drink.

Long, long past midday, when the sun had floated stealthily across to the left, high above the crown, and your shadow on the right was now vying with you for speed and smartness, and the grasshoppers were making as if they would shoot themselves to death, the two men, still alone in the bar, had emptied about ten bottles of palmwine between themselves and now gawked and belched and drawled at each other across the table. There was no more space now on it. All over were bottles and a plate empty of food. This Obanua had scrounged from the woman with as much importunity as secured him the drinks, though this time he aroused more pity than contempt because he got the woman to picture, as often, the helplessness of his domestic plight. The entire stuff now littered the table. Occasionally one item tottered and nearly fell, but was again steadied by the same fumbling hand that had tipped it out of balance. At best the two men looked like two travellers who had grown tired of the way and had stopped over to refresh, but in the process had quite forgotten that a good journey still lay ahead, and guzzled away.

'Why did you laugh when I said—when I said she liked me?' Obanua was saying in sodden language.

'B-because I knew you were lying,' the other replied, then chuckled while his eyes laboured up to look at Obanua.

'Me? Me lying?'

'Yes.'

'You—you are a liar yourself!' and he stabbed his finger unsteadily across at Nwanze.

Nwanze chuckled again, then bent his head sideways and spat on the floor of the bar.

'Do you—hear me?' Obanua insisted. 'I said you—you are a *liar*!'

'Alright,' the other said. 'Let us—let us not qu-quarrel about that.'

Obanua gazed at him for a while. Then his face loosened in a full-toothed grin, and he stretched an unsteady hand to pat Nwanze on the shoulder in a show of drunken solidarity.

'That's why I *like* you! You are—you have a lot of s-sense —sense in your fat head.'

He laid the hand on Nwanze's shoulder and shook it. The other winced and nodded under the effect, then let his head stoop. Obanua let his own stoop too, and the two men now looked as though they had been thoroughly discomfited in a self-imposed contest and had now decided by mutual consent to give up.

Shortly after Obanua raised his head again.

'You are *sleeping*!' he dizzily accused Nwanze, stabbing an unsteady finger towards the other's face.

'Me?' Nwanze knocked his chest in denial. 'Me? Sleeping? You are *mad*!'

Again Obanua grinned gratuitously.

'Do you know—do you know—what my mother was asking me—yesterday?'

Nwanze looked up slowly to listen, and Obanua chuckled awhile, shaking under the effect.

'Women are v-very foolish! Ve-ry—'.

The barmaid briefly emerged from the room and caught his attention, and he suspended his topic.

'Come here, you g-girl! Come here qu-quickly! Come and—take away all these bottles and l-let us—have some more d-drinks.'

The girl ran across to the window and picked up what she had come for.

'Do you *hear* me?' Obanua bellowed.

'I am not giving you any more drinks,' the girl retorted sharply.

Obanua looked across at his friend with blurry-eyed surprise.

'You see this—this *rat*? These ch-children are turning into something else,' he moralised, cleaning his dripping mouth.

But he gave up the protest, then stared dimly awhile on the floor as if following the progress of an ant.

'What was I saying?' he asked, looking up at Nwanze.

The other shook his head, his face turned downwards, his eyes shut.

'I don't know. What—were you saying?'

'I said—I said—one day, I am g-going to lose my patience over those f-foolish women—those foolish women, who call themselves my wives. They *don't* know me. *You* know me —they don't know me. B-but you—you know me. Is that—not so?'

'Yes,' Nwanze replied. 'They don't know you. I know you.'

'I will kill all of them—*all* of them—'

And they both chuckled and nodded in rapport.

The woman of the bar came out of her room and walked towards them, and they stared up at her, like powerless cubs.

'Alright, you two. You have had enough. You can go

home now. I think what you have drunk should be enough for you. Come on now, stand up and go home. You have had enough. Come on!'

Obanua stared at Nwanze, his eyes large and unbelieving. But Nwanze held his face downwards, his eyes shut, his mood apparently imperturbed.

'Can't—can't we stay—just a little longer, have a little bit more rest?' Obanua pleaded, his head swaying, his mouth dripping.

'No. You've had enough,' the woman insisted. 'Come on, get up and start going home now.'

'O—oh! Now d-don't bother us—don't bother—'

'If you don't stand up I'll pour water on you.'

It was at this point that Nwanze tapped his friend on the shoulder, wistful and slightly sober, and said, 'Come on, *oba*, let us go now—'

'Go where?' the other bellowed.

'Go away—just go away.'

'B-But I don't want to go. I have a right—to stay here —here, or anywhere I like. What—what right has anyone got to tell me'—he knocked his chest to emphasise—'where to be? I have—'

'I tell you, Obanua,' the woman warned, 'If you don't go away from here I'll pour cold water on you.'

'I have a right—to be here, and—'

'Come, come,' said his friend, rising up unsteadily and taking Obanua by the arm. 'Let's go away. Don't you know—that a poor man is a wretched thing? Come, let's— let's go away.'

And he led Obanua away, still protesting and looking back at the bar with vengeful but ineffectual eyes. Occasionally they tripped upon each other and fell, then laboured up again. They would sing a raucous and discordant tune together, stopping in the middle of the way, then going on again but heading nowhere in particular. People looked at them and laughed, or shook their heads and hissed. For they knew all about it . . .

Far above on the left, slowly and stealthily, the tired sun still glided down.

10

'It was here, *here*,' Nwabunor emphasised, as she pointed under the little Hausa basket near her bed, 'I am quite sure it was here that I put the money. And you can hardly turn your eyes away from a thing in this house but it gets spirited away as if you are no longer living with human beings.'

She walked this way and that, angry and confused, sat down, and stood up again, retying her wrapper and blowing her nose. Her son sat in the corridor and watched, worried and afraid. She walked into the room again, hissing and cursing.

'I am definitely sure about it. Whoever took it must certainly have been waiting for the chance. No sooner do you look away in this house than your things start disappearing. *Here*, here was where I kept the money, and nobody is going to tell me any differently. Ubaka,' she called.

'Ma,' answered the boy.

'Come here. Are you sure your hand didn't come near any money that was left here? Are you sure you didn't take anything away by mistake? Tell the me truth, are you sure?' she stared down searchingly at him.

'I have told you, mother,' he said, half-crying, 'I did not see the money. I swear to God, mother, I didn't touch any money here.'

She left him and walked out of the room, retying her cloth once again.

'I have always known it wasn't you. You are not the type. But some devil certainly did it. I am quite sure of that—some devil in this house. And those devil's fingers will *go* with the money, that I am quite sure of.'

She flung her fingers to emphasise the curse, then cleaned her running nose and retied her wrapper yet again.

She was still cursing as she walked towards the kitchen where she was making supper for her son—her son alone, and herself. As she walked she stumbled against a careless stick that was lying across the way, and she stopped and bent down to study the stick as though meaning to read the hand that deliberately placed it on the floor. Then she hissed and walked away.

Ogugua was also in the kitchen, sitting in front of a fire that warmed the food that was meant for her alone with her three children. All this time she had not said a word, but listened intently with a hand against her chin, waiting to catch a word or phrase that might constitute a direct reference to her or any of hers, thinking, She wouldn't dare. A madman knows how far he can go. She wouldn't dare. She was tapping a foot on the ground and nibbling at her little finger from the hand that propped her chin, in an impulse she was making an effort to control.

Her two daughters were also nearby, each busy at one culinary chore or other and occasionally throwing reproachful glances at each other as though swearing, You fool. You fool.

Only Bomboy stayed outside, amusing himself. The little black 'witch-cat' sat a cautious distance away from him and refused to accept his subtle invitations. Occasionally Bomboy would call 'Puss-ss! Puss-ss!' and throw a piece of food. The cat would only crane her neck towards it and wave her tail somewhat, but would withdraw her attention once again the moment she smelled his intention. When the boy came near, broomstick in hand, the cat would get up and move further away from him . . .

Inside the house Nwabunor still complained.

'There won't be any rest in this house until the accursed rogue who took my money—fifteen shillings! Have you ever heard of such theft within a house? If that thief does not put the money back, may *Ushe* take care of her, and quickly too!'

Nobody replied. And that seemed to her even more painful. She got back to the room, sat down and stared at the floor for a while, then clapped her hands in silent horror and rose up again.

'I think the time has come when we should have a proper look at ourselves and let the thief disgorge whatever he has taken in. The time has come to really put an end to such shameless villainy as this—I cannot continue to be afraid every time I put down my property in my own house. Come, you two girls, are you sure you don't know where this money is that I have been talking about?'

At this moment Ogugua jumped out of the kitchen and confronted her.

'Nwabunor, be careful today. If you know that there is something itching you on the eye you'd better take care of it. And do not involve my children in your affairs. Do you hear that?'

'Why should I not involve your children? Do they not live in this house?'

'I am warning you, keep my children out of this—unless you want the whole town to be witness again to what will pass between you and me today.'

'I am asking you, do your children not belong to this house, and are they not like everyone else liable to be questioned if anything goes wrong? Tell me, are they not?'

'My children are not thieves, do you hear that? My children are not thieves, and if you are foolish enough not to know how to keep your things carefully you should stop pointing fingers at them any time one or other of your things get lost. Do you hear that?'

'Nobody has said that your children are thieves, but the way they conduct themselves in this house gives anybody reason to suspect their movements. And look how brightly they have been adorning themselves lately. Is this how children of—'

'Have you ever been responsible for buying them things?'

'God forbid that!'

129

'Oho! Then what business of yours is it what they put on—does anything of theirs belong to you?'

'Well, where do they get them from? Or have you suddenly started buying them things?'

By this time they had begun to talk close to each other's faces and to stab fingers across and clap their hands at each other and adjust their cloths in readiness for possible action.

A small crowd had gathered outside the door, made up mostly of children who watched for fun or in horror and fairly aged women who counselled peace but could do nothing practical to end the quarrel.

Obanua had finally left Nwanze and was trying for home, but when he spied the situation from a convenient distance he retraced his steps and headed towards some other direction. He did not wish to have any part of the confusion. For there was nothing he could do about it. And so he did not stay to watch the situation worsen. He was not there to see his two wives curse at each other until they resorted to blows, until Nwabunor quickly went out of breath again and collapsed to the ground and a different story would have been told had people not quickly rallied to her rescue and brought her back to consciousness.

Not very long after, she had gathered the cloth together around her waist, taken all the rest of the money, left the food for her son, and set out to the house of the soothsayer. Already by this time evening was a world bathed in thin grey smoke, the complaints of the creatures, the distant exchanges of pounding pestles, the smell of forgotten refuse.

She walked on, didn't look at anyone, didn't greet anyone and hardly even raised her head when a familiar person greeted. They turned to look at her, and never took offence. They understood. She is an unlucky woman, they hissed and thought, getting into a house like that. What fortune, she thought, how could this come upon me, fall to my lot? And always her eyes were to the ground, her whole frame little more than a walking mind, thinking, wondering and afraid, suspecting, blaming the whole world. They want to kill me, put an end to my life, so that they can have all the space. They would stop at nothing, my money, my life, just as much as they have planned to cover me with shame before the whole town. Only one child, never to be blessed with another. And yet they wouldn't stop at that. My man too. He knows all about it, but wouldn't do anything. True, he couldn't, but he wouldn't even if he could. Because he is in it too. Otherwise wouldn't he be concerned even for the welfare alone of my only child? They are all in it, all planning to get rid of me and my child. But my spirit is too strong for them, or they would long have succeeded. They cannot!

And she never looked up one moment. She would probably have missed the way. Only instinct, somewhat reinforced by purpose, drew her, still worried and thinking, to the door of the soothsayer who, seated pensively on a brown tattered mat and silently chewing something between his gums, seemed either to be reckoning the winnings of the day or intent on piecing together the loose ends of a projected divination.

He was supposed to represent for her the shrine of hope. But torn as she was between the desire and the dread, between the long and lingering hope of eventual triumph over the forces that threatened her and the powerful and equally lingering suspicion and fear that a conspiracy so concerted would surely drag her fighting powers to the death, she was not entirely herself when the soothsayer asked his questions and attempted what little comfort he could within the limits of his quest for money. And knowing that she still hadn't got all the amount he wanted and how far away salvation was from her reach, she was certainly not all herself as she tried to relate to him, with broken breath and a tone that bore out her distress, her experiences of today and the days past, and to plead again that the rites he performed before the demands had been completely met.

'But I have told you,' he insisted, coolly and with a show

of sympathy, 'I have repeatedly told you, that the spirits do not accept any half-measures. Or do you want me to wake the masters from slumber without the wherewithal to wash their faces? No, no, my daughter—think what you are asking and consider what kind of good you will be doing your case if you seek to rouse them thus wantonly.'

'But I am begging you,' she pleaded, rubbing her palms, 'isn't there something you can do to let them see my plight? Please.'

'What can I—'

'Please. Please! Let them see how it is in our house. I'm sure they will understand. Let them see how I am having to bear my own burdens. The father of my child would not, has refused to pay his fees, and the boy is being asked to pay up or leave. I would wear myself out to fetch the money to pay it up, but where is the health and the strength for that? And of the little I make a good part finds its way into the thievish hands of the ones that want my total shame and ruin. And who can I beg in this town? Please, can't you see? I beg you. Let them see my emptiness. I'm sure they will understand. And I promise to meet up the price from time to time so that I can at least try to help my son as well. He is the only thing I have and I can at least try to save him some of the shame and sorrow that is now my lot. Please. I beg you.'

The soothsayer shifted uneasily on the mat and scratched the nape of his neck in a gesture of disapproval.

'There is nothing I can do, my daughter. I am only a servant of those I consult and there is nothing I can do to change their minds. It seems to me you really have to decide what you want. If you still want me to do this work for you, the only way I can do anything is if you pay the price first. Not even humans can work on an empty stomach. So go home and come back when your money is complete. That is all I can say. What you are asking me to do for you is not a simple job and cannot be dismissed so lightly, just because you don't happen to have all the money yet. This is all I can say.'

'But—'

Nwabunor stopped in her breath. It was useless to say anything further. For the soothsayer's argument, like everything else, was overwhelming. Or probably the pervading fear, now heavily reinforced by the ominous words of the man, assumed a much more horrifying aspect that quite dried the language out of her. And the soothsayer in turn, noticing that he was making the required impact in the interests of his trade, lost no time in taking advantage of her defencelessness, again with that stern detachment characteristic of his trade.

'Let me tell you, my daughter. You are not the only one to have come here. People stream in here day in day out, morning, afternoon, night—with exactly the same kind of problem as you have. If you had taken notice you would have seen a man and his wife walking with fear on their faces. They had just left my house. You are not the only one who comes here. And I tell all of them exactly the same thing. I don't hide anything from anybody,' he emphasised theatrically. 'I say to them, Look, I say, my work is quite plain. If you think you are not ready to abide by my rules, then go anywhere else you like. Many people come here asking me to make them medicines with which to destroy their enemies' lives. But I tell them plainly, That is not my work. I only work to improve the lives of people and to give them new hopes. Take a look through the whole town and you will see my good work all over the place. So I say to these people, If you want to take somebody's else life, this is not the place for that. You can take your case to other people. Ese Nwozomudo, that ill-fated hunchback, is there. That is her speciality, and she has the deaths of countless sons and daughters of this town laid heavily on her shoulders and crooking her frame further still. One more death from her lethal herbs and powders will not make much difference. So if that is the course you prefer, you can find your way to her. Everybody knows where she lives—right close by the way out of the town where human and beast alike leave their waste to decay. That is what I tell them, my daughter, nothing more. My work is plain, my hands are clean. I am only telling you what will bring good to you. You can take it if you like, but if—'

He said no more, for he had noticed that Nwabunor showed greater interest when he talked about his sworn rival, Ese Nwozomudo. This was hardly the effect he had intended to achieve. For now the woman's face wore a new look. He could not quite understand what this new expression meant, whether it conveyed a new hope or revealed a vision that had suddenly been opened to it or. . . . He could hardly understand. He merely looked as Nwabunor sighed and put her hands to her waist, untying her pouch with what now seemed to him like determined urgency.

'I have heard you,' she said as she shook the money out of the calico pouch. 'I think I understand, and I thank you very much. You have no need to say any more. Thank you. Good night.'

He could not even bring himself to reply. With an uncertain hand cupping the money and a mouth agape he watched the woman make her way out.

Nwabunor pondered as she walked, one hand on her cheek, the other across her breast. Should I be alone in my suffering? she thought. To seek to deprive me of having any more children, and threaten my life as well. . . . And that of my child. . . . What other way out is there? Why should I bear the disaster alone? They will not succeed. What have I done? Why should this happen to me? God forbid it. Rather, let it be all of us. . . . Rather than that I. . . . But what . . .

Her feet stepped into a cluster of creepers, and she jumped up suddenly, thinking it to be a snake.

'Sister, sister, step out awhile,' said the first old woman.

The other emptied the pepper into a pan, folded the mat and placed it at a corner of the wall, then came slowly out in response to the elder's call.

'What is it?' she demanded, the curiosity weakly drawn around her half-open mouth and her aged eyes.

'Can you not see who is going?'

The second woman looked towards their neighbours' premises and nodded perceptively at the figure walking ahead of the house.

'The younger wife. I see she is out again, the slut. See how lewdly she wears the wrapper close to her knees—see how loosely the upper dress falls below her neck.' She shook her head, scratched her backside somewhat, and cursed, 'What a world of faeces!' a bit under her breath, yet audibly enough.

'Faeces indeed. And now that she is setting out at the fall of light, God alone knows when she will be coming back home.'

'Who is there to question her goings and comings?' the second woman corrected. 'Even if she decided to stay beyond the night, who would question it? Besides, her man will be away at work tonight.'

'True,' her sister agreed. 'Very true. But have you seen what I have been seeing lately, or have my weak old eyes been deceiving me?'

'What? About her and Odafe Gwam? You are telling me! I saw them once, one night, on my way back from Ezumezu's house—they were standing so close to each other that I began to wonder within myself if all these visits he had been making to Obanua's house had any honest intentions behind them. But what could an old man like that be fooling himself for—fancy an old goat chewing wood-bark.'

'Ask me again! What worries me is that as they grow older some people think more with their groins than with their brains. Let them enjoy themselves—only I cannot see what good it will bring.'

Suddenly there was a faint noise from afar off, the shouts of a crowd cheering and then hooting. The two women listened hard, until the noise died fitfully out.

'What was that?' the second woman wondered.

'I don't know,' the first woman said, as she listened expectantly for another short while. 'Would it be anything else but those madmen that Gwam and Enyinabo are gathering to harass us poor people? God help them. But where is my little witch? Pu-ssss! Pu-ssss!'

The little black female cat was nowhere in sight.

'Pu-ssss! Pu-ssss!' she called again.

Then looking at their neighbours' compound she saw what was going on. With a broomstick in his hand Bomboy was stealing upon the little cat which was now leaving this house of perpetual yet familiar molestation and was trotting dutifully home to the owner's call. But just as he was about to lash out at the cat, his hand was gripped from behind by Ubaka who warned him to leave the 'witch-cat' alone. Somewhat frightened by the unexpected interception Bomboy shook, and began to cry. Both of his elder sisters ran out and took Ubaka to task for 'beating the poor little child for no just cause.' The exchange of words that followed was brief because Ubaka left the two girls to themselves, took the little boy by the hand, and comforted him.

Now the cat had got home, and was rubbing her body against the leg of the woman. She waved the cat ahead, somewhat reproachfully, and joined her sister inside. Night was closing in upon the fleeing daylight, and the first hurricane lights now dappled the scene.

II

The afternoon sun threw down very strong heat. But it was not long before its presence was being menaced by some other celestial element. Droves of black cloud floated past its face now and then, defiant, as in a determined and fearless drift of protest, and the earth below was treated just as often to brief intervals of sunless calm. Not many birds played beneath the changing light and shade. The few that ventured showed against the vast celestial sheet either as swift, active, little black bolts or else like so many big charred leaves rising out of a bonfire and floating lazily across the face of the sky.

Gwam found there was very little money left for his multiple pursuits, and this worried him. The campaigns were fast approaching now. The rivalry between him and Enyinabo was becoming very hot. Each tried to outbid the other for support, spending some money in the process. But Gwam had an uphill task because he represented an 'alien' party and had to spend a lot more money lobbying chiefs and notables. Enyinabo spent just a little, in kola and drinks largely, to win back the uncertain minds that Gwam may seem to have put in doubt. The money served to buttress the convincing plea that the citizens of the town would be foolish not to identify with their 'kith and kin'.

Gwam's funds had all but run out. Very little came now from the party headquarters. Probably headquarters did not place much premium on an area where the struggle was so forbiddingly unequal. Probably too they reflected that Gwam, with so many personal projects going—a house at home, another in Warri, another in Sapele—could not have been using his campaign money to the party's advantage. So they hardly bothered about him until they saw any fresh, convincing reason to replenish his resources. He had written many letters that were either not acknowledged or at least got the ever-tantalising response that someone would be coming round to listen to candidates' problems. Thus stranded and uncertain, Gwam was a worried man.

He had held a premature rally in the town. The organisation of that rally was almost a solo exercise, for he paid very few people to help him (having hardly got the means), and most even of this few did not hesitate to cross over to Enyinabo's camp with the necessary inducement. That rally should really never have been held. It was just that Gwam was dismayed at the size of his opponent's clientele, the widespread popularity of his slogans, and the strength of the favour he enjoyed among old and young alike throughout the constituency. If this chance slips my fingers, he had thought, how will I manage? How will I tend to all these pots I have set on the fire? And so he had hazarded the rally as one last desperate measure before he would go up to headquarters and make his case. After the rally he had come back into his father's house depleted, like a woman who had hurled her pot of soup at a gang of rats just to chase them away.

In the face, therefore, of this dilemma, he was beginning to doubt seriously his capacity to carry through every other plan he had lent himself to. He was a man of unlimited aspirations, but he lacked the calm and courage to weather setbacks. And as if it was not enough that his electioneering uncertainties were costing him a good deal, he now found himself having to reconcile his financial crisis with the demands of the woman he had been making plans to carry away from her own marital home and make his wife.

'And if you seriously mean that I should organise the women for you, then understand that there are a few things we have to do in this connection. For instance, I am as you know a member of the *Umu-Agbala Society* and I should have no problem at all in getting the other members round to vote for you and even convince their husbands to join your side. All we need do is give about fifty pounds to our chairwoman to arrange a big function, and you can count on everybody. You give me the money,' she examined her fingers and picked her nails, 'and I'll know how to get it across. And then there is that other women's society, the *Iganihu Club*. This should be a good opportunity to reconcile our group with theirs. Another fifty pounds should do the work, and we could even arrange a joint affair just to—you are not listening?'

'I am. But sincerely, Ogugua, don't you—'

'No, I don't think it's a difficult matter at all. And then there is the question of making uniform dresses. Since I already have a machine there is little problem here. I reckon that we'll be needing about thirty to forty pounds to buy the clothing. Material is very expensive these days and—'

'But don't you think all this should wait yet? I'm quite short of money now, as you can see. I have already spent—'

'Yes, but how long do you want to wait—until the elections are just tomorrow? I think the trouble is that you have been spending your money on unnecessary matters. Take this question of fetching sand, for instance. Isn't it unbelievable that you should want to waste so much money on those little children? *Two and sixpence* a day, for little children! I've never heard the like before. No matter how much sand they'll have fetched, I'm sure they'd be extremely delighted if at the end of the whole thing you gave them each five shillings—or even invited them all together to a good meal instead. Why, hardly any one of them has ever laid hands on one shilling before, unless he stole it. No, I think you are merely wasting money there. You are surely wasting good money, money you could use for more pressing things like these.'

He sighed helplessly, rubbing his bare chest absent-mindedly. The bewilderment showed on his brow. She blinked and turned away her head, not satisfied that she had said all she wanted to say. But then almost at once she turned, full bosomed, to stroke his bare hairy breast, a warm liquid smile playing around her eyes and her mouth.

Her headtie and her clothes lay on the bed, near the pillow. At a corner of the room was her basket of foodstuffs which she had bought from the market and was taking home. And Gwam was beginning to reflect which now posed the greater menace for the future—defeat at the polls or life with a woman who cared more than anything else for what she wanted and did everything to insist on it—when he heard some knocking at the door. At first he didn't reply. But Okoh knocked again, hard, as though the door stood in his way.

'Who is that?' asked Gwam.

'Me,' Okoh mumbled, in a tone of frightened reverence.

'What do you want?' Gwam blared.

'They are asking for you.'

'Who are *they*?'

'The labourers.'

There was a brief silence. Gwam and Ogugua looked at each other. She made to dress up and go, but he motioned her to stay.

'Alright. Tell them I am coming.'

He shook his head and put on a shirt, and came reluctantly out.

Three men were seated outside the door of the house. They had only their loin-rags on, and the profuse sweat on their bodies showed they had either been working very hard or had come so determined on their mission that the resolution exercised both mind and body. When Gwam came down they didn't turn their faces towards him. They just sat there, looking away, waiting for him to answer their quest directly.

He knew what they wanted. He would not want to argue if he could help it. But there was nothing he could do. He smiled wryly and scratched his head, thinking, If I had bolted. And still those men said nothing.

'It is only three weeks now since—' Gwam started.

'It ish three weeksh now shinsh you made your lasht pyomish, and we are not going to take any more pyomishish.'

The leader of the group of strangers finished his statement and looked away again. He did not have the patience to say more. Anger is all the more accentuated if it lacks the means wherewith to express itself correctly.

'I know. But look—do you not know that labourers are paid only when they have completed the whole work?'

'That wasz not the agyeement we made. You pyomished to pay ush at the end of every week. Five weeksh have gone now, and all you keep making ush is pyomishish upon pyomishish. We are not pyepared to take them any more.'

Gwam sighed and moved about a bit, somewhat uneasy.

'But it is not even the end of this week yet . . .' he said. 'Look. Let me give you this last undertaking. You all, come down here on Sunday morning and I will pay you everything that is outstanding. Do you hear me? Sunday morning.'

They made him no reply. They just sat and looked away. At last their leader spoke again.

'It ish only becaush of your late fada that we have been sho shilent. When we came to thish town and had nowhere to shatay, he gave ush shelter, then let ush work on hish farm and fed ush there. He ish the one we are yeshpecting. Otherwyshe we should have stopped piling thish sand a long time ago. But we are no longer going to take thish tyeatment from you. If we come on Shunday and you do not pay ush, we are going to shtop working.'

They all rose, brushed their buttocks and left without another word. Gwam stared after them for a while, then shook his head and turned to go in. At a corner stood Okoh, who had been watching what was going on. Gwam stopped and surveyed him briefly with contempt.

'You can never be trusted to have any sense,' he told him. 'Do you not know how to say, "He is not in"?'

Then he hissed and walked in. When he got to the room he discovered that Ogugua had left through the same back door by which she had come in. But that did not worry him in the least. One problem now began to bug his mind: why stay on in the town one minute longer when there is hardly a penny? He sighed heavily and began to get dressed in haste.

Out in the mellow sun the children had settled to amusing themselves, each having done the daily number of rounds of fetching. They had all grown tired, very tired. So tired that they were already looking forward to going back to school, as the vacation drew to a close. And they were also looking forward to getting the money for the work they had been doing. Sunday, Gwam had promised them also.

The twin girls came out of the shop and, on their way home, began each to take another look at the articles she had purchased. They had been sent to the market by their mother to buy a few items of food that she had forgotten to buy, and had thus taken the opportunity to spend their loot.

Ndidi turned her two pants this way and that and was not very satisfied with their colour (red), and even thought they might be oversize. She hissed. Then she saw Ogo smiling at her own articles, obviously very happy with the purchase.

'Why did you buy scarves?' she queried.

'Why not?' Ogo wondered. 'What's wrong with scarves?'

'They are easily seen, being worn on the outside.'

'What does it matter?'

'What does it matter? How would you explain how you got the money to buy them?'

Ogo was perplexed by what looked like sound judgment.

'Well . . . I'd say I picked them.'

'Picked two scarves—are you so lucky?'

Ogo was slightly worried now. But on reflection she lit upon what seemed like a plausible argument.

'I'll never wear the scarves at home. So how would anybody know I'd bought them?'

But defeat was what Ndidi would not accept, any more than her sister.

'Suppose they are discovered lying carelessly around at home?' she asked.

'I would not let them lie carelessly around.'

'Still, mother could find them somehow.'

'And couldn't she find yours that same way?'

'Needle-tongue!'

Ogo glanced mockingly at her.

'I know what's worrying you.'

'What is worrying *you*.'

'You've realised that I bought nicer things than you have!'

By nightfall, when after supper most fathers smiled and shook their heads and told stories of past happenings and of the tricks of the tortoise to their happily curious little children, while their wives worked on in the breath of the harmony, Obanua was still trying to make his point to the woman of the bar who never ceased to shake her head adamantly each time he said a word.

'But I promise you,' he said, 'I shall repay you all. Or do you think I am lying?'

'M-m,' she refused. 'I mean it today. Not even a cup.'

'Look, just a bottle. I will certainly be paid tomorrow and—'

'I say no. I may give you tomorrow, but you will drink nothing here tonight.'

Nwanze never said a word, never opened his mouth. He merely cupped his chin on his hand where he sat by an empty table and stared with resignation while his friend laboured for the benefit of both of them.

'But—come, my dear—I am not a new person here,' Obanua pleaded on. 'Are you afraid that I will—'

'I am not afraid of anything, Obanua, you hear? I am not afraid of anything. I am only saying that the debts you owe here are enough and I am not willing to give anything away any more.'

'But you are not giving anything away. I say I will be paid tomorrow, or do you—'

'Come and drink as much as you like after you have been paid tomorrow. But before you touch anything here you have to settle all your debts. This is what I am going to keep telling you even if you beg me from now till the end of the world.'

She spat heavily on the mud floor and rubbed her sole against the spittle till a thick patch of wet showed on that spot. She was sitting on a low bench, looking unperturbed, her wrapper carefully trussed between her thighs. Presently her eyes fell on a used match lying on the ground near her. She picked it up, blew the dirt carefully from it, and started scooping her ears.

Very soon Sinkea and two friends shuffled into the bar, and there was a brief exchange of compliments. Between him and Obanua it was very impersonal. The three arrivals sat by a table and began to chat among themselves. The woman of the bar quickly rose to give them attention.

'Aliam!' she called.

'Ma!' came her maid's quick reply.

'Bring drinks for Sinkea. Bring three tumblers.'

'Yes, ma.'

Obanua moved away from the wall near the window, on which he had been leaning. He sighed hopelessly and walked to his friend, motioning to him to come away and let them leave.

'Mm,' Nwanze sighed as he rose. 'Let me go before I die like the hungry antelope who waited in vain at the bottom of the fruit tree.'

But before they walked out of the door Sinkea called the attention of his debtor.

'Obanua,' and the other turned to answer. 'The month is ending tomorrow. I just wanted to remind you that I will be here in the morning to wait for my money. This was what we agreed on in the presence of everybody—you all were here.'

'I have not forgotten.' He nearly tripped.

Obanua and his friend walked out. It was getting very dark now. Now there were no longer the harsh sounds of light, of daylight. There were only the suppressed sounds of retirement and darkness. Nearby a boy was riding home his metal bicycle-wheel with a stick and it knocked against a slow-moving old woman and she cursed him till he was too frightened to apologise and rode away fast, disappearing into the murky distance, like a scared stray dog.

Obanua felt subdued too, he and his friend, but he particularly. To be chased away from home, and now to have the door again shut against your face where you most expected it to be open to receive your poor driven self. And when you are chased again from a place like this where else do you think of going? The grim thought of home began to invade his mind once again and he sought to chase it away. But I will be paid tomorrow, he thought, and I will settle most of my debts and there will be no problems here. Yes, I will be paid tomorrow, he thought again, earnestly trying to clutch to this welcome consolation.

He and Nwanze said good night to each other very briefly. There was nothing to be happy about or celebrate. There was enough to be sorry about.

'Sleep like a rat,' Nwanze said.

'Good night,' Obanua replied.

'Where shall I meet you tomorrow morning, at home?'

'No. At the bar.'

'Alright.'

Nwanze disappeared with his halting steps.

For Obanua this was another uneventful night at the watch. Ever since the battery was spent he had ceased to use the torch. The battery had burnt so soon after it had been supplied by the priest that the latter would surely have been very unwilling to supply any more. So Obanua had procured a hurricane lamp from his house. He would light it up and place it at a comfortable distance from where he lay to watch. At least the impression was made that there was a watch on, and that was enough of a deterrent to any sinister mission. Whoever or whatever it was that was responsible for the disappearance of the stones had either taken a holiday or was shaken by these few days of the nightwatchman's bold presence. But this presence was merely an impression. For not having had anything to make him drunk Obanua had not fallen into that insensible mood that rendered him negligible to the night visitors. He was now awake to and aware of the dangers of his job and had secured himself a convenient roost at a spot some distance away from the hurricane lamp, which was only meant to make an impression of a bold presence. But the night visitors never thought of this, or at least seemed not to. Or probably they never came. And so nothing happened once again this night, and the stones remained.

The following morning the priest was impressed, and paid him his salary. Three pounds ten shillings.

12

Nwanze found it difficult to maintain a respectable presence.

'Move your leg!' the barmaid warned rudely. 'Move your leg!' and whipped the broom menacingly close to Nwanze's feet.

'Look here, you foolish girl!' Nwanze cursed as he shifted.

'Move your leg!'

'If you don't take care with that broom I'll split your head.'

'Move your leg, or I'll—'

'Aliam!' called the woman of the bar.

'Ma!'

'What is it?'

'It is Nwanze.'

'What has he done?'

'He wouldn't move his leg while I'm sweeping.'

'Is his leg standing in your way?'

'I wonder what kind of an impudent girl you have here,' intercepted Nwanze.

'It is his fault, ma. He wouldn't move his—'

'What a liar you are! Don't listen to her, my dear,' Nwanze said. 'She has got an evil tongue in her head. She has been telling me all sorts of things here. Saying I was a greedy man, that she knew I had come here to beg for drinks, that I was so greedy I wouldn't wait for the day to break, that I even crew before the cock did, that I was merely giving the town the impression that I was lame but that when it came to drinking appointments I ran faster

147

than a dog after a bone, and all other insolent language she has been turning out of her mouth.'

'*Eiii!* That is a lie, ma! I never said any such thing. He merely refused to move his—'

'Shut up!' the woman of the bar warned her. 'Can you not tell a man's leg from the leg of the table? If you know he won't move his leg can't you just sweep around it and be about your business?'

'Don't mind the rat. Do I blame her? If it wasn't for Obanua who asked me to come and wait for him here, would she have seen a target for abuse this morning, this little frog that can hardly clean her anus after she has fouled it?'

It was a bit early for a visit to the bar. But the mission of which he was a waiting representative was, if not a noble, at least in the woman's own terms a gratifying one. And he had reason now to draw his legs close, readjust his white cover-cloth, and lick his mouth from corner to corner, like a vindicated cat.

For Obanua walked into the bar and took off his cap and his heavy coat, the regular nightwatchman's outfit. But there was a conspicuous absence of cheer on his face. Nightwatchmen don't often look very bright after their night work. And though he had just been paid his month's salary Obanua had a considerable load on his mind. He had with him the sum of three pounds ten shillings, but he was unhappy to reflect how much would be left in his hands after he had paid all his debts at the bar.

Nwanze began gradually to lose the encouragement that he had felt when he saw his friend. Was it that Obanua did not after all get the money, he wondered, or did he suddenly decide at waking up from his night roost that he was going to give up his bar life? He had little knowledge of what was preying on the other's mind. Then he noticed that Obanua had in his hand a paper package a little wet with oil. And now his mind was being exercised between the call to console a cheerless friend and the hardly repressible joy of knowing, or even believing, that the morning was not going to start too badly after all.

148

'*Oba* the great!' Nwanze greeted, clownishly clearing his throat and scratching his head. 'I was beginning to wonder what has become of you in that enclosure of misers they call a mission. Whatever God they serve will never allow me to come even within smelling distance of their place. That reverend father is so miserly that, as it is rumoured through the whole town, if he could eat the feathers of a chicken he would be very glad to. They say that not a single bone is left when he eats chicken, for there is a special kind of liquid he injects into the poor thing before it is slaughtered. And that giant dog of his is so hostile that I begin to wonder if he doesn't do all that barking at visitors because he thinks they come after likely bones. I have never been to such wicked premises in all my life.' Then he looked keenly at his friend. 'What is the meaning of all this gloom on your face? Is it the usual early morning dullness, or has that wretched priest not done as he promised—I would not put it past him. Hm?'

'No—he has paid me,' Obanua replied.

'Then why does your face look like a cherry dropped in cowdung?'

'Nothing. I have a slight headache.'

'Headache—ha! ha! This must be a strange kind of headache that a man feels when money comes into his hand. I would surely love to feel this kind of headache.'

No sooner had he said that than Sinkea came into the drinking-house, unaccompanied. His face showed neither cheer nor hostility. He merely walked into the parlour, exchanged greetings with the two men without any enthusiasm, then took his seat by one table and cupped his chin in his hand.

'I have never seen so many vultures gathered over one single carrion,' Nwanze cracked. '*Oba*, I can now understand the meaning of this unusual gloom that has come upon your face this morning. When you reflect with what determination your creditors are awaiting you nobody will blame you for wearing that look. But take courage, my dear friend. It is much better that you should be called upon to pay for what you have been allowed to enjoy than

149

that you should give all your money and be greeted with nothing but the door. Cheer up.'

Then he looked across his shoulder into the room and called, 'Madam!'

'I am coming,' said the woman of the bar.

Outside, hens clucked and jostled one another for particles of food on the sand. The morning air was neat and sharp as a bamboo shaft.

Finally the woman came to meet them at the parlour. She wiped her hands on her wrapper and greeted them.

'Pardon me,' she said, 'I was only trying to tidy a few things up and wash my hands. You are welcome.'

It was Nwanze that spoke again.

'Madam,' he orated, 'you know why we are here so early in the morning. God knows that nothing in this world would bring me out like this so early, apart from the unrequited service that I do for our ungrateful old chief, summoning up everybody with the wretched gong just when sleep is sweetest, and asking his elders to assemble at his court. For that is the state of the matter. As I said, you know why we are all here—Obanua, Sinkea and myself. Just some days ago we nearly witnessed an ugly scene in which these two big trunks threatened to ruffle the ground here. Now that should never have happened but for the sake of this devil called money. They say it was because I opened my big mouth to disturb their game, but they all know very well that it was all because their eyes and their hearts were set on the money—here they are, ask them, they can't deny it.' They all chuckled. 'So—we do not want that kind of thing to happen again. And you, madam, I know you have not been very happy about all the debt that Obanua has been owing in this bar. I know—I don't like it myself. It has caused me discomfort too, and it has even exposed me to the language of that little rat there who can't even talk yet.' The girl blushed and retired inside. 'But you know how it is. There is hardly anywhere Obanua goes in this town other than this place—let us not recall any sad stories. So there can be no question of his running away. I have always known that whenever he had the money he would pay you all the debt, otherwise—'

'Pardon me, Nwanze,' Sinkea interjected. 'We have to cut this story short, because I have somewhere to go now. Ogoh's roof leaks furiously and I have made the old woman a promise that I would rethatch it unfailingly this morning. So please—'

'Alright, alright,' Nwanze quickly assured him. 'My story is not really a long one. Madam, how much do you say Obanua owes you?'

'He knows. Three pounds five shillings.'

'And you, Sinkea, how much?'

'Over a long period he has owed me no less than . . . two pounds ten shillings. Ask him. I made it plain.'

'Alright, alright,' Nwanze settled. 'There is no quarrel about it. Obanua, how much do you have?'

Obanua cleared his throat, moved his legs a bit, and replied, 'I have only three pounds here with me.'

'Hm,' Nwanze sighed, slightly confused. 'The whole affair stinks. Sinkea, let him pay you one pound, next time he can—'

'There is no talk about that,' Sinkea said. 'I made it clear to him last time that I would accept not a penny less. So let us not quarrel over that. Besides, I need all that money because I have been taking all the thatch-leaves from Okogwu's farm-land and he has sworn that I would never set foot on that place again until I paid off all the outstanding dues. So I cannot afford the kindness this time.'

Nwanze sighed and scratched his head. The problem was all the more acute because his adjudication was influenced by a reflection of how much money would be left to Obanua after all the payment—not in Obanua's own interests, but in the interests of their continued patronage of the bar. So in the face of Sinkea's apparently justified intransigence he felt his wits taxed to the full.

'Alright,' Obanua put in. 'Let me pay him his dues for our last contest. There is no trouble about that.'

He counted out twenty-five shillings and gave it to

Sinkea, who reflected a bit, hissed, then bid them all good morning and went on his way.

Nwanze looked keenly at the woman of the bar. He knew he had little reason to expect her to be understanding now. He was prepared to use all the power of speaking at his disposal to strike a convenient bargain that would leave all parties satisfied. But now Obanua had ruined his scheme by one act either of cowardice or of indiscretion.

'Madam,' he endeavoured, as the woman merely looked away and said nothing, 'you yourself were witness to the ugly scene that nearly developed between these two men recently. And who would have been able to restrain the two of them when once they came to blows—is it you, a woman, or I, a poor lame animal who can hardly hold himself upright? This is the reason I am asking you to please take what little is left in Obanua's hands now. Let him pay you one pound ten shillings—even if he has left to him only five shillings with which to think of himself. Please.'

The woman turned to them eventually and sighed in resignation.

'If all those days he had been coming to drink on credit I had said no to him, it would have been noised round the whole town that I was wicked to my customers. But you can now see what has happened. There is nobody in this town that puts himself in debt at this bar to the extent that he does. All because I have tried to be kind and understanding. What have I not done for him here—is it food? This is where he eats all the time, *all* the time. Ask him.'

'We know, but—' Obanua broke his silence to plead.

'Or did you hear that kindness hung his bag in my house, that I should continue to ruin my trade for the benefit of a man who cannot take control of his affairs? I think all this nonsense will have to stop. . . . Alright, let him bring the one pound ten shillings. At the end of this month, he will have to pay the rest or he will never set foot in this bar again.'

'Trust me to take care of that!' Nwanze swore. 'I am a poor crippled thing, but when it comes to keeping a word of honour I have no equal in this whole town. . . . *Oba*, give her the money.'

Obanua fumbled a bit in his pocket and brought out the amount. He would probably have dodged the debt, but this was the only way he knew he could ensure a continued escape from his house. Even if this would secure him the comfort of one day, that would be enough. A good thing I didn't declare all the money though, he reflected briefly.

The woman took the money and thanked Nwanze for his arbitration. Obanua and Nwanze rose and stretched their bodies. For a moment it looked as though they were set to go. But Nwanze thought briefly to himself how much really he had gained from the whole exercise. He had succeeded in making everybody comfortable, but what about himself? So having made up his mind on one last piece of craft, he stretched his body once more, yawned fulsomely, then scratched his neck with an expression on his face of practised villainy.

'*Oba*,' he said, 'every day I blame our poor old chief because he scarcely opens his mouth to ask his attendants to give me a mild mouthful of the good liquid for all I do for him. But he is a poor old fool, so old he cannot even remember that I have done anything. I am quite sure that if he did he would have ordered me a full bottle of dry gin. So do not allow me to have spent all my spittle on your behalf this morning only to get nothing in return. Put some money down and let us bid good morning to the day.'

Obanua laughed at the cunning. Besides, he was not in any great hurry to go home himself. He spread the *akara* balls before them and they fell to.

But the woman warned that no drinks would be parted with unless they paid the money down first. That wasn't any problem. And the woman hardly took offence at the trick . . .

Nwanze and the barmaid exchanged abusive glances each time she brought a fresh bottle, in full recollection of their earlier encounter and particularly of his assertion that he had not in the least come to take any drinks.

Before long the two men had eaten far into the undeclared money. Nobody asked any questions. Besides, they were already too tipsy to ask or answer or do anything but go on drinking and drinking.

The sun was making good progress.

Deep in the afternoon, Nwabunor was seated outside by her wares, looking out again into the distance as though she had some special customer in mind. Sales were slow and indeed she had only made so much for the day as would be barely enough to feed two stomachs. But her problem went beyond that, and she was thinking very deeply, with that hollow look on her face that only deep thinking could carve.

She was alone at home. Ogugua and her daughters had gone out, though where to, she did not know. Her son had gone to work for the day, accompanied as always by Bomboy, and would soon be back. Her husband had not been seen at home since yesterday, though not even that bothered her. He could be dead—what good has his living been? But her mind was being exercised by something more weighty. He must be right, she thought, that soothsayer could not be wrong. I am convinced beyond doubt, that they would go beyond bringing shame upon me and my child. They would wish to take our lives as well. But I am prepared to fight them with *every* means at my disposal, to destroy their evil designs. There is no other way now—should I wait till our lives are taken from us? What good will all I have been paying do me, if my enemies are already tying up their plans to ruin me and my child? And he keeps telling me, *You must pay all before I begin.* But I don't care any more. I will *not* be ruined, nor will my child. Rather . . . rather . . .

She blinked and swallowed hard, frightened now by the thought of what her mind seemed to counsel with so much conviction.

Slowly and stealthily the sun was gliding down towards the west and trying very hard to conceal its weakness. But her thoughts, her suspicions, her fears and her resolve never weakened.

Very shortly Ubaka came home with his bucket, accompanied by Bomboy, who held to his brother's hand and tried to keep up with his pace.

'Good afternoon, ma,' Ubaka greeted his mother.

'Good afternoon, ma,' Bomboy imitated.

'Welcome, welcome,' Nwabunor replied them. The innocence of youth is unassailable. 'How was the work today?'

'It was good, mother,' Ubaka replied. Again Bomboy echoed him.

'When do you stop working?' she asked.

'Saturday is our last day. Gwam said we should come on Sunday morning to take our money.'

'Thank God. How much do you earn a day, two and sixpence?'

'Yes, ma.'

'So for the four weeks you have worked for him you will get—let me see: six days a week gives you . . . fifteen shillings—so for four weeks you will get . . . three pounds. That is not bad.'

'Yes, ma.' Ubaka's eyes lighted with hopeful joy.

'It is not bad. At least it will help. For over a year we have not paid your fees and we owe your school . . . five pounds. But I am sure they will understand and accept the three pounds. At least they won't send you away as they have been threatening. But let us wait and see. Let us wait and see,' with an instinctive check on her enthusiasm.

'Yes, ma.'

Ubaka grew a bit gloomy. All the money would be paid into the school fees, and there would be nothing left, not even the smallest part, to buy the littlest bit of delight. And all his school mates would be sporting new things. He was not very happy about this. But he understood, and he tried to cheer up again. At least he was happy in the thought that he was helping his mother. She would not suffer very much now, and that gave him sufficient joy.

'Go into the kitchen and have your food. You must be very hungry now.'

He hurried into the kitchen. Bomboy stared at him as he ran. Young as he was, he was sufficiently aware of the domestic situation to know that he could not share Ubaka's joy too freely. So he merely stared.

Suddenly there was a clatter on the roof as of pebbles dropped, a regular feature of the season. From afar the downpour raged nearer, as of the sound of an approaching invasion. Humans and animals alike ran for shelter.

'Ubaka!' Nwabunor called, as she hastened to move in her wares.

'Ma!'

'Hurry out and bring in the clothes. Quick!'

Ubaka ran out of the kitchen and made for the clothes spread out in the sun to dry. There were two groups of clothes. He gathered his mother's hangings under one arm. Then he made for the other group hung out by Ogugua, her own clothes and those of her children. But before he could gather them his mother blared out at him.

'Leave those clothes alone! Do they belong to you? Did you hang them out? Come on, run inside before your kindness kills you!'

Ubaka rushed in, half wet, with the clothes he had taken.

'Next time learn to mind your own things and keep away from whatever does not belong to you, do you hear that?'

'Yes, ma.'

Something suddenly struck Ubaka. The feeling was probably not strong enough to be a presentiment, but at least it registered as fear of something unusual. For when he looked at his mother's face he thought it presented a picture he had never seen before. It now looked very ugly and contorted with something of venomous spite, like a disfigured mask seen in a shrine under the dim light of a candle. He quickly dropped the clothes and went back into the kitchen. Bomboy stared outside, too scared to venture into the rain, while the merciless downpour made muddy work of the clothes left outside.

From a corner of the kitchen Ubaka signalled to him and he came in. Secretly and quickly they shared his food together, then quickly washed their hands before Nwabunor could come into the kitchen by accident and find them. And then the inevitable questions finally came.

'Uba,' Bomboy asked, 'shall I accompany you to collect your money?'

'Yes.'

'Uba, will you give me some of the money?'

'I don't know. Probably I will.'

'We shall buy many things. We shall buy a pencil, and a catapult, and a pair of shoes, and many things. Shall we not?'

'Yes, we shall.'

And then Bomboy fell silent again. Maybe even he wasn't so sure any more.

The rain clattered on . . .

13

Sunday finally came.

Sunday morning, in the village, is unlike any other morning in the week. For life takes on a different kind of colour. Today most people leave off work, either in welcome relief of their vital energies or (if they feel that way) in reverence of God. Today at about eight o'clock in the morning every young boy, every young girl, feels it a duty to go to church either out of true Christian conviction or —especially when certain unhappy circumstances like lack of adequate adornment get the better of conviction—because the class teacher is sure to be there to mark down absentees and late-comers for punishment. So up to church the children troop, in their best or their most, proud of their new clothing or unhappy at their insufficiency. As the church bells clang there is a general air of hurry among them which the ringing of bicycle bells and the tooting of car horns help to accentuate. This is the rainy season and the roads are soft with mud, and if any stain from the dirt affects the dress of a child he either laments the tragedy on the spot or rushes unhappily home to get rid of the stigma. Little ones who can ill afford the hurry are either dragged along by their young elders with displeasure on both sides or left in the middle of the way to help themselves. The elders are in turn warned by their mothers that if they do not take the little ones right up to church and back they will not even so much as smell the special Sunday dish. For mothers have stayed back to cook rice, which is a food only rich families can afford and which the average family can only save for festive days and for one out of a number of Sundays. No child therefore wants to suffer such a loss, and so the elder one has to come to terms with the little one's pace even at the risk of being marked late by the ever-present tyrant, the teacher. This is all part of the excitement and the resentment that is Sunday morning.

But the rule was lost on some twenty little boys who knew no church for today. They had been fetching sand for Odafe Gwam all through their vacation and had piled up an amazing deal of it. And until the approaching end of the vacation brought the tedium nearer to their spirits they had laboured happily together, spurred on no less by the promise of rare money than the joy of playful company. So the children had gathered together on the compound of their employer, beside the sand that they had fetched. Some of them had come at the first crow of the cock, or even before then, if some chance subconscious impulse had roused them sooner. Some may have even dreamt of the coming occasion. No doubt many had scarcely touched the supper of the evening before, satisfied as they were with the fistful of hope that tomorrow offered. Thus while their mates hurried by to church in all their glamour and gloom they played happily on Gwam's compound, waiting confidently on his pleasure to rouse and give them the money. Even Bomboy came along too, and the journey with his brother to the assembly of hope had been engaged for the most part with the same inevitable questions and the same inevitable answers.

Morning wore on. The sun in its upward course along the celestial arch was now acquiring greater confidence and a more certain brilliance, at the same time chasing the last traces of dullness from the face of the earth. In place of the uneasy groans of a working weekday came the distant but cheerful praise songs of worshippers in the Christian churches, or the more spirited testimony of the Jehovah's Witnesses, or the less ordered but equally inspired cacophony of revellers at the fun-places of town . . .

Even after midday the children in Gwam's compound had not been attended to. But, still confident, they continued to spend their waiting in play. Some of them had contrived a deficient soccer team with a fallen orange, and the excitement streamed down their faces and soiled their clothes. Some swung on the branches of a nearby tree and a few wrestled in mock contest.

Ubaka and the usual hostile trio played their *koso* in rapt earnest. The common hope of today had apparently been set aside meanwhile. The contest was long and tense. Nobody said a word. Everyone was seriously determined to win. No one took any chances that could cause his elimination or mark him down for the final punishment. Each spun his *koso* with caution and plied it with scrupulous neatness. The established superiority of Ubaka was now being seriously and unyieldingly challenged. After a time their fingers ached and all four of them agreed to observe a truce. And though they maintained their separate camps, the fact that they were able to achieve even this limited understanding was no less a tribute to the general mood of today than a triumph of a determination that had no chance to be petty. By the same tamed sense of purpose they were able to agree when to resume the contest, and for each one of them the game could last the whole day so long as victory was the goal, or at least a determination not to lose, the guiding fever.

The sun itself could well have been sweating as it glided down the first third of the other half of what started as a merry journey. Gradually the glamour of Sunday began to fade, the tone to falter, and people moved about now as homeward from a funeral dance. And as the children waited on, little bothered by hunger or monotony, there was still no sign of either employer or foreman.

Suddenly Gwam's three labourers appeared round a corner of the house. They stopped just to look at the huge heap of sand in the premises, then walked towards the door. The little boys stopped their several games and looked up at the men with inquisitive hope in their eyes. One of the men walked up to the door and knocked several times, but there was no reply at all. He looked round at his fellows, who wore the same surprise as he. They said nothing. He turned to the door again and knocked harder and harder, several times. There was still no reply. He shook the door hard. Maybe somebody was asleep inside, he figured. He shook harder still. And still no reply from anybody. He turned round angrily to his fellows, whose faces showed the same expression. They released a welter of language in their native tongue that sounded like curses. The children looked on, motionless, somewhat apprehensive now. Cheer and hope began to give way in their hearts to fear and doubt.

Inside the room Okoh had lain and dozed on a bed, while the children were wasting their Sunday outside. With the visitation of these men he was startled into apprehension, then panic. He struggled out of the bed, with the cloth hanging loosely round his loins. He breathed hard, looking this way and that, up, down and around as the knocking and the shaking continued. He tried to peer through a crack in the window, but stumbled stupidly back as the clatter came there too. And now he fevered for an escape as the three men released with hostile fists a frenzied chorus of commotion on door and window. The situation got too much for his nerves and he yelled in panic.

'Opin de daw!' the men yelled back automatically.

'Who are you?' he asked in excitement.

'Opin de daw,' they replied as they stopped thawing awhile.

Okoh hesitated for a few seconds, then fumbled excitedly at the bolt until he finally confronted the three looming terrors who now bristled like three terrible spirits demanding full settlement of a vow long overdue.

'Whia ish your mashta?' they demanded.

'He has gone—he is not in!'

'Whia ish he!'

'He has gone out!'

'Whia?'

'He has gone away—travelled.'

'Tyavel? He hash tyavel?'

'Yes.'

'You aah lying!' they charged.

'True—I swear, he has travelled.'

At once they pushed him aside and charged into the house. They looked frantically round every corner of it, inside and outside, then came back again still bristling and panting like three massive hunting dogs whose tempers could hardly keep pace with their quest.

'Whia has he tyavel to?'

'I—I don't know. By God, I don't know,' Okoh swore as he frantically fulfilled the entire formula with his finger.

The three men stared menacingly at him, as though wanting to force him to give them the answer they expected.

'I swear by heaven and earth, I don't know where he has travelled to. He took his bag three—four—three days ago and said he was going away but would be back soon. He didn't tell me where he was going. You can ask anybody.'

He looked round at each one of them, his eyes nervously begging mercy.

The three men looked at each other, then sighed heavily and shook their heads and withdrew gradually into the open. Outside they held a brief conference in their tongue, and again their language rose in what certainly sounded like determined threats. Then they readjusted their cloths and strode quickly away.

The little boys could scarcely recover from their speechless shock. Neither could Okoh from his agitation. He blew his nose repeatedly and wiped it just as often. On his way over the threshold he slipped and fell, and the boys just managed to stifle the laughter that unconsciously came upon them. But Okoh turned round and read it on their faces. He was just about to bawl at them when he spied the three men striding back towards the house with spades in their hands. He took to his heels at once and ran into and beyond the house to some uncertain safety, far, far away, trampling, stumbling, falling, rising again, and striving to disappear, like an awkward beast breaking loose from a pen. The boys retreated apace to some convenient distance, where they stood and watched keenly.

The three men ignored everybody. They walked right up to the heap of sand, brandished their spades and scattered the heap far and wide till the compound merely acquired an additional layer of soil, till all the sand was lost and it seemed useless ever to attempt to bring it together again. Then they knocked their spades free of any sticking particles, cleaned their brows and walked back home together with only as much feeling of satisfaction as a just indignation would allow such hungry and helpless men that had toiled dutifully only to be cheated.

The little boys had stared through the entire exercise with unmitigated shock, too frightened to even protest their own case within their hearts. They merely looked at each other as though none could attempt an explanation. Then they began to walk gradually home, saying very little on the way.

Only one boy could not quite get over what the incident meant for him. All the other boys could well walk back home. For them the impact of an agitated moment and the feeling of relief from what only just now seemed a big scare could take the place in their hearts of a hope they had long cherished. Besides, they scarcely had anything to lose other than the dainties and the novelties that they had confidently named their promised payment for. But for Ubaka it was a different case. He thought of his mother, he thought of his schooling, and fear and sadness sat heavily where hope had leaned but lightly. He put his *koso* in his pocket, took his little brother by the hand, and walked slowly homeward.

Bomboy looked up at his brother's face, and didn't feel encouraged to say anything yet. But he could not let the impulse bother him much longer.

'Uba,' he started, 'will they not pay you today any more?'

The other was in no mood for exchanges. Instead the passion rose gradually up to his face, like slow steam, and now overwhelmed his eyes.

'Uba, will they pay you tomorrow?'

Almost at once the impulse overcame Ubaka, and the

tears streamed down his face as he wept disconsolately.

Bomboy looked up at once, rather afraid, easily touched with sympathy.

'Uba, don't cry, you hear? Don't cry, Uba, you hear? You hear? You hear, Uba . . .'

And he joined the sorrowful strain. It was now late in the day, and women and children had begun to take in their hangings. The fugitive sun was struggling frantically to find its homeward way behind a determined drift of dark clouds. Elephant grass rustled restlessly in the reckless wind, and the rumbling sounds from above drowned out what cheer was left underneath as the day made its retreat in a depressing diminuendo.

To Nwabunor the news of Gwam's bad faith had much greater meaning. As her son wept and sobbed she hardly felt an inclination to console him. For her heart was burdened with more inward tears, complicated the more because her mind battled with the terrors of the course towards which she now seemed to be irrevocably tending, thinking, So she thinks she can succeed. She thinks I will just sit idle and watch while she carries through her evil designs. But she is making a mistake. She is making a costly mistake. En-hen. . . ! So this is why they have been holding all those clandestine discussions, thinking they were fooling me! I see. . . . But they couldn't fool me. I knew all along what they had been hatching. I knew she had all along been against my son's employment in the labour. She knew my son was going to be paid some money. But she would be the last to see any good come to us. I knew it all along. And now she has secretly advised him to get out of town, run away. So that my son doesn't get paid. She did not care that many other children were going to be affected by her plan. No. All she was bent on was that my child and myself should suffer. All she cares is that we be ruined. She would do anything, descend to any step. Plot against my life. Plot against the life of my son, too—the soothsayer could not be lying. Do anything.

164

Descend to anything. But so would I. So would I. I would sooner ruin her than she me. Yes, so would I . . .

Night was growing strong. Darkness was now a total shield against the light of day, against the light of reality and of sanity. Very soon all life would have retired, and all that would remain would be the unfathomable emptiness of gloom. And as Nwabunor rose from her bench to retire into the house, she could feel the words of the soothsayer re-echo above the maze of her thoughts, determined yet afraid of her resolve, thinking, *Ese Nwozomudo . . . right close by the way out of the town. . .*

'Out!' the woman of the bar shouted. 'Throw him out before he makes a further nuisance of himself. Throw him out!'

The two men rose from their seats and grabbed Obanua by the hands and feet. In his drunken delirium he could hardly offer them any resistance. They lifted him clear of the floor, toted him to a comfortable distance and, to the rhythm of a work-song, merrily swung him and deposited him on the ground with an impressive thud. From here at least, they reckoned, he would have enough sense to decide to go away rather than keep on bothering other people drinking in peace in the bar.

He cursed lavishly but incoherently as he clawed at the sand in an effort to get up. Midway up he would fall back again, curse, claw, and fall back again, until he decided to take a little rest on the ground before thinking what next to do.

After he had gone the two men who had thrown him out eyed each other conspiratorially, finished their drinks quickly, and hurried away in different directions. . .

On a stormy night you can hear many noises. There is the sound of the breeze howling through the trees and indeed convulsing itself in a roaring turmoil. There is the sound of branches wrenched from the parent trunk as if in forced rebellion and crashing with a deafening din on corrugated zinc roofs. Then there are the terrified screams of little children as the thatched roof is torn off, stakes and all, as though by some horrid hand from above, and sent wafting away. And again you can hear the feverish blasts of wooden doors and windows either under the lash of the raving wind or because nervous householders are aware that this is the kind of advantage that the agents of dark generally thrive under.

But these are all sounds for wakeful ears. Obanua had long since been overcome by the alcohol. How he got to the church must have been a miracle, for his sense had been blurred and his vision clouded. He must have reached his place of work only by the triumph of a final instinctive sense of direction and a lingering compulsion to work. He had sung and acted all the way to the church, sometimes stopping to accost a passer-by unheeded, or to spread his arms and bare his chest just to drink in the wind while he grinned like a roasting goat, or even to toss a fist-ful of sand into the air and feel it whip against his face. Sometimes as he stood or walked his head would reel in a fit of dizzy weightlessness and he would drop heavily on the ground, then scratch his way up again and try to steady his tottering frame before he sauntered ahead. It all made him feel indifferent or at least saved him from the different kind of feeling he would have got if he was sober . . .

By the time he reached the church he had just enough self-control, or instinct, to find his way to the little corner where he made his roost every night of the watch. As soon as he found it he slumped heavily down on the floor without even the consciousness to remember to light up the hurricane lamp. And in no time at all he was dead asleep, sprawled on the floor like a body washed up from the waves.

The wind was still raving mad, still struggling to turn itself inside out. The Reverend Father could be heard blaring out his orders to his steward, then appeared briefly over a window on the top floor of his residence, drew the curtains close and withdrew his bulky frame into the room.

After the night prayers were over and the men and

women had gone away, the Reverend Brother quickly put out the lights except the little red one, closed the windows and the main door of the church and hurried home with his large hurricane lamp in one hand and a chaplet in the other. As he passed by the nightwatchman's corner he stopped briefly to stare at the figure on the floor, then shook his head, made a sign of the cross, and hurried away. Not long after there was a deafening crash of thunder, in the wake of which a torrential downpour overwhelmed the earth.

Obanua snored on, unmoved.

Even after midnight he had still not changed his sleeping position. The wind blew wildly and sprays of rain flew to his corner and drenched his skin and clothes. That only had the effect of rousing him into a brief spell of drunken consciousness. He huddled up lazily on his haunches, looked blurrily around him for a while, then roared out into a song. But something caught in his throat and he didn't go on for very long. He stopped singing, smiled and chuckled down at himself, and sank dully down once again into another stretch of sleep. His body was now used to the cold and indeed had begun to withstand it with an almost automatic shield of drunken numbness . . .

In such fearful weather you had to be terror itself to be able to venture out into the gloom. And whatever the night visitors were, they seemed at least to be moving comfortably in the whipping rain. All they had on them was the white loin-cloth tied round the waist, sufficiently visible against the background of deep black in the pouring distance. They moved in the usual manner, as in a ritual ceremony. In an unbroken single file they walked, in their full number. They moved up to the stones, lifted them up on their heads, and walked back again towards the river whence they came, in the same formation. They made their journey several times, at the very early hours of the morning.

By this time sensation had gradually begun to creep into the limbs of the nightwatchman and the cold was beginning to make its impression. His reflexes were gradually coming alive. As the winds howled his subconscious was being recklessly exercised:

Is he running to the river? Chase him, break his neck!

Is he running to the farm? Catch him, blow his head, blow his head, blow his head!

Catch him! He is trying to sink into the ground!

Grab him! Blast his head! Hack his legs! Smash him! Kill him!

Kill him!

Kill him!

There was a sudden blast of thunder. Obanua woke up, shook his head, and blinked hard a couple of times. And as he cast his eyes towards the stones over which he was supposed to be keeping watch, what he saw put more cold into him than the rainy wind ever did all through that night. The funereal procession of white could be seen in the distance, retiring towards the direction of the river. The rain had now thinned down into slight drizzles and the white of the figures was more visible.

He could hardly believe his eyes. For a brief moment he thought of lighting up his lamp, but just as quickly the thought was chased off his mind by fear. He crouched back further into his corner and stared on, until the figures went finally out of sight. They never came back again. And for the rest of the night, until the light of day began to steal gradually into the scene, he spent his time staring in their direction and longing for the first signs of human life to restore reality and freedom.

In the morning the Reverend Father was too angry to say anything to him. But the look on his face was so hostile that, had Obanua been a member of that church, he would have been well advised to stop even coming to worship there. So that when the Father said 'Go away' Obanua knew at once how much the order meant.

14

Monday morning came with the unwillingness, irritation and fears that children usually feel on the day school resumes. The child who has not got his books complete pictures another term of unfriendly relations with the teacher and certainly can't look forward with joy to the resumption of schooling. The holiday has been spent in relative ease and unbothered freedom, and acknowledged trouble-makers cannot be very happy to be going back to a place where their every movement is watched by the headmaster. Today there is no rush to school, unless by latecomers who know what will be coming to them. There is a general dullness in the atmosphere. The school bell seems to have lost the regularity of its sound and now clangs out its compulsion with an irritating randomness.

Ubaka walked to school with very little hope. He had scarcely touched his breakfast this morning before he left, though his mother had tried to cheer him and relax his mind of the fear that burdened it. In his absence of mind he had put his shirt on inside out, and would have gone to school in that fashion had Bomboy not laughingly pointed out to him at the door that his shirt-pockets were hanging out. As he walked along now the only thing that engaged his mind was the general assembly that the head-master was due to convene at resumption. When he finally got to school he carried his satchel to the assembly, though he should have left it with the others at the door of his own class. And when his mates stared at him in wonder his spontaneous reaction was to drop it at once on the ground.

Again in the classroom he didn't seem to be with the rest. The headmaster had failed to come to the assembly to deliver his address and call out the appropriate penalties to those whose names he had listed in his roll of dishonour. So the fear kept hanging in his mind, and his mind itself kept hanging with the fear. In the history class it was questions and answers time. The teacher finally got to him.

'What day is Nigeria's Independence Day?'

The teacher stared at him for a reply. But Ubaka was not aware it was he that was being questioned. He had not even stood up. Though his eyes were fixed on the teacher he was really not looking at him. He was not thinking of the question, or maybe he was thinking beyond it. The two boys sitting beside him nudged him out of his trance and he suddenly jumped up.

'Tafawa Balewa!' he shouted, echoing the reply to the previous question, which happened to be the last thing that had registered on his mind.

The whole class laughed. The teacher screwed his brows and fixed a querying stare on him.

'What is the matter with you?' he asked Ubaka.

In shame and frustration the boy looked down . . .

By the middle of the session the school had its normal recess. The headmaster had not addressed the assembly in the morning, but he would do so after recess. Out in the school grounds the boys passed the time in play, or spent pilfered pennies on groundnuts and *akara,* or fought over old grudges and messed up each other's uniforms.

Ubaka too had an old score to settle. Once again he sat down to the *koso* game with his three regular opponents. The last time they had played (which was the day before) the game had been undecided because it was broken up by the presence of Gwam's stalwart labourers, but even in that game it was clear that Ubaka's superiority was ceasing to be a matter of fact. And today, when his mind was ill at ease and total concentration was thus not possible, the chances were much less that he would succeed in keeping that superiority. He tried quite hard, and had even eliminated the first two boys. But the fathead proved impossible to overcome, and in the end Ubaka lost the game and showed his knuckles for punishment.

The victor could hardly believe the result. He took time to gloat over Ubaka's defeat which to him looked at best like a pleasant dream that may never repeat itself. At last! The other two boys felt the same way too. They had nothing tangible to gain from Ubaka's subjugation, but the feeling at least was a great one.

'Stretch your fingers properly!' the fathead shouted at Ubaka.

The victim, feeling considerably subdued, was powerless against the taunts. But he was ready to take them all. The little smile on his face was wry and false. Otherwise his bearing was that of defiance. He kept his hand stretched on the ground and looked away. The victor stood up and made a great show of his victory. He stretched both his arms wide, thrust his chest forward, beat on it with both his fists while his friends laughed to cheer him and mock the loser.

'Remember,' the winner said as he sat down to deliver his punishment to Ubaka, 'if you make the mistake of even spreading your fingers—not to talk of raising your hand from the ground—the penalty will be tripled.'

'Who will let you do that?' Ubaka asked him with an unpleasant look.

'I am telling you I will do it—you are defeated and you have no choice.'

'What is the rule?'

'I don't care about the rule. Come on, keep your hand on the ground!'

Ubaka merely eyed him briefly and laid his hand on the ground once more.

One!
Two!
Three!
Four!

The fathead looked at Ubaka's face and saw that his punishment had still not made any impression.

171

'I don't think he feels it yet,' observed one of his two friends.

'Yes,' agreed the other. 'Put all your power into it and let's see if he'd still look unperturbed.'

The fathead got on his knees and took a good aim. He set his hand carefully, held the *koso* tightly between his thumb and his index and middle fingers, then let fall on Ubaka's knuckles a solid rap that sounded as on a small hollow bamboo stick. Ubaka flinched and fanned out his fingers in the process.

'Did I not warn you?' his victor asked menacingly.

'About what?' retorted Ubaka.

In reply the fathead rapped the *koso* on Ubaka's head. A fight ensued.

The convent school was also at recess. Some girls sang and played, some tossed balls between themselves, others skipped with ropes, yet others played at clapping-the-hands-and-matching-the-feet, and a few bought food and ate it.

The twin sisters confronted each other like two angry cats and each seemed undaunted by the other's threats. They had stolen three packs of Ovaltine biscuits from Nwabunor's stock and an argument had arisen. One of the packs had been crushed in Ogo's satchel and Ndidi was determined to lay the burden of the damage on her.

'I will not agree,' Ogo insisted. 'The biscuits were crushed by mistake while we were both hurrying to school and it is not my fault that—'

'How could they have been crushed by mistake,' Ndidi asked angrily.

'But they were lying among my books. If you knew you could have kept them better why did you not take them?'

'You don't know what you are saying. You are going to take the crushed pack, and then we can divide the third pack into two.'

'You will have to kill me to do that,' Ogo stood her ground, poised aggressively to claim her right.

Ndidi looked at her and scowled.

'Don't do anything that will bring a fight here.'

'I don't care. The only way to prevent the fight is for you to throw away the crushed pack and let us take one each of the remaining two.'

'You are deceiving yourself—after wilfully damaging a whole pack of biscuits!' She held out the crushed pack to Ogo, almost thrusting it on her, and said, 'Take it!'

'Not me. We must divide the biscuits fairly, or we won't go away from here today.'

'Alright,' Ndidi challenged, 'come and touch me.'

And she started to move away.

Ogo sprang forward at her, held her dress and almost caused her to fall. But the other regained balance and held the biscuits tighter in her hands. She swung back and stared fiercely into her sister's face and was about to push her away.

But the encounter was interrupted. The noon angelus tolled and the recess was over for both the boys' and the girls' schools.

It was at the end of that day's session that the headmaster finally addressed an assembly of all the pupils in the school, with each teacher standing close to a collection of boys in his own class. The scene was anything but peaceful, and the old man strove to achieve a hearing over all the noise in a room where children of between six and sixteen (or more) years of age did everything from fighting for sitting space to laughing at a teacher that dozed as he stood.

'. . . And it has been brought to my notice that some of you are in the habit of busting the fence into the Reverend Father's garden and plucking his mangoes and oranges—*keep quiet at that corner!* If I hear any noise from there again I will make all of you in that section kneel down.'

A little silence. Then the headmaster continued.

'Any boy that is brought before me for venturing near the Reverend Father's garden will be severely punished—'

The noise rose again, as from a huge boiling pot covered and uncovered at intervals.

'*Who is that over there? Keep quiet I say!* If any boy is reported for going near the Reverend Father's garden he will be severely punished. Also don't forget that there is a huge dog in that compound and I won't be held responsible for whatever happens to anybody.'

The noise again.

'Who are those fighting in that corner? Come out here, both of you, come out. Come on—here. Kneel down here before me.'

There were a few giggles from the audience, then quiet again.

'Now—listen all of you. A few boys have been given double promotion. They have shown themselves quite brilliant and superior to all the others in their separate classes. So I am going to move each—*quiet there!*—I am going to take each one of them to the next class for the rest of this year. The boys are as follows. Sunday Otuedo, moves from Class Two to Class Three. Obi Jibunoh—*quiet!*—Obi Jibunoh and John Umukoro, from Class Three to Class Four. Godwin Ijomanta and Ediale Odiase, Class Four to Class Five. These boys will move from their present to the next classes ahead of them for the rest of this year.'

There was some peace, as the headmaster paused briefly. During this interval some of the boys let their passions sink into them as they regarded their mates just glorified with speechless jealousy. Ubaka was untouched by all that. He stared on, alone and afraid, at the headmaster and watched his every movement and almost followed his every breath as well, thinking, Maybe he will do it now. He will surely call me out now.

'Now,' continued the headmaster, '—*keep quiet!* Mr. Oguma, there is a great deal of noise coming from your class, will you look into it?'

174

There was brief silence as the teacher let the cane fall on the heads of two boys.

'I want to warn all of you about behaviour in church. I have seen many of you playing or sleeping or talking while everybody else is in prayer. Some of you even put your hands in your pockets when you are going to receive holy communion at the altar.'

One of the boys kneeling in front of the headmaster dozed off and nearly fell on the floor, and all the boys laughed.

'*Quiet!* Now stand up both of you and go back to your places. If you are caught fighting again you will receive a more severe punishment. . . . Now you should behave like responsible children while you are in church, and let me not catch any of you doing any of these things again. The church is the house of God and you should not behave as if you were in your homes. And now—'

He looked sternly over the audience for a while until the murmuring died down.

'And now, I think I have to do something quite drastic.'

Dead silence. Everybody listened hard.

'A number of boys have not paid their fees for some time now. I have repeatedly warned them that if they do not worry their parents and get their fees paid I am going to send them out of the school. By this morning they still hadn't paid their fees. So there is nothing I can do about the matter any longer but to ask them to cease coming to school henceforth until they can pay their fees. The boys are as follows: Samson Agbare, Class Three; Currency Akpoveta and Ubaka Ozoma, Class Four; Emmanuel Egbo, Class Six. Because of his very good performance I am going to let Godwin Ijomanta, Class Four, stay on in the school for the rest of the term. If in the end he doesn't pay his fees I am going to send him away too. But these four boys I have called should never come into this school again until they have paid their fees. And let me warn them that if they fail to pay by October, they will have to repeat their present classes. I hope this is clear and that they will also make it clear to their parents. Where are those boys—come out here, the four of you.'

The boys came out slowly and downcast.

'Tell your parents plainly that I do not want to see you here again unless you come with your fees. And I do not want any fathers or mothers to come to my house and beg me. I will send them away. Tell your parents that also. Alright. All of you:

School is over—'

The children joined in loud disharmony, happy to be released:

School is over
School is over
For today
For today
May God bless our teacher
May God bless our teacher
For our sake . . .

They crowded out of the room in the midst of shouting, singing, banging of chairs, and other assorted noises that generally accompany dismissal. Ubaka took his bag up slowly, and slowly walked out of the room. While most children ran home in pursuit of lunch, he picked his steps gradually because he knew he was not going to get much comfort when he got home. His heart could hardly bear the weight of the pain and half-way home he broke into tears. It was a very hot afternoon, and again the cicadas chirped so loudly you would think they wanted to die.

15

Ogugua sat in the yard, chugging away at the machine. She seemed to be working hard at the clothes but in reality her mind was busy with other important calculations, thinking, He should not have left the town like that. He should have told me. Or could it be that the business was very pressing? I should think so. But he should have told me all the same. He knows how much I am depending on him, how much I would be prepared to do because I depend on him so much.

She stopped briefly to rub her eyes, as they were becoming somewhat misty. Then she thought again, as if from a nagging need for self-vindication, And why should I not? What could one look forward to in a house like this?—

She passed the threaded needle of the machine through the wrong side of the dress. She hissed, stopped the machine, and unthreaded that part of the work. Then she set it all right again, and continued thinking, Why should I not depend on him? Who else would I depend on? Do people take care of themselves and their children with cowries or sand? Making or mending clothes for people can hardly supply a living for me and my children or pay their fees. The fool who calls himself my husband can go jump into the river if he thinks he can expect any respect from me when he does nothing to deserve it. Should I look helplessly on while my children and I suffer and starve to death? Not me. God forbid! But where could Gwam have gone to? The matter must be urgent. But he should have told me. Still—

She cast her eyes towards the other side of the compound and blinked away viciously, thinking, Poor senseless fool!

Nwabunor was by her wares, looking blankly again into the distance and seeming still to be looking forward to a particular customer who never came. Now and then she shook her head and sighed, then murmured something, thinking aloud, almost swearing audibly. She was struggling hard to keep in check the anxiety that tormented her mind. Her son had gone to school without fees and she was scarcely in doubt what was going to happen to him. She could very clearly picture the impending discomfiture, and her mind was gradually but steadily working towards the stage where she could hardly cope with the shame and the frustration that comes from defeat at the hands of a declared enemy. She saw this day as a last chance, the final test of strength between her and Ogugua. She was like one waiting with choking anxiety for the verdict of condemnation, thinking, Is there any other way? Do I have any choice?

Inside the room Obanua lay on the bed, worried by the thoughts that came into his head. Now and again a parched feeling caught in his throat, now and again his stomach rumbled. For he had not smoked a cigarette for some time now and possibilities of food had become narrower. Not that he was looking forward to feeding in his house. He had given that up long since. As a matter of fact he had lost count of whose turn it was to cook for what week, for now it mattered very little to him. What bothered him now more than anything else was the loss of his job. If only the priest had given me a few token shillings when he threw me out of the job! I need every penny I can get. And now where can I go in search of a job? I need something to do, somewhere to stay, just to get away from this hell of a home. Anything, anywhere will do. If only I could safely get away, away from these two devils. So long as I have something to engage me satisfactorily, somewhere I can conveniently retire to, it would not matter one bit if these two devils tore each other to death or got eaten up by their own vicious passions. I will not have a hand in it. Anything, anywhere would be fine. I am sure I can take care of myself. Certainly much better care than to stay here and bear the shame of having to beg to be fed in my own house. He hissed and got out of the bed.

The day was very hot and the air was tight as in a room too small for the number of people it held. Obanua threw his shirt across his shoulders, took his cap, and left the house without saying a word to anybody.

No sooner had he left than Ubaka came in by another way, still weeping. As soon as his mother saw him she knew what the matter was, and her heart sank. She almost wept herself, feeling suddenly now the full weight of her problems converge upon her and knowing all too well that there was little she could do to get rid of any one of them. With difficulty she sought to console the little boy.

'Come, come, my son,' she said, 'come here.'

Ubaka sobbed on but came only within reach of his mother's questions and remarks.

'It is the headmaster, isn't it?'

Ubaka nodded, still unconsoled.

'I know. He has sent you away, hasn't he?'

The boy nodded again, raising a finger to wipe a tear that itched as it ran slowly down his cheek.

'What did he say? Come—tell me, my dear. Was there anything else he said besides asking you to go away?'

In halting speech the boy replied, 'He said . . . he said I should never set foot . . . foot near the school without my fees or . . . or send my parents to go and worry him in his . . . in his house.'

'Never mind. All will be well. Don't worry. Stop crying. Go into the kitchen and take your food. Don't you worry, you hear? Don't cry any more. All will be well.'

But even she did not believe herself. For now every way seemed closed to her and all she could feel was her grudges coming back upon her and her heart aglow with a passion of reproachful anger. She decided to let it all out.

'Ogugua,' she said, rising from her seat, 'I think the time has come when we should stop deceiving ourselves.

We must have to open our hearts completely today, and I don't care what comes out of it. You have been doing a lot of things in this house and thinking that you can get away with them. Let me tell you to your face that you are responsible for what has now happened to my son—'

'Have you started again today?' Ogugua threw in.

'I am going to say it, and I don't care what happens.' She fastened her wrapper and stepped closer. 'You and Gwam could have conducted your accursed affair somewhere else without having to involve anybody else. And now see what you have done. You have cheated him of his only hope of earning money for his fees. He has sweated for nothing. I should have known he would never get the money from Gwam. I only wish that all the sand that my son has fetched for you and your accursed lover should block your groins forever!'

'Nwabunor, check your tongue!' Ogugua rose too, fastening her wrapper as well.

'And that's not all. You and your children will have to come out today and declare yourselves openly. My money and belongings have been disappearing from this house and we must know who the ghost is that spirits them away. You must all declare yourselves, shameless people!'

'Please, Nwabunor,' Ogugua was drawing closer, 'I beg you in the name of everything you cherish. Please, leave me out of your troubles today. I beg you sincerely. You are already in the hands of death and I do not wish to help you in further. Do you hear me?'

'Indeed! I say you and your children have to come out into the open and clear yourselves of the wickedness. I have noticed plainly the suspicious behaviours of your daughters in this house—how they shuffle around behind everybody's steps and when you look at them they are swift to draw their eyes away and keep their mouths shut, like rats.'

'Are you calling my own children rats?'

'What else do they behave like? What else acts in that suspicious manner? You tell me.'

'Nwabunor, mind how you talk this afternoon. If you

180

want to commit suicide I am perfectly willing to help you do so. I want you to know that. Do not think—'

'You can say what you like, spit out all the excrement you have in your mouth, but you have to prove that you and your children are not responsible for—'

'Alright, come and hold me then and make me do that —are you just going to stand there and issue empty threats? Come and make me do it now—if they won't carry your dead body away from here.'

'*Hiei!* Hear her talk about dead bodies. Who between us two is rotten inside but you. Is there anybody in this town who does not know that much, or do you want to say I said the fowl has fouled the air?'

'Since you know so much, why don't you prove it? Or are you afraid of—'

Ogugua stopped short. For a few yards away from the house she could see her two daughters being dragged homeward with difficulty by her mother-in-law. Their clothes were trailing in shredded pieces and even those pieces had nearly lost all traces of the original white and now looked like unfinished paintwork in dapples of muddy brown. Ogo was weeping disconsolately and asking to be left to finish the fight, and Ndidi was protesting furiously at Ma Nwojide's effort to take them home. Their satchels were not there. Their noses were running. Ma Nwojide had difficulty in dragging them both and her wrapper was almost free of her waist. Now and then she put one girl on the ground and subdued her by spanking her a few times on the backside.

'What is it? What is happening?' Ogugua asked, perplexed.

Ma Nwojide drew close with her warring prisoners and finally let go of them to enable her to tighten the wrapper around her waist. But no sooner had she left them than Ogo darted across and grabbed Ndidi, who tried to ward her off, warning, 'Hold her now—o! Hold her now—o! I will kill her—o!'

The girls were separated once again by the old woman

181

who held them each on one hand while they panted and bristled like two little wild animals.

'What is the matter?' their mother asked again, her face now wearing a look of horrified tartness as she scanned the body of each girl.

'These children want to kill each other,' Ma Nwojide explained. 'I was going to the market when I saw them fighting furiously. It took me a long time to be able to separate them—I have never seen such powerful children in all my life. I kept asking them what was the cause of their quarrel but they wouldn't tell me. My daughter, they are wonderful children.'

'Leave them alone, ma, let them go. Come, Ndidi, what's the matter between you two?'

Ndidi was ashamed and afraid at the same time. She kept panting and wouldn't give a reply.

'Isn't it you I am asking?' her mother bawled at her.

'She was abusing me, calling me a rogue.'

'It's a lie!' shouted Ogo, who was still sobbing fiercely. 'I'm going to say it. She stole three packs of biscuits from Nne Ubaka's—'

'Who stole?' interrupted Ndidi.

'You did!'

'E-eh! Mama, it's a lie! She stole the biscuits and brought them to the school.'

'Mama, don't mind her! Alright, you remember you told me not to let—'

'So because of three *wretched* packs of biscuits you have done this to yourselves? Three *worthless* packs—'

From where she had retired to look contemptuously at Ogugua and her two daughters, Nwabunor darted forward and bawled.

'Have you seen yourselves now?' she confronted Ogugua. 'Have you seen that now? The breeze has exposed the chicken's rump—have you seen that now? Tell me, shameless woman, do you need any further proof of the wickedness of you and your children?'

Ogugua was shaken by what she was witnessing. She tried to avoid Nwabunor's taunts and come closer to her children, who were now backing away for safety. But Nwabunor interposed herself once more, clapping her hands on the other's face.

'Come and defend yourself, you shameless woman. Have you seen what you and your children have been doing? Come, and let the whole town be judge today of all that has been happening.'

She clapped again on Ogugua's face, this time about three or four times at once. This threatened Ogugua's vision. In a flash of anger she swung her face away and pushed Nwabunor out of her path.

'Nwabunor, keep your trouble to yourself this afternoon, you hear me?' she stopped to warn.

'Have you two started again today?' Obanua's mother shouted at them. 'What if I did not drag these two girls home fighting, would this have come up?'

'Mama,' Nwabunor snapped, 'this matter is not going to end here today, do you hear what I'm saying? It's because of all this wickedness that my son has been thrown out of school. We shall know where this matter will lead us, the two of us. I will not be the only one to suffer in this house. No more!'

With that she rushed to where Ogugua had her sewing machine and clothes. She picked the machine up by the trunk and flung it heavily on the ground. Then she picked up a couple of dresses and tore them into shreds. Ogugua looked away from her disappearing daughters and saw Nwabunor ruining her trade. A sudden shaft of anger shot through her heart, and without stopping to consider anything she rushed to Nwabunor and greeted her back with a double-fisted blow. Nwabunor slumped on the ground. But almost at once she rose up and engaged her assailant, and both women locked each other in a limb-flailing encounter in which everything that could be torn or exposed had its due treatment.

Obanua's mother, an old woman of over sixty but still strong enough to want to be listened to by her son's wives, shouted up and down but could not get the two women to abandon the fight. She even tried once to separate them physically, but when one of the stray blows caught her arm she decided to stay aside and let madness take its course with them and to leave violence to stronger limbs.

A few people had gathered round the scene, but hardly anyone had the mind to give a hand. Some, among them fun-loving children, found the fight something of a spectacle, while others had no wish to be in need of rescue themselves while trying to bring rescue to other people.

The struggle raged on. At one time Nwabunor was sent reeling down. Ogugua seized the opportunity and rushed to where the other's wares were set up for sale. In one sweep she threw everything to the ground in revenge for what Nwabunor had done to her own things, then set about to trample upon articles like biscuits and cigarettes. This in turn fired Nwabunor and she ran across to finish the job she had started. When amid all this savage comedy each was satisfied that she had made a good job of spoiling the other's things, they rushed back again at each other and interlocked once more in indecisive struggle.

But this time their strengths were gradually giving out. Now the blows came much slower and the breaths were considerably thicker. The weakness was much more noticeable in Nwabunor. More often now she gave herself to defence than offence. And then it seemed as if she was seeking to run away from the fight, and to hold her arms blindly up in surrender. And suddenly, with a long gasp, she slumped heavily on the ground like a cow that had lost all the fight in her, then started to pant heavily and writhe as if she had been stoned half-dead.

There was a sudden flurry. For some of the children the spectacle became too much and they immediately took to their heels. A few other people discreetly left the scene to avoid being called up as witnesses in some judgment or other. Only about three people had the stout heart to rush to the fallen woman and offer a hand. Ogugua was bewildered and frightened, rushing here and there around the scene and yelling excuses and seeking to throw the entire blame for the fight upon her mate. Two of the spectators who remained, together with Obanua's mother, carried Nwabunor to her bed. The third spectator ran to call Nwosisi. When they finally got to the scene Obanua's mother and the others had stripped Nwabunor completely and thrown the window of the room wide open to let in air, leaving the door shut nevertheless. Ma Nwojide had taken charge of the situation and asked everybody else to leave the patient in peace. Now she had got hold of a fan and was blowing generously over the body to supplement whatever air was managing to come in through the window.

'I hope nobody has given her anything to drink,' enquired Nwosisi as he put down his bag of medicines.

'Has she even opened her eyes?' Ma Nwojide corrected quickly. 'We wouldn't bother to call you if she was able to take anything.'

He carefully searched through his bag and took out two bottles. He held them up to the daylight from the window and studied the labels one by one, taking good care. Then he blinked a couple of times in cautious hope, and put the bottles down one after the other.

Ma Nwojide was not satisfied with his pace. She stopped briefly in her fanning and eyed Nwosisi and his bottles rigidly. But not wishing to disturb professional procedure and thus probably endanger her daughter-in-law's life, she blinked away and continued fanning. She didn't even hiss, just blinked away and continued fanning, thinking how much better prayer would have done.

'Stop fanning awhile,' the 'doctor' said, 'stop fanning awhile.'

He examined the patient's face briefly. He laid his hands on her forehead, then on her sides. She was still breathing hard, her mouth open and her teeth showing. He cleaned the sweat off her brow with the back of his hand and tried to steady her head, which she moved this side and that under pain.

'Get me a cup of water. Cold water,' he commanded.

One of the helpers opened the door and quickly came back with an aluminium cup full of water. Nwosisi tilted the cup slightly over Nwabunor's head, and let the water run down in a thin line and sometimes in jolting drops.

The patient flinched her face lightly but relaxed almost at once in welcome relief. Then Nwosisi put the cup of water down and took up one of the bottles and looked at the label again. He uncorked it carefully. Then he poured a little of the ointment into his left palm and put down the bottle, taking care to put the cork on it. He rubbed the ointment against his palms and began to massage Nwabunor's chest rhythmically with it. She groaned each time the pressure was brought home on her by the experienced thumbs. In the end Nwosisi rose up and sighed, cleaning the sweat from his brow.

After a fairly long while Nwabunor began to breathe comfortably. She even opened her eyes wearily, looked round slowly, shut her mouth and swallowed.

'Drink some water,' Nwosisi said, holding the cup to her mouth.

She pushed the cup away and turned her head aside. But her mother-in-law took the cup from Nwosisi's hand and held it back on Nwabunor's lips.

'Drink, my daughter.'

Nwabunor shook her head, tensing her face.

'Come on, drink, it won't harm you. It will do you good. Here—come on, drink,' and she steadied the patient's mouth against the cup.

Nwabunor could hardly resist any longer, and reluctantly she let the water run down into her throat. After a couple of gulps she turned her head away, raised her hand slowly and wiped her mouth.

Nwosisi packed the bottles back into the bag and got ready to go. But before he left he called Ma Nwojide outside, out of hearing of everybody including Ogugua, and whispered to her.

'Nwabunor has to be taking a special meal from now on, and somebody has to do this for her. Now I don't think it is right for us to expect that Ogugua will do this, and I don't even think that Nwabunor will take any food if she knows Ogugua prepared it. I'm not saying that Ogugua is likely to do anything to Nwabunor, but you know how it is between two women married to the same man—'

'I understand what you're saying,' the woman reassured him.

'A-ha. Now I want her to be taking very light meals, in addition to the medicines I will give to her. Nothing very much really. Something like pap in the mornings and water from boiled lemon grass, and pepper-soup in the afternoons and evenings. Occasionally she could take some solid food like boiled yam or fried plantains, but this should not be as regular as before. So either you have to be coming to this house to do it yourself or you have to send someone else down to do it.'

The woman had all along been comtemplating the ground, one hand against her cheek and the other across her breast. When the 'doctor' had finished speaking she raised her head and hissed.

'Nwosisi, my brother,' she said, 'I have heard all you said. The fact of the matter is this. I do not mind telling you my troubles because you are not an outsider to me— why, here is your father's compound and there is my father's. This is what I'm saying. This woman has to leave this house and go back to where she came from—she has parents of her own too. It is a wretched son that I have got and there is nobody in this town who does not know that—'

'There is no need for you to blame yourself for anything,' he sympathised.

'E-hen. What I want to say is, this woman should go back to her parents as soon as God permits her to be able to move her feet. There is something seriously wrong with her and if she is going to die it will be much better for her to do so in her parents' hands. She certainly cannot have any comfort as long as she lives in this house and I think all this suicidal fighting must end today. Do you hear what I am saying? E-hen. This is what I have decided and I think this is what we had all better do. Tomorrow morning by the power of God she will pack her things together and go back to where she came from. Let us leave

187

the matter at that. Now tell me how much we shall pay you.'

'How you talk, Nwojide!' Nwosisi said, sighing disarmingly. 'If I take money from you for such a small affair I might well strip other people naked who are not related to me. Please don't talk about payment.'

'Well, I thank you very much. You have done well.'

The 'doctor' took his bag and left after he had deposited some pills and dictated his prescriptions. Ma Nwojide thanked the people who had offered their help, and after sympathising with the patient they too left. After they had gone Ma Nwojide called Ogugua into the room where Nwabunor was lying and spelt out her decision without mincing words.

'I am not here any more to ask who was right or who was wrong in this quarrel. There is no reason for all that now. All I want to say to both of you is this, that you have shamed yourselves and everybody enough and it had all better come to an end. Who knows, tomorrow we may not be as lucky as we have always been. Perhaps if Nwosisi had been out of town today we would have been telling another kind of story. You, Nwabunor—you do not need to be told any more that there is something seriously wrong with you. It may not always come up after a fight and in a house like this there may not always be people to come and help. I do not see that at all—I do not see that, and we cannot pretend any more. If you can get up on your feet this evening you should pack your things together and go back to your home town. If anything is going to happen to you—God forbid that!—but if anything is going to happen let it happen in the presence of your father and mother, rather than far away here where you are less likely to be saved by anybody. Do you hear me? I am tired of shouting and do not wish to do that any more. Tomorrow morning pack your things and go. When you are sure you are fully recovered you can then think deeply whether or not you wish to come back here. I don't want to drive you away from your husband's house. But I am sure you will agree that it is better to be alive than to die the death of a dog. Do you hear what I am saying? Nobody worships a master with as much as their life.'

She pulled off her headtie, tightened the wrapper round her waist, and walked straight into the kitchen. She did not give anyone a chance to make a reply. She did not even listen as Nwabunor sobbed over her muffled laments, or as Ogugua flung arms and issued defiant remarks in defence of her position in the affair and in stubborn determination not to budge an inch from a house in which she had as much right to live as anybody else.

When the pepper-soup was ready Ma Nwojide passed it to Nwabunor beside the bed. She took up her headtie, wrapped it round her head and took one last look at the patient on the bed, who just managed to gather sufficient presence of mind to clean off her tears and say 'Thank you.'

'Let it not worry you,' her mother-in-law said. 'I only hope that by tomorrow morning you will have had enough sense to collect your things and go back to your mother and father.'

She left the house.

It did not take her long to locate her son. When she saw him she stood at the door of the bar for a long time, her hands on her waist, the contempt vividly drawn on her wrinkled face as she stared at him. The other people at the bar observed a respectful silence. The woman of the bar had spied her from a distance and, not being in any doubt whatsoever about her mission, had withdrawn discreetly into the room to avoid any unpleasantness.

Obanua sat with his friend Nwanze in the midst of countless bottles of palmwine, almost all of which were now empty. When he saw the woman bestriding the doorway in all her imposing menace he stared at her for a short uncertain while with misty, heavy-headed surprise. When it became clear to him what it was his eyes were beholding he was thrown into a weary hysteria as his body shook in a dripping-mouthed laughter that only he seemed to enjoy.

'Look—look at that—that old woman there,' he drawled, grabbing his friend on the shoulder across the table and pointing towards the door with the other hand. 'What does she—I believe she wants to—drink with us. Ha, ha, ha, ha! Come—mother—mother, won't you come—come and drink with us? Eh? Come—come and sit here—Nwanze, drag a chair here. Come—mother, come!'

He paused to smile, then his head moved towards his friend, who pretended to have closed his eyes and not noticed what was going on.

'Ha, ha, ha!' he cackled again. 'She refuses to drink. What—woman, what do you want—what do you want here if—if you don't want to drink? Eh?'

He laughed again. His mother merely stared at him. But when the shame of it all became too much for her she advanced nearer the table and spat heavily on his body, then addressed him in a stern and steady delivery. Everybody stared.

'You vagabond!' she pronounced. 'You wretch! You disgrace! Did I not warn you? Did I not tell you you would regret it? Look at yourself now—do you not feel any shame for one moment? You toss your dead body here on the ground for all the world to see. Go back to your house and see what is happening there. Obanua,' drawing closer to him and pulling on her right ear, 'has there ever been a day that you have felt the slightest shame? Go to your house and see what your wretched living has thrown your household into. Where will it all be told? In whose ears will it all be noised?'

She stood away briefly to contemplate him with disgust, while he made every effort to get rid of what in his insensible state still managed to come off on him as a piece of discomfort.

'Well,' she continued, 'you may carry on as you and your spirit have decided. You can run your life into fire if it suits you—let it be upon your head alone. You shall not have the chance to take somebody else along with you. Your wives have been fighting each other and Nwabunor is now lying half-dead. I have warned her that I will not want to see her with my eyes tomorrow morning if God gives her the strength to rise from bed. If she is going to die she deserves to die in better hands. You may do what you like with your own life. *Tfuah!*' she spat again.

Her son stared at her blankly, chuckling. She readjusted her wrapper and turned to go away. But before she did so she turned back to the table once more and fixed the other man with a reproachful stare.

'Nwanze Onwodi, are you in this too? Do you know no better than to follow a man who is heading into hellfire, when you should wisely rest your unwholesome frame at home?'

Nwanze was sober enough, and did not lack quick reply.

'Forgive me, great mother. What unhappy cripple would not gladly trot after a man that kindly took him by the hand? I was sitting at home, with a hunger twice as big as that of the little antelope that waited till death under the ungracious fruit-tree, when Obanua came and called me up and said, *Whoa!* what are you doing here? Who is it that lets a dainty gift of fish merely rest between his gums?'

The woman hissed, shook her head and went away. After she had gone Obanua broke into another dizzy fit of laughter, then looked at his friend with wine-dim eyes.

'Who—who listens to—foolish old women?'

They both laughed and drank on.

16

The night was very quiet. So quiet that you did not need to listen very hard to hear the eaves of the thatched roof ruffle in the gentle breeze outside, or the little mice as they struggled over morsels up in the ceiling.

Nwabunor had regained much of her strength and ease of body. This was further reinforced by a blind stubborn will. All she knew now was one thing—*This was the end.* Why, all her fears and suspicions had now been justified. Her mind was blocked to the exercise of reason. She thought, Why, what kind of consideration has she had for me? She is responsible for the state I am in today, of that I have not the slightest doubt now. And now they want me to go home. Maybe she thinks she is winning. Hm! Well, maybe she is. Maybe she is. I suppose it will all end after I have gone home? What is the guarantee that having got home I will be safe from what she has laid for me? Does distance help, in such things? Well, it's her strength against mine now . . . her strength against mine. And let us see! She would sooner *perish* than I! And charms perish with those that weave them. That is the only way out. That is the only rescue I can think of for me and my only son. Yes, my only son. He is the only thing I have, and nothing . . . *nothing* will take him away from me. *Nothing!*

She dressed hastily, putting into her calico pouch the very little money that was left to her, some of which she was sure to need tonight. Her hands quivered under her impulse, and the wrapper hung loosely round her waist. She stepped out of the house.

'Mama, where are you going?' asked Ubaka anxiously.

'Shut up. Go in and do what I asked you to do.'

She hardly wished to be distracted from the one resolve that now ruled her mind, the one direction to which there was now no conceivable alternative—*right close by the way out of the town* . . .

In her room Ogugua reclined on her bed, one arm supporting her head as she vacantly stared at insects flirting around the hurricane lamp until they burned themselves to death. She just stared, and there was not the slightest thought in her head of either what had happened or what was likely to happen. At last she casually raised her left hand to the light and looked at her finger-nails. She sighed lightly, got out of bed, and moved towards the tiny bottles of nail polish on her window, thinking, Thank God. I think we will soon have some peace in this house. She smiled, distantly.

Her two daughters were lying on a mat on the floor close to her bed. They had not quite got over the animosities they had developed towards each other earlier on. Whenever they happened to be facing each other they would fall into a severe battle of eye-blinking until the smarter one blinked last and, feeling triumphant, turned her back to the other. Sometimes one would make the mistake of moving her leg so carelessly that it touched the other's. Thereafter a silent but furious battle of leg-kicking would take place until they saw their mother turn her head round questioningly. Even when they faced each other again with their eyes closed, mere breathing could be the occasion for another struggle. For one would feel that the other had breathed too hard on her, and thereupon they would unleash indiscriminate blasts of breath from mouth and nose upon each other until that particular episode ended with the two spitting upon each others' faces.

Bomboy had not yet slept. He had answered all his mother's calls to come in and sleep but paid no heed to any of them. He just crossed his tiny legs and sat staring at Ubaka as the latter stuffed his few belongings into a small wooden box. Ubaka's mother had asked him to pack his things because they would be leaving the house as early as possible the following morning. As he did so, he sobbed occasionally. Bomboy did not think it safe to disturb him, but he could not hold out for very long. When Ubaka threw away an item, Bomboy would walk across and pick it up, and would only throw it away in turn if he himself was uncertain to what use that article could be put. If Ubaka threw it away it had to be useless—so much was his loving respect for his elder brother, deepened all the more now by the thought that he would soon be gone.

But the little boy could hardly come to terms with the impending departure of his brother. If there was anything definite he felt now, it was puzzlement. Puzzlement at what this was all about, where else Ubaka and his mother could be going when, in his own limited reckoning, there was only one home and that was this. He was not even rescued from this perplexity when Ubaka began to give away to him items of play like *koso*, whistle, stringed bottle-tops, and the like. The gifts strengthened his wonder, and he could not help breaking the silence that surrounded the whole scene.

'Uba, where are you going?' he asked at last.

'Home. We are going home. That's what my mother said.'

'Where is that?'

'I don't know. It is in another town.'

'In another town?'

'Yes.'

'Where is that?'

'I don't know. I have never been there before.'

There was a short interval.

'Uba, will you come back when you reach there?'

'I don't know. Perhaps I will.'

There was another brief pause. Then Bomboy resumed.

'Why not let your mother go alone?'

'She won't let me stay here.'

The little boy puzzled.

'Uba, will your mother let me come along with you?'

'I don't know. I don't think so.'

194

'Uba, I promise to be peaceful. I won't trouble you. Won't you ask her for me?'

'She won't let you.'

Bomboy tried to hide his sobbing. But it finally burst open and he cried until he was finally whisked away to bed by his mother, who beat some more weeping out of him because he could not 'leave other people alone to mind their business'.

It was past midnight before Nwabunor came back, amid pouring rain. She was soaked right down to her skin, water dripping from all over her body, a mixture of rain and cold sweat. Beneath the fold of her wrapper she had securely wrapped a little package. In this was contained a tiny calabash phial, tightly corked and even tied around the cover with a string, for certainty. This calabash held some powder.

There was hardly any sound around, besides that of the pounding rain and the howling wind. She stepped close to the door and listened. No sound. Not even of feuding rats. She walked round the house, picking her steps gently, careful not to knock against anything or even kick a tiny broomstick. She came to the window of Ogugua's room and stopped. She listened. Again not a sigh. She did not bother to walk to the window of the room she shared with her husband. Even in her caution she was sure he would not be at home. So she made to walk away towards the—! She stopped dead. For a creaking sound came from Ogugua's room. She froze. Ogugua coughed and rolled noisily on her bed. Nwabunor's heart pounded faster as her legs quaked where they stuck to the ground. But the noise subsided. Still she waited until she was absolutely certain. Then she moved away, slowly, slowly, feeling her way towards the door of the kitchen.

She walked in. Stopping by the door she looked round at objects along her path. She could see rather clearly, for her sense of mission had in turn kindled the other senses. Once more she picked her way, towards her enemy's section of the little kitchen. She knew where Ogugua kept her pot of soup, on a wooden ledge above that corner. She felt her way along the rafter and touched the pot. She brought it down, gently. As she deposited it on the floor the metal cover slid off and fell away. *Eh!* Her heart almost popped out. She waited in fear, bent over the pot.

Suddenly the little dog in the house began to bark. Nwabunor was thoroughly frightened, thinking, How can I explain. . . . What can I say I'm doing here, over her pot? What kind of luck is . . . could I not have . . .

The dog was barking ceaselessly. It would probably have run out after the object, but all doors were locked, including the one that led out from the house into the kitchen nearby. And then came the voice of Ogugua.

'Bingo! Shut up! Bingo, Bingo! Shut up!'

She coughed and sat up on her bed.

'Bingo! Shut up and come here. Bingo, Bingo! Shut up. Come here, and stop disturbing people.'

She lit her hurricane lamp.

The dog whimpered towards her, wagging his tail. She smacked him once on the head.

'Shut up and stop making a noise.'

The dog coiled up beneath the bed, and Ogugua put off the light and rolled into bed again.

Nwabunor had been breathing fast, poised motionless over her enemy's pot of soup. When she saw that all was quiet again she sighed briefly in relief. Then quickly she loosened the fold of her wrapper and brought out the calabash phial. She untied the cork, removed it, and emptied the contents of the phial at once into the soup. She quickly replaced the phial under the fold of the wrapper. Then she picked up the pot's metal lid and covered the pot again with unsteady hands, causing another tinkle.

The dog growled once more, raising his head and opening his half-shut eyes. Again Ogugua cautioned him.

'Shut up, Bingo,' then somewhat under her breath, 'wonder why common rats interest you.'

She settled finally.

Nwabunor lifted the pot and placed it back on the

rafter. Slowly she picked her steps once more away from the kitchen, muttering under her breath, 'Let us see now. God knows I'm doing this to save myself and my only child.'

She walked boldly now, and came round to the main door. She knocked a couple of times. No reply. Then she went round the house to the window of her room. She knocked again.

'Ubaka! Ubaka!'

'Wish I had let the dog loose on you,' Ogugua murmured, as she recognised the voice.

'Ubaka!' Nwabunor knocked again. 'Ubaka!'

'Ma!' Ubaka rolled lazily in half-sleep.

'Ubaka!!' his mother knocked harder.

'Ma!!'

'Open the door for me!'

Ubaka got up and went to the door. He was not quite awake, and rubbed his drowsy eyes as he shook on sleep-weakened legs. Lazily he unlatched the door. His mother came in and locked it after her.

'Go back to sleep.'

Together they went into the room. Ubaka slumped back to his mat on the floor, covering himself up once again with his cloth.

Nwabunor went straight to bed. It did not occur to her to take off her wet clothes. She was still breathing fast, eyes switching this way and that. She tried to close her eyes and sleep. She couldn't. She rolled round on her side. Her eyes kept scanning the darkness, her heart poised between an elusive feeling of triumph and a fear she was not yet settled enough to understand. She rolled over again and tried to close her eyes. And still sleep would not come.

The rain was still pouring heavily outside. It seemed it would never stop. It seemed the night would never end.

17

Early the next morning Ndidi and Ogo got up and performed their chores—sweeping *their* room and *their* part of the kitchen and fetching water from the stream twice each. At the stream, in the course of the second round, they took their baths.

It was normally Ndidi's responsibility to warm the soup every morning and make the food they ate before going to school. She therefore went over to the kitchen and made the fire. She brought down the pot. Then she noticed that the lid was improperly balanced on it. She was somewhat perplexed.

'Ogo!' she called.

'What is it?' her sister replied from the room.

'Go away and stop disturbing me!' warned their mother, who had still not got up from bed.

Ogo went across to the kitchen reluctantly.

'What do you want?'

'Who opened this pot of soup?' Ndidi queried.

'Why do you ask me?'

'Why shouldn't I ask you?'

Ogo hissed and made to go away.

'Look at her—glutton! Maybe you stole some piece of meat from the soup and were unable to cover the pot properly because of your haste.'

'Shame on you! Who among us is a thief?'

'*Hoo! Hoo!* Thief!' Ndidi mocked, as she bent down to take off the cover.

'Take a look at yourself. Your life is bent already—let me tell you, if you don't know it.'

'See what you have done? Because you could not cover the pot properly you have allowed soot from the rafter to fall into the soup. See what you have done, you thief?'

'Shame!' Ogo mocked in return. 'You are only recounting what—'

'Have you started again this morning, you crickets?' their mother bawled at them as she appeared suddenly at the kitchen door. 'What is the matter?'

'Nothing, ma,' Ndidi said, as she hurriedly stirred the soup with the ladle.

'Now don't let me hear one more word from you.'

'Yes, ma.'

Ogo had stolen away.

Their mother left the kitchen and went back to bed.

Nwabunor was nervously stuffing her belongings into her box. She had not had the slightest sleep during the night, and could not even bring herself to wash her face this morning. Her preparations betrayed all the disorder that confused thinking could impose.

'Come on, quickly,' she hurried Ubaka, who was equally busy packing in the last few things that he had not assembled the previous night.

'Quickly,' his mother came upon him again. 'Will it take ten years?'

He blinked with displeasure . . .

Now and then Nwabunor would leave the room and wander round the kitchen, just to be sure that things were happening as she planned. She had been a bit perturbed when she listened very attentively and heard the exchanges between the twin sisters. But her heart settled again when their mother came out to put an end to what appeared a precarious diversion.

She was not ready to leave yet. She did not wish to leave yet. She had now got all the packing done, but until she was sure and could see clearly that what she had laid was taking the desired course, she would not leave the house.

Gradually it all began to happen. As she stalked into the

kitchen once again she met the twins rushing over their *eba* with aggressive gusto.

'Stop nipping at the fish, you rogue!'

'What about the one you just carried off in your morsel?'

Nwabunor nodded to herself. But she was not satisfied yet. Her main target was their mother. She's the one who's got it laid for me, she thought. Her turn will come yet.

She left the twins in the kitchen.

Just then Ogugua called out from her room.

'Ogo!'

'Ma!' A hurried morsel gave the girl's tone a slight tremolo.

'Make sure you set my bath water before you go off to school, do you hear me?'

'Yes, ma.'

The school bell was already ringing at the mission. The two girls finished their food, and washed a plate each. While Ndidi ran in to get dressed, Ogo grabbed a bucket and drew her mother's water quickly from the huge drum. She set the bucketful down at the back of the yard, and ran in to dress up for school.

Bomboy had woken up by this time. He had gone over to his brother Ubaka, and together, out of view at a corner of the house, they were exchanging words of farewell.

'Will you come back tomorrow?' Bomboy asked.

'I don't know. Maybe,' Ubaka replied, slowly, sadly.

'Tell your mother to let you come back tomorrow.'

'Alright. I will try.'

'Or ask her—ask her to let me come along with you.'

'I don't know—she may not agree.'

Bomboy lowered his face and stared at the inscrutable distance. Sadness played around his tender eyes. Ubaka looked at him, and held his little hand in his own. Tears stole from the corners of his eyes. Bomboy caught his mood by telepathy, and looked up. Quickly Ubaka rubbed his eyes clean.

'Are you crying, Uba?'

'No. I am not crying.'

Bomboy looked away again, pinching absent-mindedly at an ear of his jumper. Ubaka held his tears with effort, and tried to change the subject.

'Try hard to master the *koso*,' he said.

'I will learn it very well. I will play it this morning. When you come back I will know how to play it very well.'

Ubaka nodded in half-hearted approval, sadness stealing upon him again.

'Uba, when you come back tomorrow, will you bring—will you bring me a catapult?'

'I will try.'

'Please bring me a catapult, and a ball, and a *blow-blow*, and a catapult, and—.'

'I will bring them.'

The tears came again into Ubaka's eyes. Bomboy caught him this time, and his face became heavy.

'You are crying.'

'No, I am not,' rubbing awkwardly at his eyes.

'Bomboy!' Ogugua called from inside.

'Ma!'

The boy walked away reluctantly. The call barely stopped him from breaking into tears.

Having lost their uniforms in yesterday's fight, Ndidi and Ogo had dressed up in other clothing. They picked up their satchels, which they had later recovered from the scene of that fight, and rushed out of the house on their way to school. Ubaka stood at the corner of the house to bid them farewell.

'Ndidi. Ogo. Goodbye!' he called out to them, waving his hand as the tears sparkled in his eyes.

They stopped briefly to look at him.

'You are going today?'

He nodded.

They looked at his eyes, then at each other. They knew that some change was taking place. The boy was leaving.

Maybe he should have stayed, after all. But such tenderness did not endure. So they quickly waved and ran away again. He lingered a bit longer as he waved back after them. Once again he tried to check the tears. His mother called him, and he walked in to meet her, without actually answering.

Ogugua finally came out to take her bath. She seemed to be in a hurry to go off somewhere. As she walked towards the bathroom she passed Nwabunor, and neither of them said a word to the other.

After her bath Ogugua put on some home clothing and went into the kitchen. She rekindled the fire and brought to boiling the water that her daughters had left in the pot after making their own food. As soon as the water had boiled she brought it down and made *eba* for herself and Bomboy. She served out some soup, and they settled down to eat.

Nwabunor came into the kitchen and peered round as though she was looking for something. She left shortly, nodding to herself with satisfaction and thinking, Very good. You are only getting what you were intending for other people.

Ogugua swallowed a couple of morsels, and didn't like the taste of the soup.

'Worthless children,' she cursed her daughters. 'I'm sure they didn't warm this soup last night. Look how it has almost gone sour.'

She hissed and ate on. Bomboy was eating with juvenile relish. After a few more morsels and some fish and meat Ogugua left the rest of the food to him and rose to get dressed.

'Eat up quickly and pack the plates into that corner.'

Bomboy nodded and carried on with his concentrated picking.

And now after the first few moments of a feeling of victory, Nwabunor was not quite certain of herself. She sat down for a while on the bed and stared at the floor. What does all this amount to now? she thought. A number of such questions knocked in her head and she could hardly feel her way through the maze. Very likely the new feeling came as a result of doubts as to whether her action would merely achieve the desired result, or whether it was now going to lead her into the path of further discomforts and perhaps danger. But then she looked at her son, and felt once again, with some relief, that this was something that had to be done for an ultimate good.

'Go and set me water for a bath,' she told Ubaka as she rose from the bed, refusing to be held down to any more disturbing thoughts.

Ubaka picked up a bucket and set the water ready.

While his mother was taking her bath, he went across to Bomboy, who was still working on his food. He put his hand in his pocket and brought out a penny.

'Take it.'

Bomboy stretched his hand and smiled.

'Thank you,' he said.

Then he in turn felt an instinctive desire to do something for his brother, who would soon be leaving.

'Uba, eat some of my food, you hear?'

Ubaka looked down tenderly at him. He did not want to appear to be cheating the little boy of his meal. But he felt it was only an act of affection to take a gift from his little brother, whom after all he would be leaving very soon. Besides, he had not had any meal and was hungry. So he bent down and cut a morsel of the *eba*, dipped it into the soup, and threw it quickly into his mouth.

'Take some fish,' Bomboy again offered.

Ubaka was about to do this when he heard Ogugua coming from the room. He quickly rose and walked away from the spot . . .

Nwabunor finished her bath and came in, taking the bucket along with her. Before long she had dressed up and brought all the rest of her things together. Then she and her son prepared to leave. She made a pad quickly and heaved the big box onto her head, taking another bag in her hand. Ubaka put his little box into the bucket, and took the load on his head also. He and his mother left the room. He quickly went round to the next room and greeted.

'Nne Bomboy, goodbye.'

'Goodbye,' Ogugua replied indifferently.

Bomboy had been standing around, watching the departure. Ubaka rubbed him on the head and smiled with pain.

'Goodbye. I will try to come back again.'

Then he ran after his mother, towards the motor-park. Bomboy began to weep at once, and to trot after him. Ubaka looked back at him with tears in his eyes and waved reluctantly.

'Don't cry,' he sobbed at his little brother, who was now weeping with increasing vehemence.

Ogugua came out and grabbed the disconsolate little boy by the collar of his jumper, and whisked him away into the house. Ubaka turned round and walked on after his mother.

A slight breeze murmured in the air. Grasses swayed as if in resentment. Over in the horizon, just beneath the spectrum of the ascending sun, horizontal bands of red cloud hung menacingly above the tips of trees, and the morning air smelled of burnt clay.

18

When finally he got tired of weeping, Bomboy sat down under the shade of a tree in front of their house. He was whimpering quietly, and his nose was running. Sitting peacefully with legs crossed, he was fingering the three *koso* that Ubaka had given him and staring absent-mindedly in the direction that Ubaka and his mother had gone. The little dog had coiled himself up near him, fighting off flies that played around the sore ears. Denied of attention, the 'witch-cat' had left them and walked back home.

His mother had left him at home to go to the market. His sisters had long gone to school. After a while, for want of anything to do, he started practising on the *koso*. He picked up one and tried to spin it on the sand. It slipped off his fingers and fell away, for he had held it too close to the bottom. He tried again, and again the *koso* slipped off. He then held it near the tender top, but he pressed it a bit too hard and the *koso* cracked to pieces. He frowned with displeasure.

He picked up the second *koso* and tried to spin. The same errors re-occurred, and his untutored fingers once more destroyed the *koso*. In anger he threw the sherds on the ground and smashed them further with his heel. The dog tried to sniff the pieces over and he rapped the dog's head with his knuckles. Then he picked up the last *koso*. He took a look at it, but would not make any further attempt. To him it represented the last link with Ubaka, and he did not want to risk having it destroyed. Sad thoughts came upon him once more, and he began to cry.

And then his crying gradually increased. For he was beginning to feel some pain within his stomach. He put his hands under his jumper and rubbed at it. The pain grew stronger and stronger. Still crying, he rose from the ground and went into the house. He walked up and down the place, screaming louder as the pain bit harder inside his system. Finally he climbed upon his mother's bed, clawing now at his whole body and trying in vain to fight the torment that steadily sought to overwhelm him. It became too much for him, and with one last convulsive cry he threw his arms apart and fell silent. His right hand still clutched the last *koso* in an eternal fold. His face was calm as a sunset cloud.

The little dog toddled up and down the place, whimpering impatiently. An infernal hood fell over the scene.

Ndidi and Ogo were sitting under the shade of an umbrella tree outside the school gates. They had been turned out of school for appearing in colours instead of uniforms, but they did not yet have the courage to go home for fear of encountering their mother.

For a long while they sat in silence, each fumbling her satchel until they both got tired of keeping quiet.

'If you had not been too clever for yourself,' Ndidi accused, 'this would not have happened to us.'

'Stop trying to blame me,' Ogo retorted.

'Why shouldn't I blame you?'

'Because we are equally at fault.'

Ndidi eyed her, but the argument overwhelmed her and she merely hissed and kept quiet. Life went on as usual around them. People passed by, cars tooted their horns, leaves fell on the ground. After a while they spoke again.

'Ubaka and his mother should be on their way now,' Ndidi said.

'Yes. I am beginning to pity them. Something inside me makes me sorry they left.'

Ndidi looked at her and blinked away, instinctively trying to fight a feeling of self-pity.

'It is Ubaka I miss,' she said.

'I miss him too. He was a good boy.'

'He hardly ever got angry with us. If you tried to quarrel with him he would merely walk away. And he was very good to Bomboy. Maybe he should have gone with him.'

Ogo blinked regretfully at a distant picture of the boy, but quickly shook her head and looked down, playfully smoothing the pleats on her frock.

'It's his mother I never liked.'

'Yes,' Ndidi agreed. 'She is a wicked woman. She would kill us if she had the chance.'

'Still,' her sister sighed, 'I am sorry they left.'

'I am sorry too. But why did they have to leave?'

'I don't know.'

They looked briefly at each other, unwilling to voice any guilt. A few more minutes passed in silence before Ogo spoke.

'Ndidi,' laying a hand on her stomach, a squirm on her face.

'Mm?'

'I feel some pain in my stomach.'

'I've been feeling some pain too. Are you hungry?'

'No.'

'I'm not hungry myself. The pain bites.'

'Yes. Let us go home.'

'Yes.'

They took their satchels and rose. The pain increased as they went, and their pace slackened. No sooner had they got home than they threw down their satchels carelessly to battle with the growing convulsions.

It was not market day, but there was a fair amount of bustle. Ogugua picked up the yams one by one and examined them sourly, to put herself in a good bargaining position.

'How much is each bundle?'

'How much do you want to pay?' the owner, an elderly woman, returned.

'Two shillings?'

'Put them down and pass on.'

'Well, tell me your price then.'

'Two shillings! Do you think I stole them?'

'Tell me your price then. Or don't you want to sell them?'

'Three shillings, and nothing goes out of that,' and the woman looked away nonchalantly.

'Take two and six.'

The woman made her no reply. Ogugua picked up her bag and was about to go away.

'Bring the money,' the woman called her back.

Ogugua turned to examine the yams again. The woman watched her coldly.

'I'll pay you two and three. They are rather lifeless.'

The woman screwed her brow and looked hard at her.

'Can you boast any more life than those yams?'

'Why are you abusing me?'

'Why shouldn't I abuse you? Do you think I have come here to stretch my legs and watch people talk about my yams in that way?'

'And is that why you should pout your mouth at me? Please take your rotten yams away.'

'And take your rotten self away.'

Market disputes are hardly ever more than this. Ogugua picked her bag once more and walked away, while the old woman gave her an eyeful of scorn.

She stopped at the next yam stall.

'How much is this bundle?'

'Two and nine, nothing more, nothing less.'

'You won't take two and six?'

'I said "nothing more, nothing less",' as decidedly in looks as in tone.

Ogugua sighed.

'Alright, I have no strength for argument. Here is your money.'

She hurried through the rest of her purchase for the day, hardly attempting any bargaining. She was beginning to feel a gripping pain in her stomach, and quickly left the market as the pain grew stronger.

On getting home she threw down the bag, and flung her headtie upon the bed. She did not stop to look at her children. She hardly noticed them, though she had stumbled against a leg by the door of her room. Gasping and groaning she hastily picked up an orange and ripped it in two, squeezing the juice crudely down her throat. Next she gobbled down two cups of water in agitated succession, so overwhelming was the torment. She waited for a relief. But it never came. She clenched her teeth as she gasped furiously and writhed. Her agitated face shook out numerous beads of sweat, and her eyes wore the vengeful glare of a viper in the throes of a fatal blow.

But she merely fought like the others . . .

'Who is at home?' Ma Nwojide greeted as she knocked the sand off her feet at the doorstep. 'Ogugua! Who is at home?'

As she came in the little dog ran up to her, sniffing and wagging his tail in greeting. She went first into her son's bedroom. He was not in—she was not surprised. And then she saw that Nwabunor had truly cleared her things and was gone with her son. She reflected a bit on the emptiness, then hissed and shook her head.

Leaving the room she walked over to Ogugua's room. At the door she saw Ogo sprawled out on the floor face up, and Ndidi coiled up ahead with one leg crooked over Ogo's head.

'What kind of sleep is this?' Ma Nwojide fretted. Then she looked on the bed and saw Ogugua and Bomboy. 'Ogugua, weren't you here when—'

She looked closer and saw that Ogugua herself was not very respectably postured. She was even fully dressed but for her headtie by her side on the bed.

'Ogugua! What kind of sleep is this at this hour of the day? Ogugua!!'

209

She went close to the bed and shook the dead woman. 'Ogugua! Ogug—?'

She laid a hand on the woman's arm. Cold as a fish. She felt her breast. No beat. A sudden shock ran through her. She stared in dumb silence. As a last test she pushed one of Ogugua's eyelids up with a finger. The cold piece of flesh slid passively back.

'What am I seeing?' she screamed, as she stepped back in terror.

She shook all the children one by one. Their bodies merely rolled back and forth in lifeless response.

'E-weh!! Ozala come and see—o!!' she yelled in wild agitation.

In her excitement her headtie loosened and fell off her head. She ignored it, but fastened back her wrapper, which was also coming off. She ran this way and that, near-demented. Then she came back again at the corpses.

'Ogugua! Bomboy! What kind. . . ? E-weh! Ozala, come out in your numbers and see-o!!'

Presently a handful of people came and looked at the scene. Most recoiled in horror. Gradually the number of people increased, and the house was teeming with men, women and children, some of whom had only yesterday been witness to another spectacle in that house.

Ma Nwojide left the crowd as they surged in with excitement and out with wide-eyed fright. She retired to a little corner, beat her breast and cried quietly. For an explanation of the whole thing was now coming clearly into her mind and she needed no aid to the unravelling, thinking aloud, So this is what it has come to? Could it be because I asked her to go home? I thought that was the only remedy. Au! Au!

She wiped her eyes and came back to the scene. She was trying to make her way through the insistently curious crowd that kept growing. Her heart was heavy and her face was grave. Around her people were crying and yelling. Others were talking excitedly. One or two were beginning to ask where Obanua was.

But the speechless woman bent down over Bomboy's

cold body, lifted it clear of the bed, and walked straight out of the house, heading for the palmwine bar with unmitigated gravity. A small crowd walked after her with affrighted curiosity, giving her some distance.

'I tell you,' Obanua whispered languidly into Nwanze's ear, 'I got—the news from a v-very reliable—source. She gets the best—wine in town b-because she—let's the tapper—' he made lewd movements with his fingers, looking aside in the direction of the bar-woman '—you—understand what I mean?'

'Liar! I will tell,' replied Nwanze. The wine had also gone to his head. 'I will tell!'

'What—will you t-tell?'

'You said—that the tapper—had three legs, one—'

'*Sharrap!*'

And they both laughed awkwardly over the topic. After a short while Nwanze spoke again.

'You haven't yet—asked me how—how I got this money—that has blessed our day.'

'I—was coming to that.'

Nwanze swallowed three gulps and cleared his throat, then stared down on the table.

'Akpolukwu and Nwoji had just—paid their fines for failing to attend—yesterday's meeting at the chief's court. There were a lot of p-people. The chief took the money, not really—knowing how much it was, and put it by his—his side. I was sitting close to him. In the general confusion—' he belched loudly '—in the confusion, with everybody shouting at the tops of their voices, I just—just slipped my hand quietly towards the money, and took five shillings out—out of it. And before anybody could—'

He stopped talking immediately. He had vaguely spied Ma Nwojide and the crowd coming ahead, and recoiled in spite of himself.

Obanua too looked back towards the street, and saw his mother approaching with a crowd. He could not quite make out what she was carrying in her arms, and stared hazily on. The cup was shaking in his hand, and his mouth was gaping in delirious wonder.

The old woman walked straight to their table and, her face still contorted with a combination of pain and reproachful scorn, laid the body of Bomboy on Obanua's lap.

'Here is your son. I hope it pleases you now.'

And that was all she said. She simply turned and walked back the way she came, looking straight ahead with the same tragic grandeur she had worn all along and making every effort to keep back the tears that welled up in her eyes. The crowd stood dumbfounded.

The cup had dropped from Obanua's hand. He stared down at the body of his little son, and was quickly shocked out of his delirium. The body was very cold. He shook it roughly.

'Bomboy! Bomboy!'

He stood up at once from the chair. He tried to stand the boy on his feet, but the body was slumping down. A tremendous fear overcame him.

'Bomboy!! What is wrong?' he looked questioningly at the crowd, who began to shift backwards. 'Will nobody tell—Bomboy! Bomboy!!'

He was breathing fast. He looked round in horror-stricken wonder. The world looked empty, in spite of the crowd. Without another word, he lifted the boy clear of the ground and ran. Now and again he stumbled and almost fell. He was running back to his house, from which he had long been running away.

In no time at all the horror of the event gripped the whole town. For all that, some people could not resist the itch of curiosity, and fluttered with wide-eyed apprehension round the scene of the tragedy. Mother made certain that child was well within their premises, like the agitated hen when the eagle visits. If she didn't find him around she would hurry to Obanua's house, and on whisking him away would take a good exploratory look at the woman near whom he had been standing, just to make sure. A great fear was about the town.

chased off by a nagging doubt as to the good faith of a man who demanded a price with such intemperate and implacable gusto. Then she thought of herself and her son writhing in the torment laid upon them by her 'enemy'. But the exact nature of the charm proved difficult for her to visualise, and her mind was confronted yet again by that picture of death on the faces of children who were now being swallowed up in a destruction intended for their mother. Little by little, but by a steady process of mental torment, she was beginning to drift further and further away from self-control and from sanity.

'Mama!' her son called again.

'Ehn?'

'I don't know what has been worrying my stomach.'

Nwabunor's eyes lighted with sudden fright, and she stared down at her son.

'How long have you been feeling it?'

'Since this afternoon. As soon as the lorry stopped.'

She stopped to think for a while. Then a cold feeling suddenly struck her.

'How . . . where . . . how does it worry you?'

'It bites.'

'Bites?'

He nodded in discomfort. Nwabunor tugged at his shirt, unmindful now of the cold. As she pulled it carelessly over his head a button came off.

'What happened to you?' she asked uneasily.

He made no reply. Beads of sweat were running down his face.

'I am asking you! What happened to you?'

He still couldn't say a word. He was breathing rather fast. Nwabunor looked quickly at the woman near them, whose child was still sporting a smear of banana and orange around her mouth. The woman returned her a perplexed look, and Nwabunor addressed her.

'What did you—have you given anything to my child?'

'Me?' the woman quickly countered. 'Have I finished feeding my own child, that I should give to yours?'

Nwabunor was extremely worried.

215

'Ubaka! Ubaka, answer me!'

'Ma,' the boy muttered.

'Did you eat anything?'

The boy was panting excitedly.

'Isn't it you I'm asking?'

Ubaka shook his head wearily. People in the lorry were beginning to feel concern and came over to the scene. They helped to strip the boy completely and laid him on the bench. Somebody fanned him while another brought water and laid the cup at Ubaka's lips.

'Don't give him anything!' Nwabunor screamed, her mouth quaking with agitation. 'Don't give him anything yet! Ubaka, did you eat anything at all this morning at home?'

'Stop questioning him,' somebody said, 'and let him drink some water meanwhile.'

'No! He's my son, and you can't tell me how to handle him. Ubaka!'

The boy's lips opened slightly in an attempted reply.

'Ubaka! Did you eat anything at home? Ehn?'

'Bom . . . Bom . . . Bom,' Ubaka stammered. But his lips failed him.

'What?'

'Bom . . . Bom-boy.'

'Bomboy? Bomboy did what? Tell me, what did Bomboy give you?'

A grim picture quickly came into Nwabunor's mind and she broke down and cried. The man holding the cup took the opportunity to administer the water to Ubaka's mouth. But the boy in his uneasiness turned his mouth away.

The rain had now thinned down to a drizzle. The driver, who had been one of the crowd around the agonised boy, jumped down from the lorry and stood by the road to stop an approaching vehicle. But the vehicle paid him no heed, and sped by. Moments passed and seemed hardly to bring any relief. It was a long time before another lorry came by. The driver waved and the lorry drew to a halt.

'Osual, na you?'

'Wetin de happin?'

'My motor get complain, and 'e get one small pickin wey de sick bad bad inside here. You go fit carry 'im and 'im mama for me?'

'I no know wedda I get chance-o. Where dem de go?'

'Na for Aje yonder.'

'Oya, tell dem make dem enter for back quick quick. I done late kpata-kpata.'

Two men lifted Ubaka out of the immobilized lorry, Nwabunor wailing frantically after them. But on getting to the ground they looked at the boy and halted awhile. Ubaka had stopped moving, and even breathing. His body was hopelessly limp.

'I think the boy is dead,' one of them remarked, a frightened look on his face.

'What?' Nwabunor screamed upon the man, as she tore forward to look at her son. 'What do you say? What has happened?'

She began to rave uncontrollably, her hair dishevelled and her cloth falling loose off her waist. The rain had stopped completely, and only her ululations broke the quiet expanse of the emptiness around. Beneath the sky an ash-coloured screen of cloud hung motionless like a permanent shroud, severely weakening the light of the departing sun. In the adjacent shrubbery a lone finch fluttered noiseless, without any visible mission, until it finally disappeared and was blotted out of view in the smoky distance.

19

The little frame of the old woman shook under a severe fit of coughing, as she bent weakly to keep it under control.

'Bless you. Bless you,' her sister sympathised.

The woman finally raised her head, revealing the tears that slowly ran down the age-drawn ducts of her face.

'Bless you,' her sister repeated. 'I have often wondered whether Mgbushe really does a good bleeding job on your back, for how is it that this fever keeps coming back on you ever so often? Surely the bad blood has not gone off you completely. But since you trust her so much I think it will all be well before long. Bless you.'

The other spat heavily on the ground and nodded.

'Carry on with what you were saying,' she said.

'So after I had bought the snuff and was walking back home I decided to stop by and give the morning's greetings to the chief. But as I came into the court I met him presiding over a very tumultuous council. For Dimgba Ononenyi and Asielue Okoawolo had risen from their seats and were stabbing their fingers at each other in the midst of a heated argument. So I retracted my steps, and as I turned to go who should I meet but your old friend Ada Odiwe, the chief's third wife. I asked her what all the fuss was about and she said it was over a complaint that Nwojide had brought to the chief. For it was reported that Akpuko the soothsayer had whispered into her ear that if she wanted to know the cause of the disaster that struck her son's household she should look to Ese Nwozomudo, whose hands could not in the least be clean about the matter unless the spirits had lied to him. So the distressed woman, who ordinarily would not pay any heed to such matters but would rather believe it if the misfortune had been said to have come from God, had gone over to the chief and demanded that both Akpuko and Nwozomudo be banished from the town. The chief had therefore called his councillors to discuss what should be done to these two people who had done so much mischief in the town already. There the councillors began to take sides, and nothing seemed to have been agreed between them. But something that Ada told me made me cast my mind back and think deeply. Do you know that the night before that disaster I had had a dream?'

'You have narrated so many frivolous dreams to me that I am beginning to wonder if there is any point in listening to more of them.'

'Listen anyway. Every evening, as the sun goes down and darkness begins to fall, I look pitifully on as your goat runs frantically about in search of her only kid and I wonder what she would do if one day she finally lost him. That night I dreamt of a big storm. Trees and houses were being rooted from the ground and even our wretched roof had been torn off. The little kid was standing on a high wooden pedestal in a lonely spot, unruffled by the storm, spotless and glittering like the noonday sun. But your goat was busy foraging in somebody else's backyard, chopping off the vegetables and trampling over the whole place. The owner of the farm came out of the house and, seeing the waste, was filled with anger. He aimed a fat stick at the goat, but missed. Then he saw the kid on the pedestal, took a burning piece of wood from within the house, and set fire to the entire structure, destroying kid and all. Your goat bleated endlessly and could hardly get over the distress. I did not wish to narrate the dream to you, knowing how much you would resent hearing it. But it all came back quickly to my mind when this morning Ada told me that Nwabunor's son had died and the poor woman had run mad and was now a sad spectacle on the streets of their town. Sister, sister,' shaking her head distantly, 'what things I have seen!'

The second woman's mouth drew slowly open in speechless wonder. A slight breeze was blowing. Some distance away a coconut fell down from its tree and two hens rushed to the prize. But on getting to the spot they pecked at the coconut only to find that the bark was thoroughly dry. They went back their different ways.

'Thank you for the news,' the second woman said with a touch of subdued resentment. 'But save your sympathy for me and my goat. I hardly see any connection between my goat and people who are merely victims of their own fire. Still, I think it's a terrible thing.'

'Indeed. Indeed,' her sister agreed.

'But it's more than a week now since the fearful event took place in that house, and I have been watching closely to see what has become of the man. I have scarcely set eyes on him since that day and I am beginning to wonder what could have happened.'

The first woman pushed a fingerful of the snuff into her gums, and grimaced accordingly.

'What do you expect to see?' she replied, bearing her head up in a posture of knowledgeable authority. 'Is the disaster that has visited him not enough to teach him a severe lesson, or do you still expect to find him indulging in the sort of thing that has proved the ruin of his entire household? No, sister. It is unheard of. When a thing of this kind happens, then the time has come for a man to take a good look at his whole life and reflect, under the weight of his sorrow, how best to correct his ways. I think he will be a very sober man for a long while yet. I think that somewhere within that house he is brooding deeply and thinking what to do to rub the shame off his face. Of that I have not the slightest doubt.'

No sooner had she said that than they saw Obanua approaching from a distance. Heavily drunk and holding a tattered shirt in one hand, he was sauntering unsteadily towards his house as unintelligible notes issued from his dripping mouth. His lips looked swollen and so too his eyes. And from his shouts he appeared to be—singing.

The two old women glanced at each other. The second

one rose without a word and walked into their little hut, unwilling to reveal either the mockery or the scorn that now showed on her face. Soon after her sister rose too, her face drained off all self-assurance and cheer, as she hissed emphatically and picked up her snuff bottle. The little female cat trotted dutifully ahead of her, but she paid her no mind now and indeed almost stumbled against her. And again the male cat, huddled independently away on the mud dais, blinked with distrust and distaste.

The sun had gone down. Above and beyond the silhouetted trees in the horizon black cloud figures drifted westwards, homeward bound, like the sad profiles of a retreating menagerie.